The Mobile Library

Also by Ian Sansom

The Truth About Babies
Ring Road

IAN SANSOM

The Mobile Library

THE CASE OF THE MISSING BOOKS

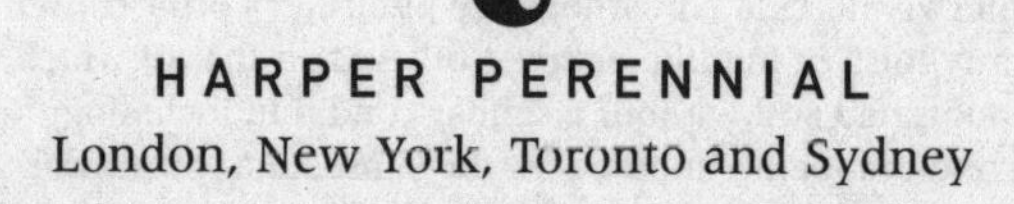

HARPER PERENNIAL
London, New York, Toronto and Sydney

Harper Perennial
An imprint of HarperCollins*Publishers*
77–85 Fulham Palace Road
Hammersmith
London W6 8JB

www.harperperennial.co.uk

Published by Harper Perennial 2006
1

A catalogue record for this book is
available from the British Library

ISBN-13 978-0-00-720699-5
ISBN-10 0-00-720699-2

Set in Meridien

Printed in Great Britain by Clays Limited, St Ives plc

For the librarians of Ongar, Epping, Loughton,
Romford, Harlow, Cambridge, Oxford, London,
Bangor, Belfast, Dublin and New York.

1

No. No, no, no, no, no. This was not what was supposed to happen. This was not it at all.

Israel was outside the library, suitcase in hand, the hood on his old brown duffle coat turned up against the winter winds, and there he was, squinting, reading the sign.

> **DEPARTMENT OF ENTERTAINMENT, LEISURE AND COMMUNITY SERVICES**
>
> **LIBRARY CLOSURE**
>
> It is with regret that Rathkeltair Borough Council announces the closure of Tumdrum and District Public Library, with effect from 1 January 2005. Alternative provision is available for borrowers in Rathkeltair Central Library. A public information meeting will be held in February 2005 to examine proposals for local

library and information services and resources. See local press for details.

Further information is available by contacting the Department of Entertainment, Leisure and Community Services at the address below.

The following associated planning application and environmental statement may be examined at the Town Hall Planning Office, Rathkeltair between the hours of 9.30 a.m.–10.30 a.m., Monday to Thursday. It is advisable to make an appointment before calling at the office.

Written comments should be addressed to the Divisional Planning Manager, Town Hall, Rathkeltair BT44 2BB, to be received by 5 February 2005. Please quote the application reference number in any correspondence.

Applic No: X/2004/0432/0

Location: Carnegie Public Library, Hammond Road, Tumdrum

Proposal: Proposed mixed-use development including residential, live-work units, class 2 use (financial, professional and other services), class 3 use (business), class 4 shop and community facilities.

T. BRUNSWICK, BA, MBA,
Chief Executive and Town Clerk
Rathkeltair Borough Council, Town Hall,
Rathkeltair, Co. Antrim BT44 2BB

Unbelievable. That was just ... unbelievable.

He couldn't take it all in; his eyes seemed to skid across the lines.

He had to read it all again and still the only words he took in were 'Library' and 'Closure' – and they hit him hard, like a blow to the head, literally rocked him back on his worn-out old heels, the worn-out old heels on his one and only pair of worn-out best shoes, his brown brogues, too tight and permanently unpolished, shoes that had done him since graduation for all and every special occasion, for weddings, funerals, bar mitzvahs and for the interminable and unsuccessful job interviews.

Israel had a headache and he was tired from the journey, his whole body and his one and only best brown corduroy suit wrinkled and furrowed from the coach and the ferry and the train and the bus, and he put down his suitcase, shrugged his shoulders a little to wake himself up, and he read the sign again more carefully.

'Library', 'Closure'.

Oh, God. He took another Nurofen and a sip of water from his water bottle.

He'd read and understood the whole now – that greasy little 'with regret' and the weaselly 'public information meeting', the obfuscating 'proposed mixed-used development' – but it was the two words 'Library' and 'Closure' that really carried all the meaning, that hit hardest. He shook his head to clear his mind and pushed his mop of messy home-cut curly hair from his eyes and his little round gold-rimmed glasses up high onto his furrowed forehead and he took a long, wobbly step back and lifted up his face and looked at the building in front of him: two storeys of unforgiving bluff red brick, blinds drawn, big oak doors locked, no lights, no sign of life.

He looked up high and he looked up hard, and then he dropped his head down low. This place was definitely closed. Permanently. And for good.

There was a stray dog then, a little terrier, sniffing around Israel's old suitcase while he stood there, and around his corduroy turn-ups, and he really didn't do well with dogs, Israel, he didn't get on with dogs at all – he was a typical vegetarian – and this thing was a mangy flea-bag, and half-blind by the look of it, and scraggly and arthritic – it reminded Israel a little too much of himself, actually – and he shooed it away: 'Go on, go! Get away!' Then he rubbed his eyes and glanced around and behind him, to see if it was for real, this grim, godforsaken place, to see if he'd made some terrible, simple, idiotic mistake, had come to the wrong library maybe, or the wrong town, too tired after his long journey to be able to see that people were in fact flocking into some secret, fabulous library entrance, some little tunnel or nook, some rabbity-hole known only to the locals.

They were not.

No one was approaching with armfuls of books or tickets in their hands: there were no sour and pear-shaped OAPs; no straggle-haired young mums at their wits' end with smeary, miserable children dragging along for story time; no one clutching important-looking unimportant documents to be photocopied in triplicate for their solicitor or the DSS; no wrinkled, stubbly, fragrant winos; no schoolkids half-heartedly working on projects about ancient civilisations or the Second World War or the processes of human digestion. No madmen. No one. None of them. The building was empty. The car park was deserted. The library was shut.

There is a terrible poignancy about a building intended for the public that is closed to the public: it feels like an insult, a riposte to all our more generous instincts, the public polity under threat, and democracy abandoned. Back home in London, Israel had always found the sight of Brent Cross shopping centre at night depressing enough, and his girlfriend Gloria, her family's swimming pool when it was drained in the winter, but the sight of the big red-brick library with its dark windows affected him even more deeply, in the same way that the sight of a derelict school might affect a teacher, or an empty restaurant a chef: a clear sign of the impending collapse of civilisation and the inevitable bankruptcy, a reminder never to count your chickens, or to overspend on refurbishments and cutlery. No one likes to see a shut library.

But for Israel Armstrong the sight of this shut library was more than just an omen or a mere unpleasantness. For Israel, this was personal. For chubby little Israel Armstrong, in his brown corduroy suit and his best brown shoes, all the way over from England, first time in Ireland and first time in the north, the sight of this particular shut library was an absolute disaster. This was unmitigated. For Israel, far from home and in a country not his own, this was the punch that comes out of nowhere and sends you heading for the canvas. For Israel, this particular shut library meant that he was out of a job. It also meant, as the cold December winds lashed around his legs and blew up litter all around him, that he had absolutely no idea where he was going to spend the night.

He hadn't exactly expected a welcoming committee. He hadn't expected the whole country, or even the whole of the north of the country, or the whole of County Antrim even to turn out with flags and banners, he hadn't expected an all-Ireland green and orange, Guinness-sponsored celebration, but some kind of acknowledgement of his arrival would have been nice, some recognition that finally he was here, that the new Tumdrum and District librarian had arrived. But no. There was no sign of interest or excitement in Israel's presence in the town of Tumdrum in the county of Antrim late on that cold December afternoon. He had arrived and no one cared.

So. He did the only thing he could do under the circumstances. In the face of rejection he attempted to maintain his dignity and his pride. He turned his back on them, the whole lot of them – on the library, on the dog, on the faceless, faithless people of the north of the north of Ireland – he turned his back on the big empty building, picked up his suitcase, pulled his big flapping duffle coat tighter around him, his pockets bulging neurotically with emergency paperbacks and newspapers, just in case he was ever caught short without something to read, and he sighed a sigh, and prodded his glasses boldly back, and stepped forward. And into the huge, hot, curling turd left behind by the fat, half-blind, arthritic *Irish* dog. Israel groaned and he cursed and he limped over to a muddy patch of grass near the library entrance and wiped his soles.

That was just his luck. That was just bloody typical.

He managed to wipe most of it off on the grass, and

used the *Guardian* to scrape off the rest. He shrugged again and trudged down the cracked concrete disabled access ramp and through the empty car park and back down to the road.

This was definitely not supposed to happen. No. This was not it at all.

2

Israel Joseph Armstrong, BA (Hons), had arrived in Northern Ireland on the overnight ferry from Stranraer. It was his first experience of sea travel, and he had found he did not agree with it, or it with him.

In his rich imagination, Israel's crossing to Ireland was a kind of pilgrimage, an act of necessity but also an act of homage, similar to the crossings made by generations of his own family who had made the reverse journey from Ireland to England, and also from Russia and from Poland, from famines and pogroms and persecution to the New World, or at least to Bethnal and then Golders Green and eventually further out to the Home Counties, and to Essex, and similar also to the fateful trip made by W. H. Auden and Christopher Isherwood on board the *Champlain* in 1939, say, or Robert Louis Stevenson sailing the South Seas, or the adventures of Joseph Conrad the mariner, or the young Herman Melville, or similar, at the very least, to the adventures of Jerome K. Jerome's eponymous three men rowing in a boat on the Thames.

He'd read far too many books, that was Israel's trouble.

Books had spoilt him; they had curdled his brain, like cream left out on a summer's afternoon, or eggs overbeaten with butter. He'd been a bookish child, right from the off, the youngest of four, the kind of child who seemed to start reading without anyone realising or noticing, who enjoyed books without his parents' insistence, who raced through non-fiction at an early age and an extraordinary rate, who read Jack Kerouac before he was in his teens, and who by the age of sixteen had covered most of the great French and Russian authors, and who as a result had matured into an intelligent, shy, passionate, sensitive soul, full of dreams and ideas, a wide-ranging vocabulary, and just about no earthly good to anyone.

His expectations were sky-high, and his grasp of reality was minimal.

The big white ferry that had carried Israel over to Ireland, for example, he realised sadly and too late, was not the boat of his imaginings and dreams; it was not like the *Pequod*, or Mark Twain's Mississippi riverboat; it was more like …

It was more like a floating Little Chef Travelodge, actually, full of Scots and Irish and possibly Scots-Irish lorry-drivers, men profoundly pale of colour and generous of figure, men possessed of huge appetites and apparently unquenchable thirst, and Israel couldn't understand a word they said, and they couldn't understand him, and he couldn't believe how much they were drinking. They were drinking gallons. Literally. Enough to sink a ship.

He'd never been a great one for the drink himself,

Israel, although he wasn't entirely averse; he found that two glasses of red wine was usually about his limit and seemed to have approximately the same effect on him as a dozen pints of super-lager on his peers and contemporaries. Any more and he was usually violently sick, as he had been on the ferry a little earlier actually, although without so much as a sip of red wine and only coffee and snacks inside him: he wasn't sure if it was nerves or the swell, or the after-effects of the ten-hour coach journey up from London Victoria, and a couple of vegetable samosas on the way, a 10% Extra Free! pack of Doritos, two Snickers, two hard-boiled eggs and a souvenir packet of 'Olde London' fudge bought on impulse from a kiosk at Victoria moments before departing.

He had tried to regain his sense of balance and his composure in the ferry's bar – the unfortunately named Sea Dogs – with a glass of Coke to settle his stomach, but by eight o'clock things were getting a little rowdy in Sea Dogs, and a little choppy, and he had no desire to add further to the mess and the confusion, so he moved on to the television room, where he had to endure a charity reality TV show in which people were forced to compete for the chance to have their houses redecorated by their favourite celebrities by entering a lookalike karaoke competition.

Trying to sleep upright in a chair, next to men twice his not inconsiderable size dribbling burger juice, with Sky TV at full volume: this was not how his new life and new career in Ireland were supposed to begin. His new life in Ireland was supposed to be overflowing with blarney and craic. He was supposed to be excited and ready, trembling on the verge of a great adventure.

But instead Israel was just trembling on the verge of being sick again, and the journey had given him a headache, a terrible, *terrible* headache; he was a martyr to his headaches, Israel. He'd probably had more headaches in his life than most people have had hot dinners, assuming that people these days are eating a lot more salads and mostly sandwiches for lunch. It was all the books and the lack of fresh air that did it, and the fact that he was a Highly Sensitive Person.

When the ferry finally arrived in the grey-grim port of Larne, hours late, and disgorged its human, pantechnicon and white-van contents onto the stinking, oily, wholly indifferent harbourside, Israel had a bad feeling, and it wasn't just his headache and the sea-sickness. He was supposed to be met at the ferry terminal, but there was no one there and no one was answering the phone at his contact number at the library, so he had to use what little remained of his money and his initiative to get the train out of Larne to Rathkeltair, and then the bus to Tumdrum, and through the long grey streets end-on to the hills and to the sea, and all the way to the library – to the big shut library. It felt as though someone had slammed his own front door in his face.

Israel had grown up in and around libraries. Libraries were where he belonged. Libraries to Israel had always been a constant. In libraries Israel had always known calm and peace; in libraries he'd always seemed to be able to breathe a little easier. When he walked through the doors of a library it was like entering a sacred space, like the Holy of Holies: the beautiful hush and the shunting of the brass-handled wooden drawers holding the card catalogues, the reassurance of the reference books and the eminent *OED*s, the amusing little troughs of children's books; all human life was there, and you could borrow it and take it home for two weeks at a time, nine books per person per card. By the age of thirteen Israel had two pink library tickets all of his own – you were only really allowed one, but his dad had had a word with the librarian and won him a special dispensation. 'More books?' he could remember his dad proudly saying when he used to stagger home from the library after school with another sports-bag full of George Orwells and specialist non-fiction. 'More books? That's my boy!' he'd say. 'He's read hundreds,' his father would boast to the librarians, and to teachers, and to friends of the family, and to other parents. And 'Hundreds?!' his mother would correct. 'What do you mean, hundreds? Thousands of books that boy's read. Thousands and thousands. His head is full of books.'

And so it was this Israel Armstrong – this child of the library, his head full of books and a little overweight perhaps these days in his brown corduroy suit, portly even, you might say, but not stout, and not yet thirty years old – who had found himself barred and locked out in the fishy-smelling, grey-grim town of Tumdrum on that cold December afternoon, and who found his way eventually to the Tumdrum and District Council offices, after having had to ask directions half a dozen times, and who was finally being ushered in, old brown suitcase in hand, to see Linda Wei, Deputy Head of Entertainment, Leisure and Community Services, to sort out the apparent misunderstanding.

'Ah! Mr Armstrong' said Linda Wei, who looked as though she might have been quite at home on the Larne–Stranraer ferry – she was a big Chinese lady wearing little glasses and with a tub of Pringles open on her desk, and a litre bottle of Coke, half its contents already drained; you wouldn't have blinked if you'd seen Linda behind the wheel of an articulated lorry, honking on her horn while offering a one-fingered salute.

'We meet at last,' she said; they had previously spoken on the phone. 'Come on in, come on in,' she motioned to him, rather over-animatedly, and then again, for good measure, because Israel already was in, 'Come in, come in, come in!' She gave a small Cola burp and extended a sweaty, ready-salted hand. 'Lovely to meet you. Lovely. Lovely. Good journey?'

Israel shrugged his shoulders. What could he say?

'Now, I am sorry there was nobody to meet you at the ferry terminal this morning ...'

'Yes,' he said.

'You were late, you see.'

There was an awkward silence.

'But. Never matter. You're here now, aren't you. Now. Tea? Coffee? It'll be from the machine, I'm afraid.'

'No, thanks.'

'Erm? Crisp?'

'No. Thanks.'

'They're Pringles.'

'No. Thank you.'

'I missed breakfast,' said Linda.

'Right.'

'Sure I can't tempt you?'

'Absolutely sure. Thanks anyway.' This was not a moment for Pringles.

'Well. OK. So. You're here.'

'Yes.

'And you've been to the library?'

'Yes.'

'Ah. Then you'll be aware that—'

'It's shut,' Israel said, surprised to hear a slight hysterical edge to his voice. 'The library. Is shut.'

'Yeeees,' she said, drawing out the 'yes' as though stretching a balloon. 'Yes, Mr Armstrong. There's been a wee change of plan.'

Linda paused for a crisp and rearranged herself more authoritatively in her padded black-leather-effect swivel-seat.

'So. You probably want to know what's happened?'

Israel raised an eyebrow.

'Yes. Now. Let me explain. Since your appointment as the new Tumdrum and District branch librarian I'm afraid there's been a little bit of a resource allocation. And the library—'

'Has been shut.' Israel tried to control the quavering in his voice.

'Temporarily,' said Linda, raising – almost wagging – a finger.

'I see. So you no longer need my—' began Israel.

'No! No, no! No! Not at all, not at all!' Linda licked some crisp crumbs from her lips. 'No! You are essential, in fact, to the ... planned resource allocation. We are absolutely delighted to have attracted someone of your calibre, Mr Armstrong. Delighted.'

'But there's no library for me to work in.'

'Not exactly.'

'Not exactly?'

'That's right. You see, it's not a cutback in our funding, or anything like that we're talking about – no, no, no! It's more a re-targeting of our resources. Do you see?'

Well, to be honest, no, at that moment, Israel did not see.

'No. Sorry. You've lost me.'

'Well, yes, of course. You've had a long journey. London, was it?'

'That's right. Ten hours on the coach, eight hours on the—'

'I've a sister in London,' interrupted Linda.

'Oh.'

'Southfields? Would you know it at all?'

'No. I'm afraid not.'

'She's a project manager. For – what are they called? Something beginning with D?' She struggled for the answer. 'The mobile phone mast people?'

'No. Sorry. I haven't come across them.' Israel was not interested in Linda Wei's sister who lived in Southfields and who worked for a mobile telephone mast company which began with D. 'And getting back to the library?'

'Yes. Erm. The library. Well, first of all I want to assure you that we at Tumdrum and District Council are absolutely committed to continuing the public's free access to ideas and resources.'

'To libraries.'

'Yes. If you want to put it like that.'

'Fine. But you've closed the actual library?'

'Yes.' And here she ballooned out the 'yes' as far as seemed possible without it actually popping and deflating and turning into a 'no', and she reached up high to a shelf behind her and took down a fat ring-bound report, which she handed to Israel, and gestured for him to read. 'Here,' she said. 'This'll explain.'

The report had a title: *The Public Library: Democracy's Resource. A Statement of Principles.* Israel started flicking through. It was all output measures and graphs and tables – the usual sort of thing. He turned to the recommendations at the back.

'In the opinion of the Information Resources Steering Committee,' recited Linda Wei, who seemed to have memorised the key passages, 'it is important for the borough to continue to provide information resources with a high service proposition combined with increased competitive flexibility. The overall aim should be to minimise cost per circulation, and to maximise number of patrons served.'

'Right,' said Israel. *High service proposition*? *Increased competitive flexibility*? 'Which means?'

'Do you have a current British driving licence, Mr Armstrong?'

'Yes.'

'You do! Grand. That's grand!' She clapped her hands together, delighted.

'Because?'

'Because, the position we are now able to offer you is really very exciting. Very, very exciting. If, admittedly, *slightly* different to what you may have been expecting.'

'I see.'

'It's more ... mobile.'

'Mobile?'

'Yes.'

'You mean a mobile library?'

'Exactly!' said Linda Wei. 'That's it, that's it.' She was so delighted with Israel's powers of deduction that she helped herself to a handful of Pringles. 'You're like Hercule Poirot!' she said. 'I knew we'd picked the right man for the job. Although these days we don't call it a mobile library. We call it a mobile learning centre.'

'Right.'

'Pringle?'

'Thanks,' said Israel. 'But no. Thanks.'

Linda leaned to one side slightly in her chair then, and smiled, and audibly passed wind.

Oh, God.

It would probably be safe to say that the mobile library is not considered by many people in the know to be at the pinnacle of the library profession. At the pinnacle of the library profession you might have, say, the British Library, or the New York Public Library, or the Library of Congress, or of Alexandria. Then coming down from those Parnassian heights you have university libraries, and private research libraries, and then maybe the big public libraries, and then district and branch libraries, and school libraries, hospital libraries, libraries in prisons and long-term mental institutions. And then somewhere off the bottom of that scale, around about the level of fake red-leather-bound sets of the *Reader's Digest* in damp provincial hotels and dentists' waiting rooms is the mobile library.

The mobile library is to the library profession what, say, chiropody is to medicine, or indoor carpet bowls to professional sport.

'No,' repeated Israel.

'I have some Tayto cheese and onion, if you'd prefer?' said Linda Wei, who was busy licking her palms.

'No. I am not going to drive a mobile library,' said Israel.

'No, no, no!' said Linda, snapping back to attention. 'Ach. Of course not. Silly! We'll give you a driver for that. To show you the ropes. At least at first.'

'No thanks.' Israel got up to leave. 'I'm not going to be a mobile librarian.'

'Outreach Support Officer,' corrected Linda Wei.

'Sorry?'

'We don't call them mobile librarians any more. You'd be an Outreach Support Officer.'

'Oh.'

'We're hoping to offer people assistance with IT, and digital photography, surfing the net, family history, that sort of thing.'

'And books?'

'Books?'

'In the mobile library?'

'Oh, books,' said Linda dismissively, 'there'd be plenty of them as well of course, lots and lots of books. Everything, we're going to have.'

'In a mobile library?'

'We'll squeeze it all in, sure: it's just a question of storage. It's like with your kitchen corner cupboards: it's amazing what you can get in a small space. I'm just after having my kitchen done. Honestly, it's like the Tardis.'

'Right, well,' said Israel, making towards the door. 'That's all very interesting, and good luck to you, but I'm really not going to be an Outreach Support Officer on a mobile library, sorry.'

'Mobile learning centre!' corrected Linda.

'Right. Whatever it is you want to call it. I'm not going to be running a mobile library, thank you. I was employed to run a branch library. So, thanks and what have you. And, er.' There was no nice way of saying this. 'Goodbye.'

'No!' said Linda, as Israel was about to open the door. 'No. No you don't!'

Israel stopped.

'Good, now. Ahem. Don't go. Sit down. Come on. Come on! Sit!'

Israel, who was too tired to do otherwise, did as he was told.

'Good. Now. Now. I think if you check your' – Linda coughed, crisps caught in her throat – 'your contract, you will find that your role is to fulfil all the duties as required by the Department of Entertainment, Leisure and Community Services.'

She handed him a copy of his contract and tapped it with a Biro. The relevant passage had already been circled. Israel read it once. Then twice. He attempted to think of all the ways the words could be interpreted and reinterpreted. But the contract was tight. She was right.

'Well,' he said, 'I'm sorry, but I'm really not interested. I'm going to have to resign from the position before I've begun.'

'Ah. Ergh. Excuse me!' Linda took a quick swig of Coke and motioned for Israel to pat her on the back, which he did, leaning across the desk, and which seemed to do the trick. 'Ah, that's better,' she said. 'Sorry. Crisp.'

'Right.'

'What were you saying?'

'I'm not taking the job.'

'Well, you have, strictly speaking, already taken the job.'

'Yes. But I resign.'

'Ah. You can't.'

'I can.'

'You can't.'

'I can,' said Israel slowly. 'And I do. I am. Right now. I resign. Now. This minute.'

Filled with sudden overwhelming despair and rage and a desire to get out, and with no feasible or logical means of expressing his discontent in this small beige office, Israel snatched up Linda's Biro, and reached for his contract, on which he began to write the words, in capitals, 'I RES,' but before he got to the 'I' Linda had snatched the pen back from his hand.

'Thank. *You*.'

She stared at Israel.

He stared back.

Now he might have had a headache and he might have had a long journey, but you didn't argue with Israel Armstrong: he had an Irish father and a Jewish mother, and three sisters, and had therefore a long childhood of often heated debate and disputation behind him, plus another three years of rigorous training in the discipline of English and American Studies at one of the best former polytechnics turned universities in the country. His body was round but his mind was honed: he could carry his weight.

But nor did you argue with Linda Wei: she was a Northern Irish Chinese Catholic with a secure job at the council.

It was a stand-off.

'Now. Calm down,' said Linda, seizing the initiative. 'Let's not get carried away. I clearly can't accept your resignation myself, Mr Armstrong, in the here and now. There are all sorts of procedures.'

'Whatever. But I'm not doing the job. I'm just going to leave.'

'Well, obviously, if that's your decision ... But it would be *such* a shame. I don't know what I would tell everyone: they'll be *so* disappointed. People were *so* looking forward to meeting you and getting to know their new librarian.'

'I'm sure.'

'They'll be just devastated. When I think of them,' said Linda, with a slight pause, and leaning her head meditatively, staring into her almost empty tub of Pringles, 'all those old ladies not able to get out any books, and the wee childer unable to do their homework, their thirst and hunger for knowledge unquenched and unsatisfied, their longing for the green pastures of learning and Internet surfing denied and—'

'Yes, all right, I get the picture,' said Israel.

'Desperate, desperate altogether.'

'Yes, that's very sad, I agree, but—'

'And dear knows it could be months by the time we re-advertise and fill the post, by which time we may have had to reallocate resources once again, which might mean' – and here Linda took a longer pause, for dramatic effect, and another quick swig of Coke – 'there wouldn't be any library service at all.'

'None at all?'

'Nope. None. At all.' She made a little moue with her mouth, and popped in a crisp. 'Which would be desperate. For everyone, wouldn't it?' She picked up the tub of Pringles at this point, turned it upside down and picked at the last few crumbs in her upturned palm. 'No library. At all. And all,' she said, between munches. 'Because.'

Munch.

'Of.'

Munch.

'You.'

Israel had absolutely no intention of giving in to this woman's attempt at emotional blackmail, and he had half a mind to get back on the bus, and the train, and the ferry, and the coach, and then finally the Underground back home to lovely, leafy north London.

Except that ... well, except that, the thing was, Israel Armstrong hadn't actually worked *as a librarian* for some time now, not since the end of his short-term contract working in a little library at a City law firm, a job that his girlfriend Gloria, who was an actual lawyer, had managed to wangle for him.

Jobs for graduate librarians are not that easy to come by – a lot of people don't realise that – and Israel's career so far had been a little ... patchy.

Which Linda Wei, being in possession of his CV, must have known: she would certainly have known, for example, that Israel had graduated from Oxford Brookes

University with only a 2:2 in English and American Studies, a mark that did not reflect his abilities, according to his lecturers and his mother, and she would have known also that after six months on a graduate librarianship course he'd drifted from short-term contract to short-term contract and that in fact the longest he'd worked anywhere had been in a discount bookshop in the Lakeside Shopping Centre in Thurrock, off the M25, in Essex, not the kind of a job that a successful career librarian tends to take, or to stick at for any length of time, and that he'd been there for three years, two months and five days, until last Friday, in fact, when he'd grandly shaken hands with everyone in the shop, said goodbye, and gone home to pack to come to Tumdrum, off on his great Irish adventure.

So as she sat staring him down and psyching him out in her tatty beige office gobbling crisps and swigging Coke, Linda Wei, Deputy Head of Entertainment, Leisure and Community Services, may well have surmised that Israel needed this job.

She may well have surmised, indeed, that Israel Joseph Armstrong – a great-grandson of the rabbi of Brasov, in Romania, no less, whose children and grandchildren had survived pogroms and concentration camps and had gone on to make successful lives for themselves throughout the capital cities and great trade centres of Europe and in America, and in Turkey, and indeed in Israel itself, as doctors, and dentists, and chemists, and as Assistant, Associate, Tenure-Track and Full Professors in the Humanities and in the Sciences – that he – a scion also of the mighty Armstrong clan, a breed of hard-headed, big-handed farmers originally out of County Dublin and Dublin's fair city, but also these days to be found in New Haven, Connecticut, and Toronto, Canada, and London, England, and anywhere else where there's a phonebook and where people need tax consultants, and jobbing builders, and publicans, and journalists – that Israel – this proud, dextrous, determined, committed reader, and a beneficiary of all that a childhood in London could offer – was absolutely desperate.

And if she had surmised such, she was right.

Israel really needed this job. He needed it to get away from his mother, who never let him forget that he was a genius in waiting, if only he could just settle on the thing he was going to be a genius at: working for the UN, probably, after having retrained as a doctor or a lawyer, or both, and married an all-singing, all-dancing, fertile, home-cooking and just slightly less well-qualified doctor or lawyer willing to drop everything to follow him into troubled yet not actually dangerous UN-peacekeeping-type situations. He also needed the job to prove to his girlfriend Gloria that he wasn't just a scruffy, overweight slacker who was sponging off her in order to be able to continue to afford to buy expensive imported American hardback fiction. And he needed it to prove to his old dead dad that he was proud to be Irish, or at least half Irish, and even though Tumdrum, County Antrim, was a long way away from his dad's home town of Dublin, County Dublin ('So good they named it twice,' his dad used to joke), it was the same island, after all, and a homecoming of sorts. Above all, he needed this job to prove to himself that he wasn't going to have to spend the rest of his life behind the till, ringing up *Da Vinci Code*s and Schott's *Miscellanies* at a discount bookshop in the Lakeside Shopping Centre in Thurrock.

So Israel was resolved. There was no way he was staying.

'No,' he told Linda Wei. 'I'm sorry.'

'You wouldn't even consider giving it a go?'

'Nope.'

'Just a wee go?' asked Linda, making a face.

'No.'

'A little, little go?' she pleaded.

'No.'

'Not even for a couple of months or so, just to get things up and running?'

'No.'

'Six weeks?'

'No.'

'A month, and see how you like it?' She was virtually begging now. 'Go on.'

'No.'

'Oh, go on. Go on. Go on. A couple of weeks, till Christmas just?'

'No. No. No.'

'Reduced hours? Renegotiated salary?'

'No.'

'And we'll fly you home at the end of it?'

Well.

That was it, that was the fatal Cleopatra, that was the clincher for Israel, who at this point was not merely notionally desperate, not desperate merely in the medium and the long term, but desperate also in the here and now

– in the traditional sense of being cold and hungry and fed up and far from home and completely unable to face the prospect of getting back on the ferry for another eight hours and the ten-hour coach journey back to London. Linda was offering him a couple of weeks in Ireland, and then home, no disgrace, with money in his pocket, and he could at least put it on his CV, plump it up a bit, expand two weeks into two months or even two years, and start his job search over again. It was that, or back to the bargain bookshop with his tail between his legs.

'Oh, all right then,' he said, prodding his glasses grudgingly. 'But just a couple of weeks.'

This was how most of the big decisions in life got taken, in Israel's experience, and contrary to what he'd always been given to understand from his reading of the world's great literature: you needed to go to the toilet, or you were bored, or you were just tired from arguing and you couldn't think of anything else to do, and suddenly you found yourself married, or you'd signed the petition, or you'd volunteered for something you wouldn't normally consider doing even if you were paid for it, or you'd accepted a job driving a mobile library in a godforsaken corner of the north of the north of the island of Ireland.

'Oh, that's great! That's great!' exclaimed Linda, punching the air with her salty, chubby fists. 'I'm delighted, delighted, delighted. Wonderful!' She reached over her desk and shook his hand. 'It'll be like a holiday for you.'

Israel rubbed his hand on his trousers.

'Sure. And you'll be re-advertising the post?'

'Of course. Yes. Absolutely. Right away. I'm glad we've

sorted that out. We've your accommodation and everything all arranged for you.'

'Right.'

'You're going to love it! You're going to be staying with George up country. It's lovely! And if you just get yourself down to Ted he'll sort you out with the mobile library—'

'Ted?'

'Ted Carson. You'll love Ted! He's going to be showing you round. He has his own wee cab company there in town. You know, you're going to love it here, Mr Armstrong. I really think you're going to fit right in.'

3

He was not fitting right in. In fact, on the contrary. In fact, to be honest, to be absolutely, perfectly honest – and he wouldn't have wanted to have offended anyone by saying this, particularly his long-dead father, but still, the truth hurts and sometimes it's important to speak one's mind, if only to oneself and to the familiar dead, who can take it – to be absolutely frankly, *brutally* honest, Israel had taken an immediate, huge and intense dislike both to the people and to the place of Ireland in general, to Northern Ireland in particular, and to Tumdrum, County Antrim in very particular. And he was getting to dislike it more and more all the time.

Back at the council offices Linda Wei had got him to sign several forms on the dotted line, and had issued him with papers and instructions as to his exact role and responsibilities, and details of bank accounts had been confirmed, and then it had taken him an hour – a whole hour – to find Ted's Cabs following Linda's directions, wandering up and down the endless grey-black streets of Tumdrum, which meant that in total he'd been on his vast trek now from London to here for nearly two days – *two whole days* – and when he finally made it to the so-called offices of Ted's Cabs, it turned out to be nothing more than a large shiplap and corrugated-iron shed on a patch of weedy waste ground next to a barbed-wired electricity sub-station on the edge of Tumdrum. There was a red neon sign attached to the roof of the shed, flashing TED'S CABS into the cold Northern Irish sky, and as he got closer Israel could see a faded motto painted on hardboard in a wobbly hand which hung on chains down and across the front of the shed, and which was banging forcefully in the high winter winds: IF YOU WANT TO GET THERE, announced the flapping sign, CALL THE BEAR.

He could feel another of his headaches coming on. He could have done with a chunky KitKat.

He swallowed his absolutely last Nurofen and stepped up to the shed, to a window that had an orange number-plate with the word TAXIS spelt out on it and a large arrow pointing down, and he tapped on the glass – which wasn't glass, in fact, but a thick, scarred plastic, and which slid back instantly, which made Israel gasp, not something he was much given to do; his life up until now had never given him much cause for gasping, which was pretty much how he liked it, and he nearly choked on his headache tablet.

The opening revealed a metal grille, and a man sitting up close to the window, his huge meaty face filling the space.

'Aye?' said the man, not looking at Israel.

'Hello,' said Israel, as cheerily as possibly, after his near death by Nurofen. 'I'm looking for Ted Carson.'

'Aye?' said the man again. He was busy watching a television mounted high on a wall bracket in the opposite corner of the shed.

'My name's Israel Armstrong. I'm the new librarian. Linda Wei up at the council offices said I could call in here and Ted would be able to—'

'Aye. Well,' said the man inside, turning an eye from the TV for a moment and looking at Israel. 'It's you, is it?'

'Yes—' began Israel.

The man got up from his seat and gestured for Israel to move over to the door of the shed, which Israel dutifully did, and there was the sound of the sliding of bolts and the unlocking of locks and then the door opened and the man beckoned Israel inside.

'Come on!' he commanded. 'If you're coming.' Israel stepped inside and the man locked the door behind him. 'You can't be too careful these days.'

'No. Quite,' said Israel, putting down his old brown case, turning down the hood on his duffle coat, and taking off his glasses to wipe the mist and condensation from them.

'Blinkin' head-bangers, they'd have the paint off the walls.'

Israel glanced around, but there didn't actually seem to be that much in the shed for blinkin' head-bangers to steal: a table, the chair, a Calor Gas heater, and the TV. There was no paint on the walls.

'We've been burnt out twice,' said the man.

'Oh dear,' said Israel. 'That's terrible.'

'You're right,' said Ted, looking Israel up and down, sceptically. 'So, they got one in the end, then.'

'Sorry?'

'A librarian. You're supposed to be the new librarian?'

'I *am* the new librarian,' said Israel, with some force and certainty, although to be honest he was no longer entirely convinced himself. He no longer felt much like a librarian: he felt more like someone having reached the edge of the world and himself, a bit like Scott on his last expedition to the Antarctic, perhaps, or Robinson Crusoe on his desert island.

As the man stared at Israel, sizing him up, so Israel did his weary best to stare back.

The man saw Israel – the duffle coat, the glasses, the case, the podge, the suit, the messy mop of hair – and Israel saw a man in hearty good health, maybe early sixties, with a shaven head and wearing so many different layers of clothing that it was difficult to tell where his natural thick-settedness ended and mere padding began. His bulk and his distinctly lived-in, or rather, punched-in appearance – he looked as though someone had at some time secured his fat head in a vice and hit him hard with a flat-iron – suggested that he wouldn't stand any nonsense. You wouldn't mind him driving your cab, but you wouldn't want to have to argue over the fare. Israel strongly suspected tattoos.

'You were supposed to be here earlier,' said the man.

'Yes. Sorry. I got held up.'

'Aye. Right. But you're here now and you're wanting the van and dropped off?'

'Er. Yes,' said Israel. 'Linda Wei said someone here would be so kind as to—'

'Aye. Linda …'

'Is that OK?'

'Well,' said the man, turning away and beginning to flick delicately through a large black ledger on the desk by the grille. 'I suppose it'd better be.'

'Right. Erm. Well, if not, I'm sure I can always find someone else to take me.'

'Aye.' The man laughed – just once. 'You could try. And you might know different, but to my knowledge I'm the only minicab company between here and Rathkeltair.'

'Uh-huh,' said Israel, suitably chastened. 'So you're actually Ted Carson himself?'

'That I am.'

'Pleased to meet you,' said Israel, extending his hand.

'Aye,' said Ted, shaking Israel's hand absentmindedly, and almost crushing it, and continuing to examine the ledger. 'Fortunately for you, as it happens I do have a car and a driver free.'

'Good.' Israel waved his hand to restore his circulation; it was a hell of a handshake. 'Good. Is it … Er. The mobile library. And where I'm staying. Are they – is it – far?'

'Within an ass's roar,' said Ted, 'and at the back of God speed.'

'Right,' said Israel.

Oh, God.

The driver that Ted had free was in fact Ted himself, and the car was an old Austin Allegro with a large illuminated orange plastic bear stuck on the roof – 'Ted, bear, d'you see?' said Ted. 'It's advertising,' and 'Yes,' said Israel, trying to sound enthusiastic, 'very good' – and Ted drove Israel far out of Tumdrum, out along the coast, along narrow country roads between high hawthorn hedges, with grey and white farms dotting the landscape, and hills and mountains looming, and the sea shimmering in the distance, but Israel was too tired and too fed up to be bothered about the view.

'Mind if I smoke?' said Ted.

'Not at all,' said Israel, although he did mind actually, but he couldn't say he did because he was a liberal and so instead he just slumped further down in his seat, huddled in his duffle coat and his corduroy trousers, looking at all the green and the grey outside, and feeling profoundly sorry for himself. Ted turned the heating up to full. The car felt like a pressure cooker.

'You know you've come on one of the busiest days of the year?' said Ted.

'Really? I'm sorry,' said Israel.

'No one's blaming you. First Friday in December. Beginning of the auld Christmas season. Bunged, the whole place.' There didn't seem to be that much traffic on the roads.

'Of course. Sorry. I forgot.'

'Forgot Christmas?'

'I'm Jewish,' mumbled Israel in mitigation. 'And a lot on my mind. You know, packing up, moving over here.'

'Oh,' said Ted, giving Israel a sidelong glance. 'Muhammad Ali, he was a Muslim, you know.'

'Erm ...'

'Ted Kid Lewis: he was Jewish. Ruby Goldstein. Probably before your time.'

'Erm ...'

'Welterweights,' said Ted, adding, 'Birth of Our Saviour and all that, Christmas.'

'Yes.'

'So the young ones are all out getting bladdered.'

'Yes,' agreed Israel, who could feel things beginning to rise within his gullet. 'I wonder. Erm. Would it be OK to have a window open?'

'Aye,' said Ted, winding down his window. 'No problem.'

'It's Hanukkah too,' said Israel vaguely, momentarily revived by the breeze.

'Bless you,' said Ted, turning off the main road onto a narrow road and then onto a rutted lane and pulling up outside an old corrugated-iron barn. 'Here we are now.'

'What?'

'The van.'

'Where?'

'Here.'

Here was a ploughed field, with far views off to dark green mountains one way and the dark grey sea the other, and the old metal barn set in mud and concrete between them. Ted parked, got out of the car, fiddled with some padlocks on a door, and ushered Israel inside.

'There she is,' said Ted, pointing to a massive dark shape in the centre of the dark shed. 'That's my girl.'

It was a large bus-shaped girl.

Ted stepped closer to the big bulky mass and Israel followed and tentatively held out his hand, brushing the dark, heavy, patchy fabric, which felt like a giant damp towel left on a single radiator for many years.

'This is the mobile library?' asked Israel.

'Aye.'

'This?'

'Aye.'

'Right,' said Israel. 'What's with the ... sheet?'

'The tarp?' Ted touched the tarpaulin and sniffed his fingers. Israel imitated, trying to pick up the scent.

'What's that sm— '

'Chickens,' said Ted.

'Ah!' said Israel, wiping his hands on his trousers. 'That's disgusting.'

'Well, we couldn't have let her just stood.'

'Ugh!' said Israel, still wiping his hands. 'How long's she been here?'

'Long enough,' said Ted, gazing round.

Israel looked around too. A barn more in the middle of the middle of nowhere and dirtier and damper and dustier Israel could not have imagined: the cobwebs had cobwebs; the dust had dust; and the dirt was so dirty you'd have had to clean the dirt off it first to get at it.

'The mobile library's been kept in this ... place?'

'Nowhere else for her. We had to keep her safe, when they stopped the service a few years back. The council wanted to sell her as scrap,' said Ted, screwing up his face in disgust, which was effective: he had a face that was more than capable of expressing disgust; his broken nose was pre-wrinkled. 'They were after breaking her up and selling her off.'

'I see.'

'Same as they did with me.'

'Right.'

'I drove her nearly twenty-five years, man and boy. And then they did away with the pair of us.'

'I'm sorry.'

'Ach, sure but, you knock your pan in for half a lifetime, that's what you get. They're a bunch of hoods, the lot of them.'

'Hoods?'

'Aye.'

'Right. But the council didn't break her up and sell her for scrap?'

'No. Because we hid her.'

'You hid her?'

'Aye.'

'You hid her from the hoods?'

'Aye. Exactly. We had to tuck her away, like. So they couldn't find her,' said Ted, who was now circling the tarpaulined shape, sizing it up, like a sculptor before a block of stone, or a wrestler eyeing up a worthy opponent.

Israel was struggling to keep up with all this.

'So – hang on – you hid a whole mobile library?'

'Aye.'

'In here?'

'Aye.'

'Like Anne Frank?'

'Well, I don't know about that.'

'But hidden.'

'Aye. You're the first man to be seeing her, actually, apart from myself, for nigh on three years.'

'Was that not illegal though?'

'What?

'Well, when you say you *hid* her ....'

'Hmm?'

'Is that not the same as stealing her?'

'Ach, no. Not at all. Stealing's wrong. Yous must have that in your religion, don't you?'

'Yes. Of course we have that in my religion—' began Israel.

'We were looking after her, just, that's all. She was on loan, if you like.'

'And now you've decided to give her back?'

'No. No. We're not giving her back.'

'But ... This is the mobile library we're going to be using?'

'Aye. But we're not giving her back. We've sold her back.'

'You've sold the council back their own mobile library?'

'That's right.'

'That's unbelievable.'

'It's practical.'

'God,' said Israel, trying to take it all in. 'It's quite a vindication, I suppose, for you.'

'Vintication?' Ted glowered. 'It'd take more than that for a vintication.'

'Right. So you and who sold her back?'

'A few of us.' Ted tapped his nose. 'Those of us with the interests of the wider community at heart.'

Israel knew when not to ask any further questions, and anyway some small chick feather seemed to have lodged itself in the back of his throat; he began coughing and coughing, breathing in more dust and the stench of bird and chicken shit.

'Ah.'

Ted slapped him hard on the back.

'Eerrgh. Thanks,' said Israel. 'Couldn't you have kept it, you know, somewhere a bit more hygienic?'

'There wasn't anywhere else. Here we go,' said Ted, unbolting the big double doors at the far end of the chicken shed and heaving them open. Light and fresh air streamed in. 'Freshen her up.' Ted's shaven head shone like a beacon in the winter's light.

'Where are we exactly?'

'Where? We're here.'

'Yes, but where is here exactly?'

'Well, that'd be Ballycastle across Cushleake there. What's that? North-west?' Ted pointed off into the cloudless distance. 'Then round westerly you've got yer Giant's Causeway, and Bushmills and—'

'I see,' interrupted Israel, who was still none the wiser, his grasp of Northern Irish geography being almost entirely limited to memories of the little black dot showing Belfast on the BBC news during his childhood.

He wiped his glasses on his shirt and turned back to look at the tarp – a vast, damp, mouldy sack, pocked with black and white stains. Ted was walking round and round, huffing and puffing, loosening ropes.

'I used to do all the work on her myself. She wasn't in bad shape, so she wasn't.'

'I'm sure.'

'But the tarp, you know.'

'What?'

'Not good, tarps. Moisture. Rust if you do, rust if you don't.'

'A bit like life really then,' said Israel feebly.

Ted ignored this comment. 'You helping, then, or your hands painted on?'

Israel started fiddling with the ropes. 'These are tight knots. I'm not sure if I can— '

'Quit your gurnin' and get on with it,' advised Ted.

So Israel did.

'Now. Pull,' commanded Ted eventually, and he started pulling, and Israel started pulling, and 'Pull!' commanded Ted again, and Israel did again, and 'You're as weak as water,' shouted Ted, and 'Pull!' again and suddenly the whole big damp dirty tarpaulin came off in a storm of dust and bird and chicken shit, right on top of Israel, who lost his balance and fell back onto the filthy dust and bird- and chicken-shit floor.

'Aaggh!'

'What?' said Ted. There was a muffled sound from under the tarpaulin. 'You there, you big galoot?' More muffled sounds. Ted lifted up the heavy tarpaulin and helped Israel out and onto his feet: he was covered, head to foot, in grey dust and black and white and bright green bird and chicken shit.

'Aaggh,' said Israel.

'There she is,' said Ted.

'Aaggh,' said Israel, rubbing his eyes.

The van came into focus. He could just make out what looked like the remains of a bus in a faded, rusting cream and red livery: there were rust patches as big as your fist, and what looked like mushrooms growing around the windscreen.

Ted was down on his knees, examining the wheel arches and the paintwork.

'Aye,' he said to himself, lost in rapture. 'Aye, aye.' Having eventually circled the bus and patted it fondly, as though calming a beast, he stood back. 'Well?'

'Well,' agreed Israel.

'Well?' said Ted. 'What do you think?'

'Erm. It looks like a bit like a ... bus,' said Israel. 'Except without windows.'

'You're not wrong, Sherlock Holmes,' said Ted. 'It's a Bedford. Built on a VAM bus chassis. Beautiful, isn't she?'

'Beautiful' was not quite the word that Israel had in mind: the words he had in mind were more like 'write-off', 'wreck', 'filthy dirty', 'yuck', and 'I want to get out of here and go home.'

'You are joking me, are you?' he said.

'Joking?' said Ted.

'This is not the mobile library,' said Israel.

'That she is.'

'But we can't possibly drive that ... thing. It's a wreck.'

'Lick of paint, be as good as new,' said Ted.

Israel put his hand into a rust hole.

'Come on,' he said.

'And a bit of bodywork,' admitted Ted.

And then there was the soft sound of something heavy and metal falling onto the ground and Ted got down on his hands and knees and looked underneath the vehicle.

'And some spot-welding,' he admitted. 'But she's no jum.'

'I see,' said Israel, who had absolutely no idea what a jum was. He was up on tiptoe trying to peer into the bus's dark interior.

Ted produced some keys from his pocket and weighed them heavily in his hand, as if they were precious jewels. He then placed them ceremonially in Israel's hands.

'Over to you, then,' said Ted.

'No, really,' said Israel.

'She's all yours,' said Ted.

'No. I—'

'Take. The keys,' said Ted insistently.

'Right,' said Israel.

'So,' said Ted.

'Well,' said Israel, hesitating and trying to think of something appropriately moving to say. He couldn't. 'It's an—'

'Get on with it.'

'Right.'

He went to open the door on the driver's side of the mobile library, but there was no door on the driver's side.

'Oh,' said Israel.

'Other side,' said Ted.

Israel went round to the right side and placed the key in the lock, turned, and nothing happened. He looked helplessly at Ted.

'Jiggle her,' said Ted.

Israel jiggled as best he could, but he was getting nowhere. He let Ted have a jiggle. That was no good either.

'Ach,' said Ted, examining the keys. 'Rust.'

'Oh well. Another time maybe.'

'Not at all,' said Ted, pointing up at the top of the van. 'Skylight.'

'What about it?'

'Way in,' said Ted. 'Catches wore away years ago. Should have got them fixed. Lucky I didn't. Come on.' He bent down slightly and clasped his hands together ready for Israel to climb up.

'Hang on now,' said Israel. 'Wait a minute. You want me to—'

'Come on,' said Ted, 'none of your old nonsense now,' and nodded to him to put his foot on his hands.

Israel hesitated. 'This is ridiculous.'

'Set yourself to it. Come on. Quickly. We're not on holiday, are we?'

'No.'

'So then. Come on, you big glunter.'

So against his better judgement – and partly because no one had ever called him a big glunter before – Israel did what he was told and placed a foot on Ted's big joint-of-meat hands and Ted grunted and puffed and straightened up and Israel scrambled for handholds and footholds up the side of the van, and by grappling and struggling he made it up onto the roof of the van, where there was only a few feet clearance from the roof of the barn, and he knelt down, puffing and scraping dust and rust and chicken shit out of the way.

'Eerrgh.'

'Good man you are!' shouted Ted. 'Go on then!'

'All right. Give me a minute,' said Israel, catching his breath and crawling on his belly towards the skylight. 'It's filthy!'

'Get on with it.'

'But—'

'Just pop it.'

'What?'

'The skylight. Pop it.'

Israel had a hold of the skylight and was wiggling and wobbling the Perspex from side to side.

'Got it?'

'Not yet.'

'Pop it!' shouted Ted, like a boxer's corner man.

'I can't pop it!'

'Go on!'

'I am going on!'

'Put some effort in.'

'I am putting some effort in. It's stuck.'

'Are you sure?'

'Yes!'

'Might be rusty,' granted Ted.

'Might be? It's all rust.'

'Just yank her then,' said Ted.

Israel got a hold of the two sides of the skylight and braced himself, half kneeling and half standing, and put all his weight into pulling up and back and he took a deep breath and then he pulled up and back, and the skylight gave a sound of cracking, and the ancient Perspex came away in his hands.

And Israel straightened upwards and backwards ... smashing the back of his head on the roof of the barn.

'Aaggh!' he screamed.

'You done it?' said Ted.

'Aaggh!'

'What?' said Ted.

'Aggghh!'

'What's the matter?'

'Aaggh, shit!'

'Will you mind your bloody language!' shouted Ted.

'Aaggh!' shouted Israel back. 'I nearly brained myself.'

'Aye. Knock some sense into you.'

'Ow,' said Israel, rubbing his head. 'I'm injured. My head.'

'Only part of you safe from injury.'

'I'm in agony here!'

'Aye, but you've not lost the powers of speech.'

'It hurts.'

'All right. You got a bump. Now just get on with it.'

'Get on with what?'

'What do you think? Your eyes in your arse or what?'

'What?'

'Climb in, you fool.'

'What do you mean climb in? There's no ladder.'

'Of course there's no ladder. Jump!' said Ted.

'I'm not jumping in there,' said Israel. 'It's dark.'

'Of course it's bloody dark. Just jump,' said Ted. 'What's wrong with ye, boy? Just mind your bap, eh.'

'My bap?'

'Your head, you eejit.'

'It's quite a drop,' said Israel, peering down into the dark interior of the van.

'Get on with it now,' said Ted. 'Christmas is coming, and it'll be here before we are if you keep carrying on.'

'I don't like the look of it.'

'Well, you're not going to like the look of it when I come up there and throw you down. Now, jump.'

'I don't know if I'll fit.'

'Of course you'll fit. What do you want us to do, grease

you like a pig? Get in there and stop your yabbering, will ye. Come on.'

'Ah, God. All right,' said Israel. 'But I'm blaming you if I get hurt.'

'Fine. Just jump.'

'My head hurts.'

'It'll hurt even more if you don't shut up and get on with it,' said Ted reasonably. *'Jump!'*

And lowering himself over the gap, supporting himself by his arms, Israel did.

And 'Aaah!' he cried, as he landed awkwardly on his ankle inside the mobile library.

'Ach, God alive, Laurence Olivier, that's enough of your dramatics now,' said Ted. 'Open the door.'

'I've hurt myself,' called Israel from inside the van.

'Ah'm sure,' said Ted. 'But come and open the door first.'

'I've hurt my ankle,' shouted Israel. 'I don't think I can walk.'

'Well, crawl.'

'I think I might have broken it!'

'If you've broken your ankle then I'm the Virgin Mary,' said Ted.

Israel stood up. 'I can't walk!' he cried.

'I tell you, if you was a horse I'd shoot you. Now stop your blethering and open this door before I lose the head and batter the thing in on top of you.'

Israel hopped down the bus and, after some fiddling with catches and locks, managed to open up the side door.

Ted entered.

'Ah,' he said. 'At last. Smell that.' It was not the smell

of a library – books, sweat, frustrated desire, cheap but hard-wearing carpets. It was more the smell of a back-alley garage – the smell of warm corroding metal and oil. 'That's beautiful, sure,' said Ted, sweeping his arm in an expansive, welcoming kind of gesture. 'Welcome home.'

Maybe in her day the mobile library had been beautiful: maybe in her day she'd have been like home. These days, however, she was no longer a vehicle any sane person could possibly be proud of, unless you were Ted, or a dedicated mobile library fancier, or a scrap-metal merchant, and she wouldn't have been a home unless you were someone with absolutely no alternative living arrangements; also, crucially, and possibly fatally for a mobile library, there were no shelves.

'There are no shelves,' said Israel, astonished, still rubbing his head, and staring at the bare grey metal walls inside the van.

'No.'

'None at all.'

'Aye,' agreed Ted.

'Well, I don't want to sound all nit-picky, but shelves are pretty much essential for a library.'

'True.'

'Essential.'

'You could stack books on the floor,' said Ted.

'Yes. We *could*. But generally, we librarians prefer shelves. It's, you know, neater.'

'All right. Don't be getting smart with me now.'

'Right. Sorry. But there are no shelves. And no books, as far as I can see. So … the books?'

'The books?'

'The library books?'

'Ach, the books are fine, sure. You don't want to worry about the books. They'll be in the library.'

'This is the library.'

'Not this library. The old library.'

'The one that's shut?'

'Yes.'

'You're sure the books are there?'

'Of course I'm sure. There's been books there since before Adam was a baby.'

'Really.'

'We'll take a wee skite over later on, sure.'

'A what?'

'A skite. And we'll get Dennis or someone to knock us up some shelves.'

'Who's Dennis?'

'He's a plumber.'

'Right.' Then Israel thought twice. 'What?'

'He's a joiner. What do you think he is, if he builds shelves? I mean, in the name of God, man, catch yerself on. I'll give him a call later. So, do you want to try her?'

'Sorry?'

'Try her? Start her? For flip's sake, d'they not speak any English where you come from?'

'Yes. Of course they speak English. I am English!'

'Ah'm sure. And you can drive, can you? Or do they not teach you that over there on the mainland either?'

'Of course I can drive,' said Israel, grabbing the keys from Ted's hands.

Israel *could* drive - sort of. He had a licence. He'd passed his test. But he was a rubbish driver. And he was tired and he had a headache and what he really needed now was a lie down in a darkened room, preferably at home in lovely north London, rather than attempting to drive a clapped-out old mobile library under the scrutiny of a half-mad miserable minicab driver in the middle of the middle of nowhere. Nonetheless, he wasn't going to lose face, so he climbed into the thinly padded driver's seat, the foam coming out of the leather-effect PVC, put the key in the ignition, turned the key and ...

Nothing.

Thank goodness.

'Oh well,' he said, 'we can always come back—'

Ted's heavy hand fell on his shoulder.

'It'll only be the battery,' said Ted. 'I'll take a look.'

It was the battery. And the alternator. And the air filter. And the fuel filter. And a lot of other things Israel had only ever heard rumour of – the gasket, the plug circuit, wiring looms, cylinder barrels. Ted spent a long time examining the engine.

'No. We'll have to get her into the workshop to get the guts of it done,' he concluded.

'Oh dear,' said Israel. 'That is a shame.'

'Aye,' said Ted. 'Offside coil spring,' he continued, to himself. 'Brake drums.'

'Right,' said Israel, as if he had any idea what Ted was talking about, which he didn't. 'My foot's fine, by the way, thanks for asking. And my head.'

'Aye.'

'You've not got any headache tablets, have you?'

'What for?'

'For my headache?'

'Ach.'

'That's a no, is it?'

Ted locked up the shed and walked back to the car. Israel walked back with him.

'You're wanting a lift then?' said Ted.

'Er. Yes.' Israel looked around him at the middle of the middle of nowhere: mountains; the sea; hedges; the barn. 'Yes. That would be nice. I've been on the road now for...' Israel checked his watch.

'Aye. Well. I've a couple of fares I need to pick up first.'

'Right.'

'I've to pick up George at the Strand, at the pork dinner.'

'Right. I see.' Israel had really had enough for one day. 'And what's a pork dinner, just ... out of interest?'

'The *pork* dinner,' said Ted. 'The Pork Producers' Annual Dinner. At the Strand. Same every year. First Friday in December.'

Oh, God.

4

It was dark now as they drove and Ted was offering a running commentary and pointing out interesting landmarks all along the way, although it was too dark for Israel actually to be able to see any of the landmarks, and anyway most of them were carpet factories, and canning factories, or buildings that no longer existed. Eventually, Ted pulled off the road and up onto yet another rutted lane, which led to the hotel, the Strand, which had clearly seen better days – even in the dark you could tell it could have done with a paint-job and some re-rendering, and maybe some work on the subsidence round where it stood on the cliff overlooking the sea.

As they drew up outside the hotel Israel could see through the vast, brightly lit ground-floor windows groups of men in dinner jackets and women in evening dresses talking, and smoking, and laughing, and clutching each other and glasses of champagne and barbecued spare ribs, and just for a moment he thought he could have been back in London: the romance of it, the people, the comfort, the warmth. He could almost smell the perfume without opening the windows.

'Only be a minute,' said Ted, once he'd parked the car. 'Just go and round them up.'

'Fine,' said Israel, happy to sit dozing in the passenger seat, glad that the longest and worst day of his life was finally coming to an end.

A man and woman approached the car and got into the back seat, laughing and joking. They didn't notice the heap of sleeping Israel in the front, and Israel, dozing, didn't notice them.

What woke him up was the sound of the kissing. It took him a minute to remember where he was: sitting in the front of a cab in the middle of nowhere waiting for Ted Carson to return, feeling sick, while a man and a woman on the back seat seemed to be getting to know each other as more than just good friends.

Oh, God.

There was a smell of alcohol and cigarettes and hot barbecued meats coming from the back seat, and that distinctive smell of passion; that pulse; that vibration; that disturbing hint of civet. Israel half opened his eyes, determined not to look round, and sank down lower and lower in his seat queasily, trying to remain as quiet as possible, hoping for some kind of cooling-off or reprieve, but the couple behind him were oblivious and activities were proceeding apace, and he realised if he didn't act now things could only get messier, and worse.

'Evening,' he said, in a slightly squeaky voice, in a

convenient pause, turning round as he spoke and trying to smile.

Everything happened at once. The woman screamed and reached for the door handle, the man let out a roar and reached forward with a punch that caught Israel on the side of the head, knocking off his glasses and knocking him against the passenger-seat window, and then Ted appeared, opening the driver's door.

'Ach, there you all are now. Thought I'd lost you. You've met Israel then?'

Israel was slumped against the passenger door, holding his head.

'Aaggh.'

'Israel?' said Ted. 'Are you all right?'

'Aaggh.'

'What have you been up to?' Ted clambered into his seat. 'Can I not leave you for one minute without you getting into trouble? What's wrong?'

'He hit me,' mumbled Israel.

'He's the new librarian,' explained Ted, turning round to the man and woman on the back seat.

'I don't care if he's the fuckin' Pope, Ted,' said the man. 'He gave us the fright of our lives.'

'Oh dear,' said Ted, starting up the engine and reversing out of the parking space. 'Oh dear, oh dear, oh dear. Not a good start is it?' He turned to Israel as he changed into first, and headed back down the dark lane.

'Uggh,' Israel continued moaning.

'All right, all right,' said Ted. 'Now tell me: how many fingers am I holding up? Come on. Eh? Hey? Come on!' He was holding up two fingers in the dark.

'Two,' said Israel.

'Good man,' said Ted. 'Must be a bruise just. No harm done. We'll find you a red flannel when you get back to George's. Now catch a hold of yourselves, lads, shake hands and let's forget all about it, eh?'

The man in the back seat leant forward to shake Israel's hand.

'Shake!' Ted instructed Israel, and Israel reached a cold hand round, without turning.

'There we are,' said Ted. 'Now let's settle down.' And they drove at high speed for what seemed a long time in complete and utter silence.

They skirted the coast, Israel staring with his one good eye out into the far, dark double-blackness of the sea, wishing he was anywhere else but here – even back at the discount bookshop at the Lakeside Shopping Centre in Thurrock in Essex, which wasn't a bad little job when you thought about it – and eventually Ted pulled up outside a house on what appeared to be a half-completed housing development perched on the edge of the main road and overlooking the sea. Some of the houses had roofs; some had windows; some had roofs and windows; all of them had identical bright white PVC front doors. Against the backdrop of the dark black sea the development looked like a shiny plastic clearing in the jungle.

The man in the back gave the woman a quick kiss and a squeeze of the hand, and then climbed out of the car, and Israel reluctantly unbuckled his seat belt and went to get out of the car himself.

'Where d'you think you're going?' said Ted.

'I thought I was staying with George,' said Israel.

'You are staying with George, you eejit.'

'But …'

'That's Tony, sure,' said Ted, nodding towards the retreating figure of the man, as if everyone in the western world knew Tony.

'Tony Shaw?'

'Ach, what? No. Tony Thompson.'

'Right.'

'I'm George,' said the woman from the back seat.

'Right. I'm sorry,' said Israel. 'I assumed … ' His words faded as Ted started up the car again.

Ted was silent. George was silent. Israel was silent. Everything was silence. And they drove again for what seemed a long time and eventually pulled onto a dirt track, and up a lane, past some big dark looming metal gates and some big dark looming farm machinery, and into a farmyard.

George got out of the car, and so did Israel, with his headache, and he went to get his old suitcase from the boot and then he tapped on Ted's window to say thanks.

'Hold on,' shouted Ted, having wound down his window as Israel started walking away, calling him back to the car. 'Hey! Buck Alec!'

'Me?' said Israel.

'Yes, you,' said Ted. 'Muhammad Ali. Of course you. Here. Come here.'

Israel trudged back to the car then, assuming he'd lost something, or left something behind.

'That's twenty-five pounds,' said Ted, leaning out of the window.

'What?'

'Twenty-five of your English pounds, sir. For the taxi. What, blow to the head affect your memory?'

'But,' said Israel, 'I thought, you know, what's-her-name at the council had arranged it?'

'Linda?'

'That's it.'

'Aye, she arranged for me to take you to the van, but. This is a private arrangement, between us.'

'I'm sure Linda'll square it with you.'

'Aye. Well, you may be, but I've had enough dealings with Linda Wei and the so-called council to know better. Expect nothin' off a pig but a grunt.'

'What?'

'I'll have my money now, thank you.'

'Well, I'll ...' began Israel. 'I'll have to owe you then, I'm afraid. Can we sort it out tomorrow?'

'No, no,' laughed Ted. 'Don't you be getting cute with me.' He extended a huge open hand out of the window into the cold night air: he really had tremendous fists. 'I'm not as green as I'm cabbage-lookin'. Let's see the colour of your money, and I'll be on my way. They'll be paying you good wages at the council, unless I'm mistaken. You're not working for free, are ye?'

'No.'

'Aye, well, you want to watch 'em and make sure you're not.'

'OK.'

'So, the money?'

Israel dug into his suit and duffle coat pockets and handed over all his remaining cash: £22.76. Now he was skint.

'That'll do rightly,' said Ted, counting the money, before starting up his engine and heading out of the farmyard.

'Arsehole,' shouted Israel, in a last-minute mustering of rage and defiance as the car pulled off.

The car stopped immediately and started to reverse. Israel froze. Ted reversed neatly alongside Israel's craven, apologetic form. His window was wound down.

'Come again?'

'What?'

'Did you just say something?'

'Me? No, no.'

'I thought I heard you say something.'

'No.'

'You sure?'

'Yes.'

'Well, you forgot these,' said Ted, going to hand Israel his glasses out of the window.

'Right, thanks,' said Israel, relieved he wasn't going to be bundled into the boot of the car and his body dumped in a river. 'Great. Cheers.'

And as he leant down towards the window to take the glasses Ted grabbed him by the toggles on his duffle coat and pulled him close up to him.

'If you don't want your other eye to match the one you've got, you want to watch your mouth, eh.'

'Yes,' gasped Israel.

'I don't like auld dirty talk.'

'Right. Sorry.'

'This is a Christian country.'

'Right.'

'And you'd do well to remember that.'

'Right.'

And he let Israel go. 'There you are,' he said, handing him his glasses.

'Thanks,' mumbled Israel.

'See you tomorrow morning!' called Ted cheerily as he pulled off in the car, orange plastic bear illuminated. 'Nine o'clock. At the library.'

'Right,' said Israel. 'Great.'

The farmyard was deserted and dark.

George had disappeared.

And Israel's eye was swelling like a marrow in shit, and he stepped forward with his case and trod in something soft. He bent over to sniff it.

Oh, God.

It made no difference. He no longer cared.

And then he saw a light go on in a window on the dark far side of the farmyard, and he slipped and slid his way over.

A stable door opened into a whitewashed room and George was in there, wearing wellies, her high heels in one hand, a frozen choc-ice in the other; she held out the choc-ice towards Israel as he entered.

'No, thanks,' said Israel. 'I couldn't—'

'It's for your eye, you idiot. It's all we have.'

'Right. Thanks,' said Israel, pressing the choc-ice up to his face. 'Aaggh.'

'You bring the yard in with you?' said George, pointing at Israel's manured shoes and trousers.

'Yes. Sorry.'

George tutted and then went to leave the room.

'Look,' said Israel to her retreating self. 'I'm sorry we

got off to a bad start. I mean, I'm from London. I've met lots of people with funny names – not that George is a funny name, of course. I mean, for a woman, it's—'

'It's late, Mr Armstrong.'

'Call me Ishmael – no – Israel,' he said, correcting himself.

She looked at him then with pity and stepped momentarily closer towards the light and Israel enjoyed his first proper one-eyed look at her. She was red-haired and bare-shouldered in her velvet evening dress, a dark green shawl slung over to keep her warm.

'I'll stick with Armstrong, thank you,' she said. 'This is you, then.'

'This is where I'm staying?'

'That's correct,' she said crisply. 'Goodnight.' And with that she shut the door, and was gone.

Israel stood and looked around him. At last he was home. His new start in Ireland. He sniffed. He thought he could smell something funny: fungus; straw; long-standing neglect; fresh paint; damp; and – what was that? He sniffed again.

It was chicken shit.

5

Israel had never before been woken by the sound of a cock. And certainly not by the sound of a cock in the same room, perched like the Owl of Minerva on the end of his bed.

His eye hurt. His head hurt. His back hurt. It'd be easier in fact to say what didn't hurt: his toes, they seemed fine, but that was because they were so cold he couldn't even feel his toes. He was just assuming his toes were fine. His nose, also. He felt for his nose – it was fine. But where were his glasses? He needed his glasses.

He was feeling around frantically for his glasses when the cock crowed again and started strutting boldly up the bed towards him. Any chickens he'd ever met before had tended to be already either safely roasted with their cavities loosely stuffed and their juices running clear, or well boiled in soups with carrot and onions, so this living, breathing, full-throated, fully feathered chicken was something of a shock to his already shell-shocked system.

It looked bigger than the chickens he was familiar with: you certainly couldn't have fitted it comfortably into the average-sized roasting tin or casserole. Maybe it was the feathers that did it.

He tried shooing the fat clucking chicken by flapping his hands, but it wasn't until he wobbled his tired, cold, beaten body up out of bed and turned nasty, throwing stuff from his suitcase – books, mostly, including his hardback *Brick Lane*, which he'd lugged around for years, trying to wade through – that he managed to chase the damned thing to the door and escort it outside. In the end it was his paperback edition of *The Curious Incident of the Dog in the Night-time* that did the trick. He knew that'd come in useful one day.

Outside it was drizzling rain and whipping winds again, and there were lights on in some of the outbuildings around the farmyard, and the sound of unoiled machinery, and thrumping motors, and animal noises, and Israel peered at his watch and it was six o'clock in the morning: 6 a.m.

Oh, bloody hell.

Israel had never exactly been renowned as an early riser – it was always Gloria who'd been quickest off the starting block, showered and hair-washed and away to work by the time Israel had surfaced usually – and by his own calculation he had enjoyed only four hours' uninterrupted sleep during the past forty-eight hours, which was not good. Which was torture, in fact, probably, under the UN Convention of Human Rights – he could check that with Gloria.

He needed a lot of things right now: something good to eat, a bath, more Nurofen, a new job, a plane ticket out.

But above all he needed more sleep. Lots more. Lashings of sleep.

He'd been so cold in the night that he'd got up and unpacked all his clothes from his old brown case and piled them in layers on top of himself, a kind of clothes sandwich, but that hadn't worked: the clothes had all just slid off, leaving him cold again, so in the end he'd got dressed again; shirt and jumper and his best brown corduroy suit, including the trousers ankle-deep in shit which he'd had to roll up past his knees, two pairs of socks, and the duffle coat to weigh him down. He'd used his pyjamas rolled up as a pillow – the pillow had got soaked through with melted choc-ice.

So now he was lying there again, fully dressed, warm and comfortably immobilised, and just beginning to drop off when he heard what sounded like an explosion outside.

And there was then what sounded like licking flames – that pffung! and whoosh! of flames – and so he had to raise himself again – bloody hell! – and quickly put on his shoes and ...

Bloody hell! *That's* where his glasses were; he'd tucked his glasses inside his shoes last night before he fell asleep, he remembered it now, as he felt a snap underfoot.

'Aaggh!' he yelled, and, 'Oh shit!'

And then he remembered that the building he was unfortunate enough to be staying in was now possibly on fire, so he wrenched open the door and hobbled outside, half-crippled, into the darkness.

There was no fire.

The lashing sound of the flames was in fact coming

from a man with his back to him, dressed in yellow all-weather jacket and trousers, who was using a big humming power hose to clean the farmyard, not taking care to miss wooden doors, metal milk urns and other unsecured items, hence the clatter and the whoosh.

'Aaggh!' said Israel, hopping slightly on his foot. 'Hello?'

And 'Uh?' said the man, surprised, turning round suddenly with the hose, and completely soaking Israel from the waist down.

'Aaggh! No!' screamed Israel. 'I'm! You've! *Aaggh!* I'm soaking!'

'Sorry,' laughed the man, who wasn't in fact a man. It was George, scrubbed clean, looking quite unlike she had done the previous night – she was smiling now, for example.

'I'm soaking!'

'All right, Armstrong,' she said. 'Dry your eyes.'

'What do you mean, dry my eyes? Dry my eyes? I am soaking wet. And ... Ooowww!'

'What's the matter with you?'

'My glasses! They were in my shoes!'

'In your shoes?'

'Yes! My! Shoes!'

He bent over and carefully took his left shoe off – his thin-soled, one and only best left brogue – and shook two separate pieces of what had been his glasses onto the concrete yard.

'*Look! My glasses!* You've broken my glasses!'

'I haven't broken your glasses.'

'You have broken my glasses! If you hadn't been doing

your ... spraying thing, I wouldn't have had to rush outside and ...' Israel was hopping and shaking his head in rage. 'For Christ's sake! What is this bloody place?'

'What do you think it is? It's a farm.'

'Right. Yes. I noticed. And are you all totally stark raving mad?'

'No.'

'Right! Well, if you think I'm going to settle for this, this, chicken shed—'

'Coop,' corrected George.

'Whatever! This coop as accommodation, you have got another think coming. I'll be complaining to the council about this.'

'Right you are.'

'Fine.'

'Good.'

'And now, if you'll excuse me, I had a rather long journey yesterday and I am sick and tired of you ... *people*, and I would like to go back to sleep for an hour or two. If you wouldn't mind' – he gestured towards the machines – 'keeping the noise down a little ...'

Israel turned away and began walking back to his room and immediately George turned the power hose back on again. Israel strode over to her and attempted to wrest the power hose from her hands. They struggled for a moment, cheek to cheek, hands clasped, staring at each other, like ancient warriors engaged in combat, except with a hose rather than broadswords, and in a farmyard, at six o'clock in the morning.

And in the end Israel simply let go and followed the power hose to where it met the wall, and turned off the tap.

And George marched over and switched the tap back on again. And now she was brandishing the nozzle of the hose like a gun at Israel.

'This, Mr Armstrong,' she said, 'is the sound of work – not a sound you're familiar with, clearly, although I dare say even librarians have to do something with their time to justify their wages. And if you don't like it here, I suggest by all means that you start looking for somewhere else to stay.'

'Well. Yes. I shall.'

'Good.'

'Today.'

'Fine.'

'Immediately.'

'Good.'

'Goodnight!'

'Goodnight to you. And when you're done with your carrying on,' shouted George after his retreating figure, 'if you go on into the house Brownie'll help get your clothes dried off.'

'Thank. You!' said Israel. And he slammed the door of his room – his coop – behind him.

He *hated* losing his temper. He never usually lost his temper. He never usually had anything to lose his temper about. But this, this *place* was different: it made you lose your temper.

He surveyed his surroundings: a small broken-down chest of drawers, an old sink plumbed into one corner, attached to the brick wall with wooden battens. The rug on the concrete floor. The big rusty cast-iron bed …

And on the centre of the bed, four chickens, looking at him accusingly.

He slammed back out of the door, past George, who simply pointed at a door in a building on the other side of the farmyard.

Israel walked in.

'Right!' he called furiously. 'Hello! Hello!! Good morning? Anyone about here? Anyone up in this nuthouse?'

He walked through to the kitchen, where there was a young man reading a newspaper, sitting at a scrubbed-pine table next to a dirty white Rayburn solid-fuel stove.

'Hi,' the young man said, in a disarmingly friendly manner, as Israel stormed in. 'You must be Mr Armstrong.'

'Yes. That's right.'

'Pleased to meet you,' said the young man, holding out his hand towards the sopping wet, brown-corduroy mess of Israel. 'Nice suit. I'm Brian. But everyone calls me Brownie. Hey, Granda?' he continued, apparently shouting to a heap of filthy rags piled on a ratty old armchair on the other side of the Rayburn, and which turned out to be a stubbly old man wrapped up in pyjamas and jumpers. 'This is Mr Armstrong. This is my granda, Israel. Granda, this is the fella who's going to be staying with us ...'

Israel was now regretting his rudeness – old people and polite people can do that to you, if you're not careful.

'It's really very kind of you—' he began.

The stubbly old man stared at Israel with beady, watery blue eyes for a moment before speaking.

'Surely, doesn't the Good Lord tell us that if you entertain a stranger you entertain Me.'

'Right,' said Israel. Oh, God.

'And we're being paid for it, Granda.'

'Aye, well.'

'He's the librarian, Granda. Do you remember?'

'He doesn't look like a librarian. He looks as if he's the blavers.'

'Blavers?' said Israel.

'Ach, Granda,' said Brownie scoldingly. 'Can I get you some coffee, Israel?'

'Erm, yes, thanks,' said Israel, disarmed by the boy's easy-going manner. 'A cup of coffee would be great.'

'Espresso? Cappuccino?'

'Young people today,' mumbled the old man, to no one in particular.

'I'll take an espresso if you have one—' began Israel.

'No, I'm joking,' said Brownie. 'It's instant.'

'Right. Well, whatever.' He became conscious of his dripping onto the floor. 'And I ... erm. If you don't mind, while you're ... The lady – erm – George?'

'Yes.'

'Right. Yes. George said you'd be able to dry off these clothes for me? They got a bit wet. Out in the farmyard there?'

'Spot of rain?'

'Yes,' said Israel, abashed. 'You could say that.'

'No problem. We'll just put them on the Rayburn here. That'll do it. And what happened to your eye?'

'It was just an ... accident,' said Israel, remembering now why his whole head hurt, and why he couldn't see properly.

'You've a rare 'un there,' said Brownie. 'Should have seen the other fella though, eh?'

'Yes.'

'It's an absolute beauty.'

'Right.'

'Like a big ripe plum so it is.'

'Yes.'

'Does it hurt?'

'Yes. Thanks. Well. I'll just pop and get some spare trousers and what have you.'

'It's all right,' said Brownie. 'I'll lend you some of mine, sure. You'll starve of the cold out there. You warm yourself by the stove. I'll only be a wee minute.'

Brownie left the room, leaving Israel alone with the old man.

'So,' Israel ventured, struggling to think of some useful conversational gambit to get things going. 'Is it your farm, then, Mr ...?'

'My farm?' said the old man, fixing Israel with a suspicious stare.

'Yes.'

'Of course it's my farm.'

'Right.' That was the end of that conversation then.

'It *was* my farm,' continued the old man, as if Israel was in some way to blame for this apparently sudden and parlous state of affairs.

'Right. It's a lovely...' Israel tried to think of the right adjective to describe a farm. 'Erm. Big farm.'

'Not really.'

'No,' agreed Israel. 'Of course. It's not that big.'

'Fifty acres.'

'Fifty? That's quite a lot, isn't it. I mean an acre is ...' He had no idea how big an acre is. 'Quite a size.'

'We had five hundred at one time.'

'I see.'

'Had to sell 'em all. To survive.'

Israel nodded.

'Developers,' said the old man. 'From down south. And the mainland.' He spoke this last word with some menace. 'Now we've just the fifty. Far barn's gone.'

'Well, I suppose fifty's better than nothing,' said Israel nonsensically.

'Hmm. All George's now. Signed over to her.'

'I see. And how ... long have you been farming here yourselves?'

'Since 1698.'

At which point, thankfully, Brownie re-entered the room.

'The boy here prefers his books to proper work,' said the old man, nodding at Brownie.

'Right,' said Israel, struggling to find some possible change of subject, his agricultural chat having proved predictably inadequate. 'Are you a student then?'

'Yep,' agreed Brownie, proffering a T-shirt, and trousers and socks, and a towel.

'Thanks. What are you studying?'

'Philosophy actually.'

'Oh right. My goodness. Very good. Where?'

'Cambridge.'

'Oh really? I was at Oxford.'

'Wow. What college?'

'It was the, er, other place actually.'

'What?'

'Oxford Brookes.'

'Oh, right. Is that the old poly?'

'Yes. Yes, it is ...'

'It's got a very good reputation, hasn't it?'

'Yes ...'

Israel quickly changed the subject, his less than illustrious academic career not being a subject he wished to dwell upon: he should have got a 2:1 at least.

'Can I change into these somewhere?'

'Aye. Come on.'

'And I wondered if you had a telephone I could use at all. My mobile ...'

'Ach, aye, the coverage here is terrible.'

'Yes.'

'No problem.'

'And, er, sorry to be a bother and everything ...'

'Yes?'

'But you wouldn't have any headache tablets at all, would you?'

'Granda?' said Brownie.

'What?'

'Headache tablets, for Israel here. Do we have any?'

'What for?'

'For a headache?'

'I wouldna thought so. We've TCP and some bandages just in the first-aid box.'

'That's no good.'

'It's OK,' said Israel, wishing he'd never brought it up in the first place. 'It's fine.'

'You sure?'

'Syrup of figs?' offered the old man.

'No, thanks. I'll be fine.'

'What's yon other stuff called?'

'What stuff?' said Brownie.

'Collis-Brown. That's it. Bind you rightly.'

'No. It's really OK,' said Israel.

'It'd not do you a button o' harm.'

'He's fine, Granda. Are you sure, Israel?'

'Yes. I'll be fine. And you've not got any – I really don't want to be a pain or anything – but you've not got any Sellotape, have you, by any chance? Just to fix my glasses?'

Israel took out the two halves of his spectacles from his pocket.

'Och dear. What happened there?'

'Well. It's a—'

'I'm sure we could fix them up, Granda, couldn't we? Sellotape or soldering iron or something?'

'Aye. P'rhaps.'

'And after that we'll maybe have some breakfast, Granda? No chance of a fry?'

'Aye.'

'Lovely. And you'll join us for breakfast, Israel, won't you? Room at the trough, Granda?'

'Aye.'

'Well, yes, thank you. That's very kind of you.'

Brownie then showed Israel into a dining room full of dark, miserable, heavy furniture, hung with cobwebs and family pictures, and with a large black Bible on the sideboard, open at the Book of Revelation, and an ancient grey dial telephone next to it. Israel slowly, painfully got changed out of his wet clothes and dried himself off underneath a photograph of men in robes and with drums outside an Orange Hall, looking for all the world as if they were fresh back from a lynching, and then he rang Gloria at home in London.

The phone rang for a long time before it was answered. Israel imagined the sound of it ringing in Gloria's lovely pale satinwood, soft-furnished, little-bit-of-the-Mediterranean-in-the-heart-of-the-city, inspired-by-the-*World of Interiors*-but-not-slavish-in-the-pursuit-of-fashion flat near Borough Market. He could almost smell the fresh bagels and orange juice.

'Hey!' shouted Israel, relieved and excited when Gloria finally picked up.

'___,' said Gloria indistinctly. It was a bad line.

'It's me,' explained Israel, his voice echoing round the room like a condemned man's in a prison cell.

'___.'

'Israel.'

'___.'

'Shit.'

'___.'

'Sorry. I forgot what time it was—'

'___.'

'I'm sorry.'

'___.'

'I said I was sorry.'

'___.'

'Sorry.'

'___.'

'I know. I tried. There's no coverage here.'

'___.'

'Oh. It was unbelievable.'

'___.'

'It's some farm in the middle of nowhere.'

'___.'

'No, not exactly.'

'___.'

'No. It's not a joke. It's terrible. There are chickens in my bed.'

'___.'

'Right. Yes. Ha, ha.'

'___.'

'No. But that's not the worst of it. You're not going to believe this ...'

'___.'

'No, not that. I'm serious. There's no library.'

'___.'

'It's been shut.'

'___.'

'I know they can't.'

'___.'

'They want me to drive a mobile library instead.'

'___.'

'I'm glad you think it's funny.'

'___.'

'Yes, as a replacement.'

'___.'

'No, I told her I wouldn't accept it.'

'___.'

'It's not an opportunity.'

'___.'

'What do you mean? I can hold down a proper job.'

'___.'

'Anyway. I'm coming back in a couple of weeks' time.'

'___.'

'I can.'

'___.'

'No. You don't understand. This isn't a stepping stone. You haven't seen this place.'

'___.'

'Oh. You're not?'

'___.'

'I see. Why, where are you going?'

'___.'

'Right. Well, I'm sure you'll have a great time.'

'___.'

'No, of course not.'

'___.'

'Yes.'

'___.'

'Anyway, what else is happening there?'

'___.'

'Oh, really?'

'___.'

'No. That's great. No, you deserve it.'

'___.'

'Yeah, sure.'

'___.'

'But ...'

'___.'

'Yeah, I'll try and ring you later.'

'___.'

'Yep. OK.'

'___.'

'No. I understand.'

'___.'

'Love you.'

'___.'

'OK, yeah. Bye.'

'___.'

'Bye.'

His head hurt.

It was not the most cheering and successful conversation Israel had ever had: discovering that his girlfriend was going skiing with friends on the proceeds of her more-than-generous Christmas bonus, and that there was a possibility she was about to get an unlooked-for but richly deserved promotion, while he was stood listening, shivering in a decrepit farmhouse in the middle of nowhere, staring at photographs of men in bowler hats and sashes with peculiar moustaches and glints in their eyes, while wearing someone else's combat trousers which were too tight and too short, and a hoodie, and a T-shirt saying 'Niggers With Attitude'.

He returned to the kitchen even more depressed than before.

Breakfast was on the table, Brownie and the old man patiently waiting – the old man now decked out in a festive-looking, fat-flecked Union Jack apron.

Israel was starving.

'Sorry I was so long. I ... Something smells good.'

'Yep,' said Brownie. 'Clothes all right?'

'Thanks. Yes.'

'Good. Sit down.'

'Here,' said the old man, passing Israel his glasses, which had been fixed with masking tape.

'Thanks,' said Israel politely, putting them back on. 'How do they look?' he asked Brownie.

'Fine,' said Brownie hesitantly.

'They feel a bit ...'

'Let's eat,' said Brownie.

Israel adjusted his wonky glasses as best he could.

The plate of food in front of Israel was of such extraordinary, all-encompassing shapes and sizes that it could have fed about a dozen deeply curious meat-eating men – although a vegetarian, alas, might have struggled to find much to interest and sustain him.

'Knock it into you,' said the old man, pouring out mugs of tea.

'Mmm,' said Brownie, tucking in. 'Thanks, Granda.'

'Yes, thank you,' said Israel. 'This looks ... lovely.'

Brownie was already eating.

'Grace!' said the old man.

'Sorry, Granda.'

'May the Lord Bless This Food to Us.'

'Amen,' said Brownie.

'Amen,' said Israel.

The two Irishmen tucked in.

'Erm. Could you just give me a guide here?'

'Mmm,' said Brownie, his mouth full. 'Yes, sorry. Pork chop.'

'Right.'

'Sausages.'

'Yep.'

'Bacon. Black pudding.'

'White pudding,' added the old man.

Israel had forgotten to mention that he was a

vegetarian: maybe now was not the time.

'And that's potato bread,' said Brownie, pointing out a cardboardy squarey thing.

'Ah, right,' said Israel, delighted – something he could eat. 'Yes, I know potato bread. Lovely. My father'd call it boxty.'

'Really?'

'Yes. He was Irish, my dad.'

'Really?'

'Yes.'

'Wow,' said Brownie, in between mouthfuls. 'So it's like coming home for you really?'

'Erm. Yes. Kind of. I never made it over with him when he was alive—'

'Ah,' said the old man, as if this explained something. 'Boxty, is it? The auld Free State,' he said, to himself.

'And this,' continued Brownie, 'is soda bread.'

'Yes, of course,' said Israel, his fork poised over a hard, pointy, blackened, fat-soaked triangle.

'And where would your late father have hung his hat on a Sunday, if you wouldn't mind me asking?' said the old man, with an apparent lick of the lips.

'Sorry?' said Israel.

'Would he have been of the Catholic persuasion?'

'Well,' said Israel, hovering over a bursting pork sausage. 'You see, my mother's Jewish so—'

'Ah,' said the old man again, as if all the pieces were falling into place. 'Consider Abraham.'

'Sorry?' said Israel. The bacon looked pretty good too actually.

'He believed God and it was credited to him as right-eousness.'

'I see.'

'Galatians.'

'Leave him alone, Granda. It's only seven o'clock in the morning.'

'Watch therefore: for ye know not what hour your Lord doth come.'

Israel pushed the bacon and sausage around on his plate, warding off temptation and damnation and started in on the soda bread and potato bread.

'So how are you finding things so far?' asked Brownie, polishing off a wide, glistening disc of black pudding.

'Erm.'

'You can be honest. It's a culture shock. I get it every time I come home. You're probably already missing good coffee and cinemas and—'

'Bagels.'

'Precisely.'

'Bookshops.'

'There you are. But you get used to it.'

'Do you?'

'Sure. Of course.'

'I don't think I want to get used to it.'

'It has its advantages.'

'Really? Like what?'

Israel was having to mash the soda bread in brown sauce in order to soften it enough to be edible.

'It's quiet. You can get a lot of reading done.'

'Well. Yes. That's one good thing, I suppose.' He took a mouthful of brown and black mush: it wasn't bad. 'I'm only going to be here a few weeks anyway, just to get things up and running and what have you.'

'Oh,' said Brownie, finishing off a pale fried egg. 'I thought you were a permanent appointment.'

'Well. You know,' said Israel, tapping his nose. 'I've got a few things lined up back home in London.'

'Yes. Of course. It'll be more like a wee holiday for you really then.'

'Yes. That's what people keep telling me.'

The old man scowled in his Union Jack apron at his end of the table. 'When are yous reopening up the library then?' he asked, mopping up brown sauce with a slice of wheaten bread.

'Well,' said Israel automatically. 'The actual library has closed, I'm afraid, sir. We are, though, shortly going to be relaunching the mobile library ...'

Israel was amazed to find himself suddenly speaking on behalf of the Department of Entertainment, Leisure and Community Services: proof, he realised, if it were needed, of the thesis of Daniel Goldhagen's *Hitler's Willing Executioners*.

'Disgrace,' said the old man. 'Young people today—'

'That's fantastic,' interrupted Brownie.

'I'm glad you're excited about it,' said Israel. 'There's not any more of the soda bread, by any chance, is there?'

'No,' said the old man.

'Right. Never mind.'

'I'd never have managed my exams without the old mobile library,' said Brownie. 'They should never have got rid of it. It was a lifeline. I was stuck up here all the time with my sister.'

'George?'

'That's right.'

'So she basically runs the farm then?'

'Yep. That's her idea of fun.'

'Right.'

'Not mine though,' said Brownie, finishing his final sausage.

There was a funny smell permeating the kitchen, Israel noticed. Animals, no doubt: he sensed dogs.

'D'you not want that?' asked the old man, pointing to Israel's uneaten pile of black-fried pig parts.

'No. I'm absolutely—' Israel patted his 'Niggers With Attitude' T-shirted stomach, and before he could finish his sentence the old man had whipped the plate away from him and was scraping Israel's leftovers onto his own.

'That was great, thanks, Granda,' said Brownie.

'Keep us going another half hour,' agreed the old man.

'What have you got planned for today then, Israel?'

'That's a good question. I've ... Sorry, can you smell something?'

Brownie and Israel both glanced then simultaneously at the Rayburn, where Israel's trousers were quietly scorching on a hotplate.

'Oh shit!' shouted Israel.

'Excuse me!' said the old man.

'My! ...'

Brownie had already whipped the trousers off the hotplate and thrown them in the sink.

'... Trousers.'

'Sorry,' said Brownie.

'That's ... OK,' said Israel. He fished inside the pockets of his burnt, soaking, manured trousers and took out a couple of handfuls of slightly crinkled credit and debit cards and some wet paper and started to separate them out on the table-top.

'My cards,' said Israel.

'You'll have to get new ones,' agreed Brownie, as Israel held up a far too flexible credit card.

'Oh, God.' He paused then for a moment and took a large gulp of his cold tea. 'All my instructions from Linda.'

'Oh dear. Can you remember what it is you're supposed to be doing today?'

'Erm. I'm supposed to be meeting Ted, I think, at the library.'

'Ted Carson?' said Brownie.

'The Big Wee Man,' said the old man.

'Yeah.'

'Yeah, of course, right,' said Brownie. 'He used to be the driver of the library, didn't he, Granda, do you remember, until they stopped the service?'

'Aye.'

'Have you met Ted then, Israel?'

'Yes,' said Israel, restraining his 'alas'. 'He gave me a lift here last night.'

'Aye. He was a tight wee fighter in his time,' said the old man. 'Rough enough and damn the scars. Terrible temper on him.'

'I guess he'll be showing you the ropes,' said Brownie.

'I guess so,' said Israel, wishing now he'd had a sausage.

'Mind his left hook now,' said the old man.

'Right. Thanks,' said Israel weakly. 'I'll do my best.'

6

Israel met Ted outside the old library at nine o'clock as arranged. The conversation was a little strained. 'Nice eye,' was all that Ted offered in acknowledgement of Israel's previous night's tangling with Tony Thompson in the back of his cab, and 'What's with the specs?' he asked of Israel's parcel-taped glasses, and 'Fancy dress?' he said, of Israel's too-tight and too-short borrowed combat trousers and hoodie and T-shirt, which certainly did not match his old brown duffle coat and his brown corduroy jacket and his old brown brogues and which made him look like he was on perpetual day-release from some long-since-closed long-term mental institution.

In return, Israel did not mention Ted's less than friendly farewell of the night before – when Ted had grabbed him by the coat and nearly pulled him through his car window – which was frankly now the least of his worries. Stripped of his money, his clothes, his dignity, unable to understand what people were talking about half the time, unwilling to eat the food, forced to be doing a job he didn't want to do, and threatened, beaten, and in a state of some uncertainty, confusion and tension, he was now really enjoying the full immigrant experience: this was what it must have been like for his ancestors and relatives who'd made it to Bethnal Green and to America. No wonder they all looked so bloody miserable in the photographs. Also, when he prodded his glasses the masking tape kept digging into his forehead.

'There,' said Ted.

'Sorry,' said Israel. 'What? Where?'

Ted nodded, indicating the red and cream rusting mobile library, parked down the side of the old library building.

'I thought you said it'd take—'

'Aye. Worked on her all night. Not every day you get the library back out on the road.'

'No. I suppose not.'

'Give you the tour later. Now. Tradesman's entrance for us,' said Ted, leading Israel round the back of the library, where he opened rusty metal gates which led down into an open passageway, ankle-deep in black plastic bin bags and rubbish, and they kicked their way through to a big steel door, which had been punched and hammered and stabbed and set light to enough times to make it look like the gates to hell itself.

Ted produced a big bunch of keys.

'Dante's *Inferno*,' joked Israel.

'Dan Tay?'

'He's an author. Thirteenth-century.'

'Aye, right,' said Ted, unimpressed. 'The Carson translation's the best.'

'What?'

'Much better than the John D. Sinclair or the Dorothy L. Sayers.'

'You know the *Divine Comedy*?'

'Aye,' said Ted. 'In more ways than one. What d'you think a driver does on a mobile library when they're not driving, read the *Sun*?'

'Er. I never really thought—'

'Clearly. Electric's off,' continued Ted, moving swiftly on from literature to life, swinging the door open, as they entered a dark porch.

'Did you—' began Israel, as Ted produced a torch from a jacket pocket. 'Ah. Right. Good.'

Ted then opened up another internal door and shone the torch into the dark interior – a basement storage area, full of orange stackable chairs and old display cases. No books.

'Where are the books?' asked Israel.

'They'll be upstairs,' said Ted, who pointed with his torch over to a flight of stairs on the opposite side of the room. 'In the *library*.'

'Of course.'

'After you.'

Israel made his way over to the stairs and as he began to walk slowly up the winding concrete stairwell something suddenly whipped past his leg.

'Aaggh!' screamed Israel. 'A ... rat!'

'Mouse,' corrected Ted.

'Ah!' said Israel. 'But it was huge.'

'Ach, wise up, man, will ye?' said Ted.

The stairs twisted round and round. At the top was another steel door.

'I forgot about that,' said Ted. 'Hold the torch,' which Israel did, while Ted went through the ritual of trying every key until eventually the right key caught and turned, and the door swung open and they entered the library proper.

They were under a staircase standing in the library's main entrance area.

There was natural winter light flooding in from the vast windows set high all around. There were architraves and cornices. There were complex tiled floor patterns. There was mahogany. Even under the dust and layers of paint and the scuffs you could tell the place was beautiful, that it had ambitions, and desires, and generosity, and woodworm: it was a building that breathed public service.

Ah, yes. At last. This was more like it. This was why Israel had come. This was where he belonged.

There were two large rooms off the main lobby area, one to the left and one to the right of the central sweeping staircase.

'Where does that go?' asked Israel, pointing to the top of the stairway.

'Nowhere,' said Ted.

'What d'you mean, nowhere?'

'Nowhere, as in nowhere. You understand the meaning of nowhere?'

'Increasingly I do, yes. But it must go somewhere.'

'I just said, it goes nowhere. It's a false staircase,' explained Ted. 'They say they ran out of money when they were building. It was that fella.'

'Who?'

'The architect. Whatyemacallhim?'

'I don't know.'

'The famous fella.'

'No. Sorry.'

'More.'

'More?'

'O'Ferral. Him. Ach. Anyway. The two storeys at the front are just a … what do you call it?'

'I don't know,' said Israel.

'A fac…?'

'A what?' said Israel.

'A fec…?'

'A what?'

'Fackard?'

'A fackard?'

'Aye.'

'A façade?'

'That's what I said. There's no upstairs. Just windows.'

'Blimey,' said Israel. 'Can I?'

'Aye,' said Ted. 'If you've nothing better to do.'

Israel trotted up to the top of the stairs, which branched and which looked as though they led to upper rooms, but sure enough, as he turned left, he suddenly found himself facing a wall. Turning round, he looked opposite. Another wall.

'That's weird,' said Israel, prodding his glasses, coming back down.

'Things aren't always what they seem,' agreed Ted philosophically.

Israel then went quickly through to the room to the left: the plastic laminate sign over the doorway read FICTION AND NON-FICTION.

The room was painted in several non-matching shades of white. There was a drab, stained grey carpet and big fluorescent lights hanging down on huge chains, looking like instruments of torture. The filthy windows, with their blinds high up, had knotted grey cords and strings hanging down, looking like a set of gallows. Wires were haphazardly cable-clipped to the walls; there were cracks and holes; and brackets hung down everywhere like gibbets with nothing gibbeted to them. And all around were the shadows where once the books and shelves had been, looking like the bars of a prison.

Oh yes, this felt good. This felt much more like home.

Israel went back through the lobby into the right-hand room, which was identical – the same dirty white emptiness – except for a long grey veneered built-in issues desk running along one wall.

Ted seemed to have disappeared.

'Ted,' called Israel. 'Ted?' There was no reply. 'Ted?' he called again. 'Ted!'

He went back into the lobby.

Ted emerged through the doors from the basement.

'Everything all right?' asked Ted.

'Yes.'

'Good,' said Ted, sounding relieved.

'Except for one thing,' said Israel.

'What's that?' said Ted.

'Look around you,' said Israel. 'What do you notice?'

'The library?'

'Yes, but what exactly about the library?'

'Ach. I don't know.'

'What do you usually get in libraries?'

'Drunks?'

'No!'

'Ach,' said Ted. 'I don't know.'

'Books.'

'Books?'

'Yes. Books. Books! There are no books.'

Ted looked round at the empty library. 'Aye,' he agreed.

'No books at all,' said Israel.

'Are you sure though? Are they not through there?' said Ted, pointing to the other main room.

'No.'

'That's where I thought they were.'

'Well, they're not there now.'

'No?'

'No. They're gone.'

'Ach.'

'Maybe someone's moved them?'

'Aye.'

'Or stolen them.'

'Aye, right.'

'Well, anyway, I'd better ring Linda.'

'Ach,' said Ted dismissively.

'What do you mean "Ach"? What does that mean, "Ach"?'

'Ach, it's just Linda. You know.'

'No. I don't. How am I supposed to know? What am I, psychic?'

'Now, listen, if I wanted cheek, son, I could go down to Belfast and get some.'

'Well. Honestly.'

'Aye, well, you want to watch—'

'What is it about Linda then?'

'Ach. You know what they say.'

'No. I don't. I don't know. That's the point.'

'The rotten egg keeps the nest the longest.'

'Sorry?'

'Ach, nothin'.'

'Fine. Right. Just keep it to yourself then. I'll just have to ring her.'

'If you have to.'

'Yes. I do,' said Israel officiously.

He tried to ring Linda on his mobile phone.

'Erm. Actually, Ted, have you got a mobile phone then? I can't seem to get a signal on mine ...'

Israel's conversation with Linda Wei, Deputy Head of Entertainment, Leisure and Community Services was brief and to the point and twenty minutes later she was there.

Ted was sitting outside smoking. 'He's inside,' he said to Linda, factually.

Back home in England Israel would have been at the discount bookshop at the Lakeside Shopping Centre in Thurrock, Essex, by now, maybe getting a morning coffee and a muesli bar from Starbucks, or trading repartee and bon mots with his colleagues, and chatting about the new paperback bestsellers. Instead, he was sitting at the top of the steps of the false staircase in the empty library of Tumdrum, gingerly prodding at the egg-sized bump on his head. Also, he was wondering if he was maybe getting cappuccino withdrawal symptoms. When he got back to London he'd probably have to go into therapy.

'Well,' said Linda, as she waddled in. She was wearing a tomato-red blouson leather jacket.

'No books,' said Israel, coming down the stairs.

'Hmm,' said Linda, producing a crumpled bag of sweets from her pocket. 'Fudge?'

'No, thanks.'

Linda paused and burped. 'Oops. Excuse me. I've got white mice in here as well,' she said. 'Pick'n'Mix.'

'No, thanks. You've not got any headache tablets though, have you?'

'No, what for?'

'For a headache.'

'No. Sorry.' Linda looked in her bag. 'Liquorice?'

'No, thanks.'

'Anyway,' said Linda, 'what's happened to you? Your clothes are—'

'Yes. I had to borrow them.'

'And what happened to your eye?'

'Don't ask—'

'It looks terrible.'

'Yeah. Well—'

'And you know your glasses are a wee bit—'

'Yes, it's—'

'Is that masking tape?'

'Yes, I—'

'And have you bumped your head or something?'

'Yes, Linda. But don't let me bore you with the details. Now about the books?'

Linda popped a liquorice twirl in her mouth. 'Yes. Well,' she said. 'Where have they all gone, I wonder?'

'I don't know,' said Israel. 'I was hoping you could tell me. That's kind of why I called you.'

'Mmm. They're supposed to be here.'

'But they're not,' said Israel.

'No. Ach.'

'"Ach"? What is this "Ach"?'

'Ach?'

'Yes! "Ach!" You all say it all the time. It's ...'

'Well, I do apologise,' said Linda, in a way that suggested she was not apologising at all.

'Yes. Well. What do you think's happened to the books? Someone's moved them?'

'Not as far as I'm aware.'

'So, what do you think?' said Israel. 'Someone's stolen them?'

'They must have done,' said Linda seriously, sucking on her liquorice. 'Is there any sign of a forced entry?'

'I don't know. I couldn't see anything. But I'm not an expert. Shouldn't we just call the police? They'll know what to do, won't they?'

'No!' yelped Linda over-excitedly, spraying liquorice spit.

'Sorry?' said Israel, taking a step back.

'No,' she said, more calmly. 'I meant no, that wouldn't be necessary.'

'But—'

'No. I'm sure we can sort this out.'

'But if they've been stolen?'

'I wouldn't think it.'

'But you just said—'

'They might all be out on loan.'

'What, ten thousand books?'

'Our stock is closer to fifteen thousand, actually,' said Linda.

'Whatever. They're hardly all going to be overdue, are they?'

'I don't know. People love reading round here. It's like Iceland.'

'Yes, but they're hardly going to have a hundred books out per person, are they?'

'I don't know.'

'Linda, be serious.'

'Well, maybe not.'

'So you think they've been stolen?'

'I don't know,' said Linda, rather quietly now. 'Maybe.'

'So we need to call the police.'

'No!' yelped Linda again. Israel put his hand up this time to protect himself from the liquorice spray.

'Why not?'

Linda looked furtively around and came and stood close to Israel.

'We need to keep this to ourselves. It wouldn't be good for us – or for you – would it?'

She was very close up to Israel now, almost whispering, her mouth a big black purply maw.

'It was bad enough with the library closing,' she said, looking at him conspiratorially. 'You know your eye does look terrible; it looks worse, close up.'

'Yeah, right. Getting back to the point?'

'Well, you see, if people thought all the books had been stolen ...' She lowered her voice even further. 'The council would be seen as ... incompetent.'

'I see your problem,' said Israel.

'*Our* problem, please,' she said.

'Sorry?'

'*Our* problem,' she said, swivelling round dramatically, in a way that only a fat Northern Irish Chinese lady wearing a red blouson leather jacket and holding a bag of Pick'n'Mix could be said to swivel round dramatically. 'You're the librarian.'

'Yes. But I don't have any books.'

'You're still the librarian.'

'Well, I can't be a librarian until I have some books.'

'Exactly.'

'What?'

'It's your job to get them back.'

'Now hold on, Mrs— '

'Ms, please.'

'Ms?'

'Thank you. We do try to avoid false generics and outdated sexist names, titles and categories as far as possible here at Tumdrum and District Council.'

'What?'

'We're not the back of beyond here, you know.'

'Right.'

'An apology would be fine.'

'An apology?'

'Please.'

'All right. Sorry.'

'Thank you. Anyway, as far as I'm aware, *Mr* Armstrong, your contract states that as the librarian you are responsible for the books in your care.'

'Yes, but— '

'And I think a very dim view would be taken of you being unable to—'

That was it. That was enough. Israel now went and stood close to Linda.

'No, lady, you just hold on,' he said, with a fierce prod of his glasses.

'*Ms*, please.'

'Whatever. Whatever. First of all I arrive and there's no library. Then I find I'm being put up by some lunatic in a chicken coop—'

'Oh, you mean George? I forgot to ask. How are you getting on there?'

'Terrible. But that's another issue. *Then* I find I'm supposed to be driving around in some ancient illegal rust-bucket of a mobile library.'

'How is it?'

'It's falling apart.'

'A lick of paint, I'm sure it'll be fine.'

'No. It's a death-trap. And *now* I find there's no books for the library.'

'Yes. Well. Not to worry. As long as you get the books back we'll be fine.'

'No. You don't understand. I'm not getting your books back for you. It's not my fault they're missing.'

'Now, don't be silly. No one's saying it's your fault, Mr Armstrong. You really must learn not to take things so personally.'

'I'm not taking it personally!'

'I think you are now.'

'I'm not!'

'You are, sir, actually. You are raising your voice, and you're invading my personal space.'

'Yes, that's because—'

'If you could just step back please. Thank you.'

Israel took a step back.

'Thank you. The council runs courses, actually, for our employees to address these sorts of issues – bullying and etcetera – and you'll doubtless be recommended for an appropriate course when the time comes. But' – and she raised a finger here as Israel was about to speak – 'in the *meantime* you are employed to sort out the problem of the missing books. That's your job.'

'That's not my job!'

'It is, actually.'

'I'm a librarian!'

'Yes. And you need to find your books.'

'No. I'm not Father bloody Brown.'

'There's no need for that sort of sectarian language, thank you.'

'Oh, Jesus Christ!'

'Mr Armstrong!'

'Right. OK. Sorry.'

'Good. So I'll take it that I can leave it with you then.'

'Oh yeah, sure, yeah,' said Israel, exasperated. 'Fine. Yeah. OK. I come all the way over here to this god-forsaken hell-hole to play Inspector bloody Morse.'

'Please, Mr Armstrong. That's the second time I've had to warn you about your offensive language. I'm issuing you now with a verbal warning. One more time, and I shall have to fill in a report about your behaviour.'

Israel walked away across the empty library.

'Right. OK. Sorry. Excuse me. Fine. I'll tell you what, I'll solve it for you. I'll solve it for you right now; I'll solve your little mystery. Easy. Who has a key to the library?'

'I do, obviously.'

'Right. So did you steal the books?'

'No! Of course not. Don't be silly.'

'Fine. You're eliminated from my enquiries. Anyone else have a key?'

'Ted.'

'And that's it?'

'That's it. There's only two sets.'

'Right,' said Israel. 'So if you didn't steal them, there's no sign of a forced entry, it must, by a process of logical deduction, be Ted who's stolen them. Case solved, thank you very much, ladies and gentlemen, goodnight, I'm going home.'

Israel started to walk off.

'Hold on,' said Linda, picking at something stuck in her teeth. 'Hold on, hold on. Are you accusing Ted of stealing the library books?'

'Well, he stole the mobile library van, didn't he?'

'Ah, yes.' Linda now seemed to have got a hold of whatever it was that was stuck in her teeth, and was examining it on the end of her finger. 'He told you about our arrangement then?'

'Yes, right, that was your totally bonkers arrangement where he steals the mobile library and you buy it back from him? I mean—'

'Well. That was a … difficult situation,' said Linda, sniffing the end of her finger. 'You have to understand that the people who stole the van saw it as a civil rights issue.'

'A civil rights issue?'

'This is Northern Ireland, Mr Armstrong.'

'Right. Fine. Well, maybe they saw it as a civil rights issue to nick the library books as well.'

'Really! And what do you think they'd have done with fifteen thousand library books?'

'Read them?'

'Don't be silly,' said Linda.

'Sold them, then.'

'It's possible, I suppose,' said Linda, who now delicately chewed whatever it was that was on the end of her finger and started ferreting around in her bag again. 'But why would they want to do that?'

'To buy drugs and guns?'

'Please,' said Linda. 'This is Tumdrum. Not north Belfast. Any other bright ideas?'

'Well,' said Israel thoughtfully, 'no, not really. Are they chocolate brazils?'

'Yes. Would you like one?'

'All right, yes, please. Thanks.' It might help him think.

'Yes. Well, I see. If you've got suspicions about Ted, shouldn't you have a word with him?'

'Who, me?' said Israel, cracking the chocolate brazil between his teeth: the last thing he wanted to do was have a word with Ted. 'Can't you have a word with him?'

'I hardly think that would be appropriate, Mr Armstrong, do you?'

'Why not?'

'Because you're his line manager.'

'What do you mean I'm his line manager?'

'Ted is the driver of the mobile library. You are the librarian with responsibility for the mobile library. Any issues arising concerning his performance of his duties, it's your responsibility in the first instance to deal with it before referring it up to senior management.'

'And who's senior management?' asked Israel.

'Me,' said Linda.

'Right. Well, I'm referring it up to you.'

'And as your line manager I'm advising you to deal with it.'

Ted was still sitting outside smoking. He stood up as Israel approached. 'Well?' he asked.

'It looks like they've been stolen.'

'The whole heap?' said Ted.

'Yep.'

Ted blew out a long stream of smoke. 'Och. Any idea about who stole them?'

'Well, according to Linda, there's only two sets of keys.'

'I see.'

'She has one. And ... '

Israel took off his glasses and rubbed his eyes. He felt rather bad about saying this. Ted hadn't been entirely unhelpful since Israel had arrived, not *absolutely* entirely – he *was* rude and aggressive and physically threatening, but he had a certain charm about him, a certain undeniable winningness, a kind of huge, twinkly-eyed hoggishness – and it gave Israel no pleasure to be in the position of accusing Ted of theft. He could feel his head throbbing, and his sore ankle, just at the thought of it – but ...

'What?' said Ted.

'What?'

'You were saying, about the keys.'

'Yes. Linda has one set. And you have the other one. So.'

Ted was silent.

'And we were just wondering ...'

'We?'

'Me and Linda.'

'Aye.'

'We were wondering ... You don't know anything about it at all?'

'About what?' Ted huffed.

'About where the books are? I mean, I was just thinking, because you ...'

'What?'

'Well, because you, you know, you stole the mobile library ...'

'Aye, right. I see, Columbo. Now get this right: I did not *steal* the mobile library. I *hid* her. Along with a number of other concerned citizens who were standing up for the rights of this community.'

'Yes, well.'

'And now the council have her back.'

'Yes.'

'And so now they've got her back they're trying to frame me for stealing the books, is that right?'

'No.'

'That'd be about right.'

'No, no. No one's trying to frame you for anything, Ted. I'm just asking if you have any idea what might have happened to the books?'

Ted threw away his cigarette butt.

'So you don't have any idea?' repeated Israel, rather weakly.

Ted kept his silence for a moment and then he looked

Israel in the eye, and reached a vast, hard hand towards him.

'Here,' he said, giving Israel his keys to the library.

'What?'

'Keys.'

'What do I want them for?'

'Well, if you and auld two-face in there think you can go around accusing me of this, that and the other, and expect me to sit here and take it, you've another think coming. You might be from London and what have you, but you've got a lot to learn, let me tell you.'

'Ted—'

'You want to mind yourself.'

'Hang on, Ted!'

'You put a tramp on a horse and he'll ride to the devil,' were Ted's parting words, as he turned his back on Israel, and walked away.

'What?'

'You heard me. You're on your own now, son. Good luck. You're going to need it.'

7

It's definitely easier said than done, finding fifteen thousand missing library books, by yourself, in a place you don't know, among people you don't trust and who don't trust you, and in clothes that are not your own, but the finding of the many missing books was a task and a challenge that the now permanently rough and rumpled Israel Armstrong was setting about with his characteristic good humour and fortitude.

'Oh, God. You bastard. You bloody, bloody, bastard. You fff...'

It was his first day out on the job, book-hunting, Ted-less, out on his own in the mobile library; Linda Wei had given him a few names and a few places to start rounding up overdue books and books out on special loan, a few people he might want to talk to, and he'd been edging the mobile library slowly – very, *very* slowly – towards the school gates, two traditional fat brick pillars separating the traditional rusty cast-iron railings that surrounded the traditionally low, squat grey buildings of Tumdrum Primary School, his first port of call, and he was feeling pretty confident, pretty sure that he was getting the hang of the thing now, pretty sure that he'd got the distance about right, enough room to squeeze through, at least a couple of inches to spare either side, maybe more.

Unfortunately, though, Israel was still judging distances in the mobile in terms of the dimensions of his mum's old Honda Civic.

He'd turned neatly off the main road into the approach, eased the wheel round gently in his hands, crunching his way carefully through the old gears, and then he'd glanced up and seen a man striding towards the van across the school playground, waving at him. He was shouting something to him, Israel couldn't hear what – and he kept on waving.

And so of course Israel automatically lifted a hand from the wheel to wave back.

At which point the steering slipped slightly – just *ever* so slightly.

And there was this almighty *bam!* and an unholy *crunch!* and a horrendous *eeecchh!* – horrible, huge sounds straight out of a Marvel comic, which is where they really belonged, not here and now in the real world, and the man who'd been striding across the playground was now running towards Israel, at cartoon speed, and Israel jerked on the handbrake.

Oh, God.

He'd managed to wedge the van tight into the entrance to the school, like a cork hammered into a bottle. He nervously wound down the window of the mobile library as the man approached.

It took him maybe a moment or two, but then Israel recognised that it was his old friend Tony Thompson - the man he'd met only the other night in the back of Ted Carson's cab, the man who had punched him so hard in the face that he'd given him a black eye that was still throbbing.

Tony Thompson did not look pleased to see him.

'Small world!' said Israel.

'You!'

'Yes. Sorry, about the ...' said Israel, gesturing towards the collapsing gateposts, prodding his glasses.

'You!'

'Sorry.'

'You!'

'Sorry?' Israel smiled, wondering if Tony had perhaps developed some kind of Tourette's syndrome since the last time he'd met him.

'You!'

'Sorry? Sorry. Sorry?'

The two brick pillars were leaning pathetically, like two miniature council Towers of Pisa, buckling the rusty cast iron on either side. It didn't look good.

'Look, I'm really really sor—'

'I know you're sorry!'

'Sorry.'

'Well, apology not accepted!'

'Right. Sorry.'

'Stop saying sorry!'

'Sorry. No! I didn't mean sorry – sorry. I meant OK.'

'Did you not see me waving you down?'

'Yes.'

'So?'

'Sorry. I thought you were just waving at me.'

'Why? Do you think I'd be pleased to see you?'

'Erm.'

'Of course I'm not pleased to see you. What the hell are you doing here?'

'I was just ... it's about books for the library. Linda Wei, up at the council, she said the school might have some. I'm trying to put the library back together, you see, and—'

'And destroying my school in the process?'

'Erm. *Your* school?' said Israel. 'Do you work here then?'

'I,' said Tony Thompson, flushing and stiffening, and staring Israel in the eye, 'am the headmaster of this school.'

Oh, Jesus.

It took most of the day to ease the mobile library from between the school gates. The children in the playground at their break-time and lunch-time had to be held back from all the pushing and squeezing and hammering and excitement by a cordon of mug-hugging and distinctly unimpressed-looking teachers. The children were playing a new game, which they'd just invented, which involved running into each other at high speed and falling down: they called the game 'Car Crash'. Some of the more imaginative children, pretending to be Israel, got up from the floor when they'd fallen, puffing their cheeks out and waddling, in imitation of a fat, injured person. It was a miracle that Israel hadn't been hurt, actually, and that the van wasn't worse damaged – bodywork only.

'Just a flesh wound,' joked Israel to the miserable school caretaker who'd been drafted in to oversee the rescue operation, as the two of them set about knocking down the school gates using a sledgehammer, a pickaxe and a large lump of sharpened steel that the caretaker referred to affectionately as his 'wrecking bar'.

'I feel like Samson Agonistes,' said Israel, as he set about the pillars with the pickaxe.

'Aye,' said the caretaker, digging in with the wrecking bar. 'And I feel like a cup of tea.'

After the van was eventually released Tony Thompson's secretary grudgingly arranged for Israel to visit the school library – which also served as the school's computer suite, its special needs resources room, and apparently as some kind of holding area for hundreds of small grey misshapen pottery vases – for him to pick up any of the old Tumdrum and District Library books that had been on loan to the school during the period of the library's closure.

Israel fingered his way confidently along the little shelves marked 'Poetry' and 'Easy Reads' and 'Information', plucking off books with the tell-tale Tumdrum and District Library purple sticker on the spine and their identifying Dewey decimal number.

'It's a bit like blackberrying, isn't it?' Israel said merrily to the woman watching him, who was either the librarian or the computer suite supervisor or the special needs tutor, or the keeper of the pots, or possibly all four at once: she had man's hands and wore a machine-knit jumper, slacks and sensible shoes; she looked like she was more than capable of multi-tasking. Israel, on the other hand, had borrowed another of Brownie's T-shirts – which read 'Smack My Bitch Up', and which was now covered in brick dust – and looked fit for nothing. The school librarian did not deign to reply.

'I said—' began Israel.

'Sshh!' said the machine-knit jumper woman.

'Sorry,' said Israel.

Once he'd gathered in the books from the library he went back to thank the secretary, but there was no sign of her in Tony Thompson's office, or of Tony himself, and as he stood hesitating for a minute, staring up at Tony's many certificates and awards for personal and professional excellence – including an award for competing in an Iron-Man triathlon and raising £5,000 for school funds – Israel noticed a shelf of books behind the big brown desk, with the tell-tale purple markings on their spines and he went over and sat down in Tony's purple plush swivel chair, and took down one of the books.

At exactly which point Tony Thompson entered the room.

'What?' spluttered Tony. Israel swivelled round, plushly. 'Are. *You* doing here?'

'Ah. Yes. Hello,' said Israel. 'I've finished getting the books from the library.' He held up the book in his hand. 'And then I noticed you had a few …'

'They're mine.'

'Ah. Well. I think you'll find actually they belong to Tumdrum and District Council. It's the—'

'They're my books.'

'No. Sorry. Look. They've got a little call number here, the Dewey, and—'

'Give me the book,' said Tony Thompson, approaching Israel.

'No. Now, don't be silly.'

'Give me the bloody book!' said Tony, as he moved round the desk and stood towering over Israel.

'Now, now,' said Israel. 'Let's not get carried away.'

Tony Thompson thrust out a fist then, and, given his previous form, Israel thought he was perhaps going to hit him again and give him a black eye to match the other, so he threw up his left arm in order to block the blow, an instinctive martial arts kind of a move that would have done Bruce Lee proud, if Bruce Lee had been a tousled, overweight librarian in borrowed, ill-fitting clothes and old brown brogues out collecting books in Tumdrum Primary School on a damp December afternoon.

Tony Thompson, though, was not about to punch Israel; he was in fact simply reaching forwards to grab the book from Israel's hand, and he grabbed, and Israel held on, and before either of them knew it there was a loud rip, rip, *ripping*, and suddenly Israel was standing there with the cover in his hands, and Tony Thompson with the pages.

'Oh,' said Israel.

'Ah!' said Tony.

'Sorry. *101 Poems To Get You Through the Night (And Day)*. Never read it myself. Is it any good?'

'Look!' said Tony Thompson, holding the coverless book on its side towards Israel.

'What?' said Israel.

'Look! Idiot!'

Stamped along the top edge of the book were the immortal words: WITHDRAWN FROM STOCK.

'Ah,' said Israel. 'Sorry.'

'Go!' said Tony Thompson.

'I really ...'

'*Go!*'

Israel went.

So, as he was saying, it was easier said than done: on his first day as book-bailiff, amateur sleuth and driver of his very own mobile library, Israel Armstrong had managed to crash the library van, cause thousands of pounds of damage to school property, offend and upset just about everyone he'd met, get into a fist fight with a headteacher, and he had rounded up a grand total of just 27 books, leaving approximately 14,973 to go. If he kept it up at this rate he'd be lucky to make it back home safely in one piece to north London in time for his own retirement.

He was trying to explain his predicament to Brownie and George and old Mr Devine as they sat down to eat dinner together that night.

'Oh, God. I don't know. What the hell am I going to do?' he asked, pushing his patched-up glasses up high onto his furrowed forehead and plonking his elbows firmly on the kitchen table.

'Elbows!' said Mr Devine, who was bustling with dishes and plates.

Israel politely withdrew his weary elbows and ran his fingers through his hair.

'Sorry.'

He'd just been telling them about the disaster with the school gates.

'Wide is the gate, and broad is the way, that leadeth to destruction,' said Mr Devine.

'It's tricky,' agreed Brownie.

'Champ?' said Mr Devine, pushing towards Israel a bowl of what looked like steaming hot Play-Doh with little bits of green stuck in it, like grass clippings.

'Ah yes, champ,' said Israel hungrily in recognition. 'Mmm. Now. Champ. Yes. Thank you, Mr Devine. Spring onions, isn't it?' he said, pointing at the green bits, like little sketches, in the mashed potato.

'Scallions,' said Mr Devine.

'It's the same difference, Granda,' said Brownie.

'Aye,' said Mr Devine.

'My father used to make champ when I was growing up,' said Israel, rather mournfully.

'Aye,' said the old man. 'George?'

'Thank you, yes.'

George was sitting at the head of the table, regally uninterested in Israel's tales of woe, resplendent in a man's plaid shirt (L), washed-out dungarees (XL), and a dark blue mud-stained fleece (XXL), and knee-high wellies.

'You don't think it could have been Ted then,' asked Israel of everyone and no one, 'who stole the books?'

He had been sworn to secrecy, of course, by Linda Wei not to mention the theft of the books to anyone, but Israel reckoned it would be safe to tell the Devines; frankly, he couldn't imagine them having anyone else to tell, and also, to be honest, he didn't have anyone else to tell himself. Gloria hadn't been answering her mobile for days: she was involved in a very important case at work, apparently. Mind you, Gloria was always involved in very important cases at work; he'd hardly got speaking to her since he'd arrived.

'Ted who stole them? I doubt it,' said Brownie, mounding piles of champ on his plate, in answer to Israel's question.

'He goes to First Presbyterian,' said Mr Devine, although Israel wasn't clear whether this implicated or exonerated him.

'Oh, God ...' said Israel, even more deeply mournfully.

'Mr Armstrong!'

'Sorry. I don't know,' said Israel, shifting his plate slightly, so that he could speak round the steaming mound of potato and onions. 'If Ted's not guilty—'

'We are all guilty in the eyes of the Lord,' said Mr Devine.

'I need proof, though,' said Israel.

'For we know that the whole creation groaneth and travaileth in pain ...'

'Apriorism,' said Brownie.

'Sorry?' said Israel, sniffing hungrily at the food in front of him.

'That's apriorism: you've decided he's guilty, and now you're looking for evidence to support it.'

'No,' said Israel. 'I haven't decided he's guilty. But he had the key to the library, so—'

'Now you're just affirming the consequent.'

'What? Really? Am I?'

'Events can be produced by different causes,' explained Brownie. 'It's a classic fallacy in law and logic: in the absence of any evidence, you just affirm the consequent.'

'Sorry, you've lost me.'

'Aye,' said Mr Devine. 'He does that all the time.'

'If I intended to kill you,' said George, smiling menacingly, illustrating her brother's point from the top of the table, 'I would have had a weapon. I did have a weapon. Therefore ...'

'That's it,' said Brownie.

'Oh right, I see,' said Israel.

'Ach, Ted's yer man,' said Mr Devine. 'No doubt. He's the face for it.'

'Granda!' said Brownie.

'Well, young people today,' said Mr Devine, returning to one of his favourite themes, 'sure they're all the same.'

'What?' said Israel.

'Come on now, Granda,' said Brownie. 'Ted's in his sixties.'

'Well, he's that young I can still remember him in short trousers,' said Mr Devine, conclusively. 'Mr Armstrong, chicken?'

'Thanks,' said Israel, absentmindedly. 'I ...'

Israel looked at the glistening crispy bird that the old man was in the process of dismembering – the deep brown crackling skin wisping off, with the revelation of pure white flesh underneath, and the rich, full smell of fat and onions.

'Erm.'

He hesitated and fiddled with his glasses.

Chicken was the thing he missed most as a vegetarian, although admittedly he did also miss salami quite a lot, and pastrami, and salt beef, and sausages, and Cornish pasties, and meatballs, charcuterie, that sort of thing. A Friday night chicken, though, you really couldn't beat that: his mother used to do this thing with tomatoes and paprika, and admittedly she tended to use paprika as a condiment rather than as a spice, a culinary shorthand, a way of getting from A to Z, from meat to meatball and chicken to pot by the quickest possible route, but it was so good ... Her boiled chicken also, that was good, with matzo balls and a nice side-order of gherkins. And chicken liver pâté. But that was all a long time ago, in his far-off, golden, meat-eating childhood and Israel had been vegetarian now for almost his whole adult life, and when he'd moved in with Gloria a few years ago they'd tended to eat a lot of chick peas – she was vegetarian too. There'd always been a hell of a lot of falafel and omelettes in his relationship with Gloria.

'Breast? Leg? Thigh?' asked Mr Devine.

Israel's eyes were glazed and he was busy remembering a lovely, thick, greasy turkey schnitzel he'd eaten once as a child on holiday in Israel with his parents, visiting his mother's uncle; that was the best thing about Israel, actually, the schnitzel, as far as Israel was concerned. He'd spent six months on a kibbutz when he'd first left college, and it had not been a great success – a lot of heavy metal and Russians were what he remembered, and the endless washing of dishes.

'Is it free-range?' he asked Mr Devine.

He thought perhaps he might be able to get away with free-range. He reckoned eating free-range was probably about the closest you could get to being a vegetarian; although obviously that might take a bit of explaining to the animals.

'Free-range?' asked Mr Devine.

'You know. Like, running around free in the countryside?'

Mr Devine simply raised an eyebrow.

Brownie and George were looking quietly amused.

'What?' asked Israel, noticing the silence and their smiles. 'What's the matter?'

'Nothing,' said George.

'What's so funny about free-range?'

Brownie just shook his head, stifling a laugh.

'All I'm asking is has it had a good life?'

'A good life?' asked Mr Devine, clearly bemused.

'It's a chicken, Armstrong,' said George.

'Yes, but ...'

'Chickens don't have feelings. I hate to be the first to break it to you.'

'Ah, yes, but the question is, can they suffer?' said Brownie.

'Exactly,' said Israel.

'Well, he didn't seem to be suffering this morning when I took him from the yard,' said Mr Devine.

'What? Hold on. He's ... one of yours?'

'Of course he's one of ours,' said George. 'This is a farm, Armstrong.'

'Yes. I know it's a bloody—'

'Mr Armstrong!'

'Sorry. Blinking. Whatever. I know it's a farm.'

'Well, you'll remember the chicken who was sharing your bed last night?' said George.

'What?'

'And you said you wanted rid of it?'

'Yes. But.' Israel stared at the pile of freshly cooked and quartered flesh. 'You don't mean ... I didn't mean ...'

'Lovely big bird,' said Mr Devine.

'I'll take a thigh, Granda,' said Brownie.

'And breast for me,' said George.

'I … ' began Israel, who suddenly had an image of the poor, sick, injured chicken tucked up tight in bed with him, wearing stripey pyjamas, sipping chicken soup. 'Er. Actually. No. I'm not that hungry, thanks.'

Mr Devine said grace and then they started in on the champ and chicken.

'Mmm,' said Israel, politely tucking in to the champ.

'Hmm,' he then said, as the scalding hot white mush hit the roof of his mouth.

Then, 'Ah!' he said, and 'Ergh!' and 'Ah, yes, I almost forgot,' and he got up, fanning his mouth, and hurried over to his duffle coat, which was hanging by the door.

'Are you all right, Armstrong? Not leaving us already?'

'No. Yes. I'm fine. I … Ah. I bought us some … ho, ho, ho, some … wine. To … thank you for your … hospitality.'

George and Brownie and Mr Devine looked at Israel in deep congregational silence.

'So,' he said, smiling, returning to the table, turning the bottle reverently in his hand. 'Merlot just, I'm afraid. Not a lot of choice in town.' He'd found a £10 note tucked in the corner of the pocket of his old brown corduroy jacket and had decided to invest it all in wine and Nurofen.

George and Brownie and Mr Devine continued to gaze in hush.

'Ah, yes, right. I know what you're thinking.'

He quickly darted back over to his duffle coat and with a flourish reached into his other pocket and produced a bottle of white.

'Ta-daa! A white for those who prefer.'

The gathered Devines remained silent. Israel looked at the label.

'Mmm. Chardonnay was all they had, I'm afraid.' He now had exactly seven pence to his name. 'Still. I think we have a sufficiency. Do you have a corkscrew?

'Corkscrew?'

'Erm. No. 'Fraid not,' said Brownie, breaking the solemn silence.

'You don't have a corkscrew? Well, OK. That's, erm ...What about a Swiss army knife or something?'

'No.'

'We don't drink, Armstrong.'

'You don't drink?'

'No.'

'Not at all? But what about ...'

Israel was about to point out that the other evening George seemed to have been more than happy to drink, if her exploits with Tony Thompson on the back seat of Ted Carson's cab were anything to go by, unless it was perhaps just the spare ribs at the Pork Producers' Annual Dinner that had done it, in which case Israel wished he'd known about that growing up in north London. But George was looking at Israel at that moment much in the same way she might look at a chicken she was about to pick up by the legs and swing at with an axe.

'I see. So.'

The Devines remained silent.

'Not even half a glass?'

'We've all signed the pledge,' said Mr Devine proudly.

George and Brownie were staring down at their plates.

The irony was, of course, that he didn't really drink as

such himself. He and Gloria would sometimes share a bottle of wine in the evenings, if they were together, and Gloria was partial to the various liqueurs that she brought back with her from business trips, and Israel, who liked to keep a few boiled sweets about his person and whose already sweet tooth had been getting a whole lot sweeter over the years, was not averse to trying the odd liqueur with her: a nice flaming sambucca, perhaps, now and again, or an insanely sweet amaretto. And he'd occasionally go drinking with old college friends in London – a few beers – but he was a lightweight by any normal standards. Compared to the Devines, though, Israel was virtually an alcoholic.

Certainly, at this moment he needed a drink.

'Well,' he said, gingerly setting the bottles of wine down on the floor at his feet. 'I'll save them for my own ... er ... personal use, then.'

The wine went unmentioned for the rest of the rather strained meal and when everyone had eaten their fill of chicken and champ, Israel helped Mr Devine with the dishes while George and Brownie did various farm-type things, and then he made his excuses and went across the farmyard to his room.

Reconciled to the fact that he was going to be spending at least a few days in his whitewashed chicken shed in this mad teetotal wasteland, Israel decided to try and make the place feel a little more like home. He began properly unpacking the rest of his belongings from his old brown suitcase, or at least those that hadn't already been ruined by the wayward shitting chickens: it was books mostly, some clean underwear, and then more books, and books and books and books, the ratio of books to underwear being about 20:1, books being really the great constant and companion in Israel's life; they were always there for you, books, like a small pet dog that doesn't die; they weren't like people; they weren't treacherous or unreliable and they didn't work late at the office on important projects or go skiing with their friends at Christmas. Since childhood Israel had been tormented by a terrible fear of being caught somewhere and having no books with him to read, a terrible prospect which had been realised on only two occasions: once, when he was about nine years old and he'd had to go into hospital to have his tonsils removed, and he'd woken up in an adult ward with dried blood on his face and not even a *Beano* or a *Dandy* annual to hand; and again, years later, when his father had had the heart attack and had been rushed to hospital, and Israel had rushed there with his mother, and there was that long period of waiting while the doctors did everything they could for him ... and always since then Israel had associated the bookless state with trolley-beds and tears, that demi-world of looming horror and despair, familiar to anyone who's ever sat for long in a hospital corridor with only their thoughts for company.

Israel piled the books onto the bed, erecting a kind of wall or a tower that might protect him from marauders, or the evil eye, or any remaining sneaky chickens, and then he changed into his holey pyjamas, and his jumper, and an extra pair of socks, and he prodded his glasses and snuggled down under the duvet – this was more like home now – and reached for the first book on the top of his pile ...

A loud tap rattled the door.

'Hello?' he said, a little scared.

'Only me,' said Brownie from outside.

'Oh, right. Come in,' said Israel. 'God, you gave me a fright. I'm not used to receiving visitors.'

'Sorry,' said Brownie, entering. When he saw Israel in bed in his pyjamas he started walking straight back out again.

'No, it's fine,' said Israel. He glanced at his watch. It was only nine o'clock. It felt like midnight. 'Come in. Have a …' He jumped down out of bed. There were no seats to offer. 'Ah.'

'No. It's OK,' said Brownie. 'I won't stay. I just brought you …' and he reached inside his jacket pocket and produced a small, half-full bottle of Bushmills whiskey.

'For me? Really?' said Israel.

Brownie handed over the bottle. 'I felt a wee bit sorry for you back there, you know, with the wine and all, and I thought you might like a … you know, a nightcap.'

'Well, thank you, that's very kind. Do you want to— '

'No, you're all right. I've got all this reading to do for an essay on epistemology for when I get back to college.'

'Right. Sounds like fun.'

'It is, actually.'

'Good. Well, good luck with it.' Israel raised the bottle of Bushmills aloft, admiring the golden liquid. 'Is this yours, then?'

'Aye,' said Brownie, ashamed. 'Just occasionally me and George have a wee swally, you know.'

'A whatty?'

'A wee dram just.'

'Right.'

'You won't mention it to Granda will you?'

'No. Of course not, no.'

'Because he's dead against the drink.'

'Yes. I noticed. Well. It can be our secret, eh?'

'Aye. Well,' said Brownie. 'Any inspiration yet about finding the books?'

'God. No. Not so far,' said Israel.

'Two-pipe problem?'

'At the very least.'

'Actually, I've been thinking about what I said at the dinner table,' said Brownie.

'Have you?'

'About affirming the consequent.'

'Ah, right, yes. That was very interesting.'

'I forgot about Occam's razor.'

'You did?' said Israel, sounding surprised. 'I mean, you did,' he then said, not wishing to appear as if he didn't know what Brownie was talking about. 'Yes, of course. And, er, what is it, Occam's razor – just to remind me?'

'"Entities should not be multiplied beyond what is necessary."'

'Ah, yes. That's it – took the words right out of my mouth. Which means what in my case, do you think?'

'Kiss.'

'Sorry?'

'Keep It Simple, Stupid.'

'Right.'

'You should really be starting your investigation not with Ted but with Norman Canning.'

'My "investigation", yes. Norman Who?'

'The ex-librarian,' offered Brownie.

'Yes. Of course.'

'They sacked him,' said Brownie. 'When they closed the library.'

'Oh.'

'So he'd be your prime suspect, I would have thought.'

'Prime suspect? Yes. Would he?'

'Well, he'd have motive and opportunity.'

'Right. Always useful. And ... what's he like, this ...?'

'Norman? He's ... Well, we used to call him Canning the c—'

'All right. Yes, I can imagine.'

'I don't know if he'd be that pleased to see you.'

'Oh, I'm sure I can use the old Armstrong charm.'

'Right,' said Brownie. 'Your first case.'

For a moment, the way Brownie was talking made everything seem much more exciting than it actually was: looked at from Brownie's perspective Israel's life was almost like the kind of life you read about in novels. He could quite see himself as a Sam Spade-type character, actually: chisel-jawed, wry, laconic, solving crimes. Maybe he'd found his métier after all. Maybe that's where his true genius lay. He'd have to tell his mum.

'Occam's razor,' he said dreamily. 'Sword of Truth. Many Hands Make Light Work. Miss Marple. Lord Peter Wimsey.'

'Sorry?' said Brownie.

'Nothing,' said Israel, snapping back from his reverie, and searching around for a glass for the whiskey. 'Just thinking. Anyway. Ah. Here we are.'

'Well, goodnight then,' said Brownie.

'Yes. What did you say his name was? The librarian?'

'Norman. Norman Canning. He lives up round Ballymuckery.'

'Righto. And where's that exactly?'

'D'you know the old Stonebridge Road?'

'No.'

'Ah. Have you got a map at all?'

'No. 'Fraid not.'

'Ah. It's a bit tricky to explain.'

'Well, I'm sure I'll find it. Thanks for the—'

'Lead?'

'The whiskey. Do you want to—'

'No, you can keep it.'

'Are you sure?'

'Aye, you work away there.'

'Thanks. That's great. Well, I'll maybe speak to the, er ...'

'Suspect?'

'"Suspect." Yes. The suspect. Indeedy. Tomorrow. Thanks again, Brownie. Goodnight.'

Israel poured himself a glass of whiskey and reached again for the first book on the top of his pile and he took a pencil and wrote on the inside cover of the book the word 'Suspects' and wrote down Ted's name and then the name Norman Canning. He was definitely getting the hang of this business.

8

It was no good. He was driving round and round in circles. All the roads from Tumdrum seemed to lead back to Tumdrum.

'I wonder,' he asked, pleasantly and smartly, having pulled the mobile haphazardly over to the side of the road back in the town and wound down the window and stuck out his head. 'Can you help me, sir? I'm looking for Ballymuckery?'

This was the fourth time now that he'd had to ask for directions, which was not a very detectivey kind of thing to have to do, and no one seemed to be able to help him, or indeed to be able to understand his accent, or to have any ability whatsoever in the simple explaining of how to get from A to B, or from Tumdrum to anywhere else. The first person he'd asked had told him he'd need to drive to Ballygullable first and then to go on from there, so he was now asking everyone for Ballygullable.

'Ballygullable?' Israel asked, hopefully.

'Come agin?' asked his latest possible help-meet, a man with a lively little dog and an accent so thick it sounded as though it had been freshly cut from a wheaten loaf and slathered on both sides with home-churned butter.

'Can you—' began Israel, his own voice suddenly sounding rather thin and undernourished in comparison

'Packy! Down!' commanded the man, which silenced Israel, but seemed to have no effect on the dog. 'Down! Or I'll give you a guid dressin'. That's a fierce cold, isnae it?' he continued, addressing Israel now, presumably, rather than the dog.

'Yes. It is. A fierce cold. Absolutely. Quite,' agreed Israel, prodding his glasses; the masking tape was unravelling.

'Now, son, whereareyoufor?' continued the man, leaning right in through the window: up close Israel could see that the gentleman had yellowy teeth with gold fillings, and skin as pale as a new potato – apart from the burst red veins and the flush on the cheeks – and that there were hairs growing from his nose, and not from inside his nose, but actually *on* his nose, and there was the distinctive smell of many years of cigarettes and pints, even at this early hour of the morning.

'Erm. Ballymuckery? It's just past Ballygullable, apparently.'

'Right you are,' said the old man, laughing a hollow, dry laugh – a real Old Holborn and blended whiskey kind of a laugh. 'And whereareyoufrom?'

'I'm not from round here,' said Israel rather weakly.

'Aye,' laughed the man. 'Well I knew that. Ballygullable! You nim-no.'

'Sorry?' Honestly, he couldn't understand half of what people said round here.

'Down, Packy!' the man told the dog. 'Will you stop yer yappin'? Stop! Down!' And with that he ferociously cuffed the dog, which cowered and whimpered and finally settled down. 'D'you know Abbey Street?' the man asked, smiling, turning back to Israel.

'Er ...' Israel was more than a little put off and disconcerted by the sight of the now beaten and chastised dog – he was a vegetarian, after all – and he was not inclined to disagree or to contradict the man, but he couldn't work out the logic here: if he wasn't from round here, how was he supposed to know Abbey Street, unless for some reason Abbey Street carried its name and notoriety before it, like Fifth Avenue, or Oxford Street? And as far as Israel was aware, it did not: Abbey Street might be famous locally, but word of it had not yet reached Israel back home in north London. He looked down at the cuffed dog, though, and decided not to point out the logical error.

'No. Sorry,' he said, 'I don't know Abbey Street,' and then he started to speak more slowly, in that speaking-to-foreigners-and-those-with-possible-mental-impairments kind of a voice that he'd found himself resorting to increasingly since arriving in Tumdrum.

'It's-Ballymuckery-Yes?' and he nodded his head at this point, encouraging assent, 'That's-What-I'm-Looking-For.'

'Aye, aye. Right you are,' said the man, amused. 'And you reckon it's just past Ballygullable?'

'So I've been told.'

'Aye, well.' The man coughed again, and spat on the pavement. 'They're blaggarding you, you know.'

'Oh. I see,' said Israel, though he didn't.

'Never worry. It's just the way of us,' chuckled the man.

'Right. Yes. Ho, ho.'

'I'll see you right though – just let me think.'

This took some time – time that Israel used profitably in feeling sorry for himself, because now he saw: Ballygullable! Oh, honestly. They could have had their own Friday night sitcom, the people round here. Absolute side-splitters, the lot of them.

'Aye,' said the man eventually. He pointed down the road. 'I know. D'you see yon park?'

'Yes,' said Israel, although to be honest the patch of football-studded grass in the distance didn't look like much of a park to him. Hyde Park, that was a park.

'Up to the park there, and past the memorial.'

'Right.'

'You'll see the wine team.'

'Sorry?'

'The wine team, by the memorial. Old Shuey and them. They're harmless.'

'Right. OK,' said Israel, still with absolutely no idea what on earth the man was talking about.

'If you're wanting Ballymuckery you'd be turning left.'

'Right.'

'No, left.'

'Yes. Sorry, I meant left.'

'Aye, right. Just follow the road, son.'

The man now seemed to have finished giving his directions.

'OK. Great. Thanks,' said Israel, who went to wind up the window.

But the man hadn't finished. He pushed the window down, rather menacingly, thought Israel.

'So, you follow the road, right? Past the Spar. But that's not there any more. That's gone. It's one of them hair places now.'

'OK.'

'Then there's a roundabout.'

And here he paused again, for what seemed like a long time.

Israel assumed that this concluded proceedings.

'OK. Great, thanks,' he said, going to wind up the window again.

But no, there was more – the man was just thinking.

'Steady,' he said. 'I'm just thinking.'

There was a pathetic bark from the dog.

'And it's definitely Ballymuckery you're for?'

'I think so.'

'Aye, well. That's all right. Then there's another roundabout.'

'Right.'

'Straight on,' corrected the man.

'OK,' said Israel, through gritted teeth.

'And then there's the mini-roundabout.'

'OK. And then?'

'No, that's it. And Ballymuckery's up there on the left, by the old railway bridge.'

'Right. Good. How long do you think that should take?'

'Well, it's a brave wee walk, if you're walking.'

'Right. Er. I'm in the van, though.'

'Aye.'

'OK. Well, thanks for that. So: left, roundabout, roundabout, roundabout, left.'

'Right,' said the man.

'Right?'

'Left.'

'Left?'

'That'd be it.'

'Thanks. Good. Thank you very much.'

'I'll maybe take a wee ride with you,' said the man.

'No!' said Israel hurriedly. 'No. Really. Thanks. I'm not ... erm. Insured. To carry the public.'

'No?'

'No, sorry. But thanks. Goodbye!'

'Good luck!'

'Thanks. Bye. Bye!'

Israel finally wound up the window, and set off.

They were the wrong directions.

He did find it eventually though, Ballymuckery, and the home of Norman Canning, Tumdrum's former librarian.

Norman, it turned out, lived in a maisonette, a part of a group of twenty or thirty two-storey pebble-dashed buildings clustered around a patch of grass which forbade ball games and which had long ago turned to mud. It was a place too small to count as an actual estate but too big to be simply a cul-de-sac: it was as if the houses had been cut adrift from the rest of civilisation and left floating in a dark sea of ploughed fields. All the kerbstones had been painted red, white and blue – some time ago, by the look of it, and by people using very broad brushstrokes – and there was matching, tattered, red, white and blue bunting hung from lampposts, giving the place the feeling of a sinister floating pleasure-boat. There was no one around. The whole place had the air of a loyalist *Marie Celeste*.

Israel walked up the concrete steps to the front door of Norman's maisonette, which looked down over a small garden where there were rose bushes dug into a deep triangle of dirt, hacked and grown into standards, like blackened skeletal fingers, like the buried body of the countryside had been crushed by the buildings and was grasping up towards the winter sky. There was no other greenery or attempts at pleasantness: just pebble-dash and concrete and red, white and blue bleeding into the dark black earth.

A net curtain hung at Norman's window. There was no bell.

Israel took a deep breath and tried to think like Miss Marple.

He tapped on the white UPVC and presently a man in late middle age answered the door; he had pinched, bitter features, as if someone had gripped a hold of his face with their hand and had not let go for many years, until the lines had deepened, and he wore small round glasses not dissimilar to Israel's own, and his grey, thinning hair hung down over the collar of his worn but neat and ironed white shirt: he looked every inch the ex-librarian.

'Hello,' said Israel. 'Norman Canning?'

'Hmm,' said the man non-committally.

'Erm. My name's Israel Armstrong. I'm ... the new librarian, in Tumdrum. Well, the new librarian with the mobile library. If you see what I mean.'

He pointed back towards the road, at the mobile library.

'I see,' said the man, his eyes narrowing.

'And it is Norman, is it? Pleased to meet you.' Israel went to shake hands.

The man ignored Israel's hand and looked over his shoulder, towards the street.

Israel had parked the mobile library outside the maisonette, managing to get it surprisingly close to the kerb.

A group of young children had appeared out of nowhere and had gathered around the van, and were banging on the sides.

'Hey! Get away from there!' shouted the man, shaking his fist at the children, who ran off, shouting abuse. 'Go on! Go!'

'Thanks,' said Israel.

'They'll be back,' said the man. 'Your hubcaps'll be away.'

'I'm sure it'll be fine,' said Israel blithely.

'Aye. You'd know?'

'Well ...'

'You'd better be quick.'

'Right. I was just wondering if I could ask you a few quick questions,' said Israel. 'About the library.'

'It's shut.'

'Yes. I know. I'm ...' Israel began, but the man had already turned his back on him and walked away. 'Norman?' called Israel. 'Norman?'

'Come, if you're coming,' called the man who was presumably Norman, retreating down a narrow hallway piled up with dozens of empty bottles. 'In here.'

He led the way into a small, spotless kitchen – 'Kitchenette,' he said, as if cataloguing his own home, as they entered – the laminated surfaces pristine, the walls free of even a single spot or stain, empty bottles lined up neatly in rows: green glass; clear glass; brown glass.

'I'm preparing my breakfast. You'll forgive me if I continue?'

'Of course. Go ahead.' Israel sniffed. 'Something smells good,' he said encouragingly.

'I'm boiling an egg,' said Norman.

'Ah.'

'Take a seat.'

'Thanks.' Israel sat down on the kitchen's one and only chair, which was next to a small fridge, whose hum was much grumpier than its size. Norman went and stood by the stove.

'I—' began Israel.

'Sshh!' said Norman, raising a finger. 'About to boil.'

He nodded down towards the saucepan and stood with an egg-timer in his hand. Israel remained silent; the sound of the boiling water; the ticking of a wall clock; the humming of the fridge; the steam in the room beginning to mist the windows.

'Right!' said Norman, turning the egg-timer upside down. 'Three minutes.'

Israel wasn't entirely sure whether Norman meant him or the egg.

'Well. I suppose I should say straight away that I hope there's no bad feeling between us.'

'Bad feeling?' laughed Norman, in a not entirely friendly

and more than slightly bonkers kind of a way. 'Why should there be bad feeling?'

'Well, you know. You used to be the librarian. And now ... well, *I'm* the librarian.'

Norman snorted.

'Believe me, sir, I bear you no ill feeling. On the contrary. I pity you, actually.'

Norman swept his arm, indicating the room around him and a door leading off to another room – Israel glanced through and saw further dark, depressing depths: an imitation-flame-effect gas fire; piles of books and empty bottles everywhere.

'This,' said Norman, 'is what you've got to look forward to.'

Israel had to admit, it was hardly an encouragement to go into public service.

The egg-timer was running down.

'I worked for the Library Board for over thirty years,' said Norman. 'Did you know that?'

'No. I didn't.'

'I introduced computers. That was me.'

'Very good,' said Israel.

'And who do you think introduced the children's reading hour on Saturday afternoons?'

'Erm ...'

'Me.'

'Right.'

'And the refurbishments? Who oversaw the refurbishments?'

'You?'

'Correct. Me. The carpet?'

'You?'

'Correct. Carpet! In a library! And the toilet facilities – who was that?'

'You?'

'Exactly. Me. Me. I did everything they told me to, and more. Do you know that? All their dictates. And their reports. I was in the middle of transferring the last of the card catalogues when they sacked me.'

'I'm sorry,' offered Israel.

'Don't you be sorry,' said Norman, laughing his little laugh again. 'You don't want to be sorry for me. You want to be sorry for yourself, Mr ... What did you say your name was?'

'Armstrong. You can call me Israel though.'

'I don't think so.' Norman glanced at his egg-timer. 'See me?'

Israel looked shyly up at Norman standing by the sink.

'See me? I was the top of my year at school, d'you know that? Hmm?'

'No.'

'The Grammar. And this is where it gets you. This where you're heading, *Israel* Armstrong.' Norman emphasised the Israel with some distaste.

Israel glanced around nervously. Norman noticed his gaze.

'D'you know what I do now?' He nodded towards a box of cleaning products by the front door, and a large industrial vacuum cleaner.

'No.'

'Have they not told you what I do now?'

'No.'

'Contract cleaning. Do you know what that is?'

'Er.'

'Cleaning for businesses, and the middle classes, because they can't be bothered to pick up their own shit.' He pronounced 'shit' with the same emphasis he'd used for *Israel*. 'Like people who couldn't be bothered to buy their own books.'

'OK.'

'That's what you've got to look forward to.'

Israel remained silent.

'You know what they used to say, when I was at college?'

'No,' said Israel.

'Old librarians never die,' said Norman. 'They just become *ex-libris*.'

'Right,' said Israel, trying to raise a small laugh.

'It's not true, though, is it? Old librarians never die. They just become cleaners.' He laughed.

As jokes went Israel thought it was pretty poor: Norman probably wouldn't have got his own Friday night sitcom on the strength of that.

'Not fit for anything else, are we? Librarians!' He laughed again. 'Look at us! Look at the two of us. Useless, eh?'

'Yes,' agreed Israel nervously.

Norman looked at the egg-timer. 'Time up.' He turned off the gas.

'Actually, it's the library I needed to talk to you about, Norman.'

'Time up, I said,' repeated Norman. 'Time's up.'

'But ...'

'*I* am not interested in *your* library, Mr Israel. Do you understand? I don't care about libraries any more. Do you know the last time I stepped into a library?'

'No.'

'The day they sacked me. I vowed I would never again use a library. And I haven't.'

'Right, well, that's, er, a bit sad, isn't it?'

'A bit sad? A *bit* sad? I dedicated my life to the library service, sir. My *life*. Do you understand that?'

'Yes, I, er, I think I do.'

'Ach, you're not old enough to understand what's holding up your trousers.'

It was his stomach, unfortunately, that was holding up Israel's trousers.

'No, well,' he said. 'But I do sympathise. And I take your point. But I was wondering if you might at least be able to answer a couple of questions about the library?'

'Answer your questions?'

'Yes.'

'I suggest you take your questions to the town hall. They seem to have all the answers.'

Norman had fished the egg from the pan with a spoon and had placed it carefully in an egg-cup.

'Well, it was more of a, you know, personal kind of a question, actually,' continued Israel. 'Librarian to librarian. It was about the books.'

'What about the books?'

'They've gone missing.'

'Missing?'

'Yes.'

'Ha!' Norman took a knife from a drawer. 'Books go

missing all the time. How long have you been a librarian?'

'On and off. A while.'

'Well. You know what happens when you're dealing with the public. Overdue. Lost. Theft.'

Norman took the knife and sliced the top off the egg.

'Actually, we've lost the whole lot,' said Israel.

'The whole lot?'

'Yes.'

'Ha!' Norman laughed. 'Boys-a-boys. The whole lot! All of them?'

'I'm afraid so.'

'Oh, that's good. That's excellent. You must be even more stupid than you look.'

'Erm ...' There was no simple response to that.

'How did you manage that then?'

'They were missing before I arrived actually.'

'I see.'

Norman had picked up the saucepan of boiling water and was moving towards the sink.

'And I was,' continued Israel, 'I was wondering maybe if you knew anything ...'

Norman stopped in his movements and then slowly turned around.

'Me? Knew anything? Why?'

He was holding the saucepan of boiling water in his hand.

'Well, something's happened to the books. And ...'

'Are you insinuating, sir?'

'Insinuating?'

'Are you suggesting I have anything to do with these missing books? Is that your in*sin*uation?'

'No, Norman, no. No, no. I'm not insinuating anything. It's just, you would have had access to the ...'

Norman had stepped closer to Israel now and was standing right over him with the saucepan of boiling water. Israel could see his hand shaking slightly with rage. He didn't like the way this was going.

'Norman,' he said nervously. 'I don't like the way this is going ...'

'The way this is going? The way this is going? That's rich! You come in here under false pretences and accuse me—'

'No. No one's accusing you, Norman.'

'Mr Canning, please!'

'Sorry. Mr Canning. No one's ... I really don't like the way this is going, Norman ...'

'The way this is going! I'll tell you the way this is going, sir! You're getting out of my house, now, and you're never darkening my doorstep again, that's the way this is going. D'you understand?'

Israel was edging himself off his seat.

'Do you understand?'

'OK, yes, that's fine.'

Norman stepped closer, clutching the saucepan unsteadily. Israel could see his nostrils flaring and vibrating.

'I'm going, it's OK.'

'No, it is not OK! You come round here insinuating: it is not OK!'

'No. Fine. Sorry. I was just ...'

'I'll tell you what you should do, sir, about your missing library books, shall I? Eh? I'll tell you what you should do. You should ask your borrowers – huhn? – or your customers – customers is it? – that's what you call them now, isn't it? – ask them what happened to your books. Rather than coming and bothering me. It's the borrowers who are the problem around here. Not me. You want to find out what they know! Prise the books out of their greasy little paws, eh? Eh?'

'Yes. Thank you. That's ... good advice,' said Israel, who had edged himself off the seat and was moving back slowly towards the front door.

'And I don't expect to see your face ever again!' called Norman, looking down on Israel, the saucepan still in his hand, as Israel scurried quickly down the concrete steps and towards the sanctuary of the mobile library.

'Well,' said Israel, to try and calm himself, once he was safely back behind the wheel of the van, 'that went well.' Except for the hubcaps: Norman had been right about the hubcaps.

9

He shook all the way back to Tumdrum, his guts and his glasses jiggling and his nerves jangling, thrashing the old van up to 50 mph, and he did his best to park up neat and straight in Tumdrum's town square – there was quite a bit of play in the steering wheel, and the brakes were a little sloppy but he managed finally to bring the van to a halt across three bays at a slight angle – and when he turned off the ignition he took a long deep breath, a swig from his bottle of water, and a couple of Nurofen.

Maybe he wasn't cut out for life as a private investigator after all. He probably needed to drink more, or have some more interesting quirks and tics and characteristics: it was a shame he hadn't done time in prison or been a former heroin addict. He had done detention a few times at school, and he'd once been in a room where people were smoking dope, years ago – Russians, in the kibbutz – but that hardly seemed sufficient. By the time he'd mulled over his lack of extraordinary tics and quirks and composed himself and was ready to get out of the van, though, Israel was faced with a more immediate and more pressing problem: a queue had formed at the back of the mobile library, a dozen middle-aged and elderly women with carrier bags waiting to get in.

Israel saw them in his wing mirror, so he got up and out and shut the door to the van quietly behind him and tried to creep away unnoticed round the front.

'Hey?' called a woman, peeking round. 'Mister? Are yous not opening her up here?'

'Who, me?'

'Yes, course you. You opening her up?'

'No. Erm. Sorry,' said Israel. 'I'm just parking here for a moment.'

'This is the mobile library?'

'Yes,' agreed Israel.

That was true. There was no avoiding that. It was incontrovertible: the sign on the side of the van read MOBILE LIBRARY, with a witty coda painted across the back in a style and font last seen in the late 1970s, THE BOOK STOPS HERE!

'You can't just be parking up the library and not expecting us to want in,' continued the woman, who was now joined by her cohort of carrier bag-clutchers.

'No,' agreed Israel. 'I suppose you can't. No. It's just, the library's not quite ... ready, at the moment.'

'D'you know how long we've been without a library, but?' asked another woman, waving a blue plastic bag of fruit and veg accusingly towards him.

'Gosh. No. Quite a while though, I believe,' said Israel.

'Aye, right. And we pay rates just like them other yins,' chipped in another.

'Aye. Why should we not have the services they have?'

'Good question,' said Israel. 'Couldn't agree more, ladies. But I can guarantee that just as soon as the library's ready for action we'll be— '

'Aye, save your breath,' said another woman. 'We've heard it all before. Sure, you're all the same.'

'I can assure you, madam, that—'

'Who you calling madam?'

'Erm.'

'Are yous the new librarian?'

'Who?'

'Yous?'

'Me?' Israel looked over his shoulder: were there more of him?

'Yous!'

'Well,' said Israel, 'yes. Mes. Me, I mean, yes it is. I am. Although actually I'm what's called an Outreach Support Officer these days.'

'Aye. Right. A librarian?'

'Er. Yes,' agreed Israel.

The women stood and scrutinised him for a moment and came to their own conclusions.

'You don't look like a librarian.'

'Sure, it's him. Iqbal or Ishmael he's called, isn't he, or something?'

'Jamal?'

'No.'

'What are you called, love?'

'I thought he was Egyptian, isn't he?'

'It's Israel, actually,' said Israel, prodding his glasses in as authoratively librarian a manner as he could. 'My name. And I'm English.'

'Aye, well.'

'That figures.'

'Yes. Quite. Well. Good to have cleared that up. Anyway, I would love to chat more, and it's a pleasure to meet you all, but I am in a bit of a rush at the moment. Lots of books to collect.'

And here Israel had his brainwave – his means of escape.

'In fact, ladies,' he said, pressing his stomach threateningly out before him, 'if you do have any outstanding books that are overdue, and for which fines are owing, I would be glad to collect both the books and the monies from you now ...'

And at the mention of library fines a hush fell over the little crowd of jostlers, and they began suddenly to drift away and before he knew it, Israel was alone again.

He'd have to remember that for when he was back home in London, although maybe it might not work with muggers.

He was in search of a mid-morning snack now, something to steady his nerves after his encounter with Norman, and pretty soon he found what he was looking for: a café, on the corner of Tumdrum's central square. In bold gold lettering on red the sign above the entrance said ZELDA'S. He stepped inside.

The café was packed but it was eerily quiet except for the dense, wet sound of munching and the accompanying clacking of dentures, and the thin, slippery, slapping sound of the turning of the pages of books – almost everyone seemed to be reading. You might almost have been in a café in turn-of-the-century Vienna, or in 1960s Paris, except you very clearly were not, because people were reading large-print Catherine Cookson, for example, rather than Karl Kraus or Jean-Paul Sartre, and the air was thick with that distinctive, ever so slightly incontinent smell of provincial tea-rooms and community halls and garden centre cafés, rather than the smell of fresh coffee, Gitanes and freshly made pastries.

Israel squeezed himself onto a thick-varnished bench next to an elderly man who was wearing a combination of casual sports wear and a flat tweed cap, a curious but common combination locally, Israel had noticed, and not one that he had ever come across before, except in half-remembered *Sunday Times* black and white photo-spreads of Romany musicians and the aspiring middle classes of some of the former Soviet republics.

'Do you mind if I ...' Israel said, indicating the seat.

The man regarded Israel suspiciously. 'S'free country,' he said. He may well have been a touring Romany musician; he was certainly enjoying his vast, Grauballe pavlova.

'Thanks,' said Israel. 'It's busy, isn't it?'

'Aye,' said the man factually, and then proceeded to pretend that Israel was somewhere else entirely and not in fact squeezed up close by him, thigh to thigh and cheek by jowl. He was reading *Bravo Two Zero* by Andy McNab.

A woman, who was presumably Zelda herself, came hurrying out from behind a high counter at the rear of the café to serve Israel. She was in her seventies – at least –

but she strode purposefully and not a little menacingly across the marble-look lino floor towards him. She was wearing a white polo-neck jumper under a nylon, unnecessarily tailored black trouser suit, was in full make-up, and her nail varnish was a vivid – one might almost say a ghastly – green. Her long hair was dyed black, but still somehow streaked with grey, and piled high on her head, like an old, erect beaver's tail, possibly stuffed, or fixed with some kind of glue-mount.

'Sir?' she said. 'What can we do you for? Cup of coffee?'

Israel had not had a proper cup of coffee since leaving London, and he was getting withdrawal symptoms. He wasn't sure whether he could face another cup of instant.

'Well ... ' he began.

'Sure, it wouldn't choke you,' said the woman. 'And what would you be having to eat with that?'

'Erm ...'

'Big lad like you, you must be absolutely famished,' she said, patting Israel on the shoulder with affectionate distaste, much as if she were plumping a favourite dog-haired cushion. 'Tray bake? Pavlova? Black Forest gateau?'

'It's a little early in the day, actually, for me for, er, Black Forest gateau.'

'Each to their own. So, you're wanting something savoury? Today's specials are ham and eggs, ham and cheese omelette, baps, a fry we could do you ... '

Israel glanced around and picked what seemed most popular. 'A scone?'

'Is that it?'

'Yes, thanks.'

'For your lunch?'

'Well, it's more just a—'

'Och, come on now. Big fella like yerself, you can't have just a scone. You have to have some soup or something with it.'

'Do I?'

'Of course you do.'

'Right. Well. Er. What's the soup?'

'Today? It's lentil.'

'Hard to whack,' murmured the man squeezed up cheek by jowl next to Israel, glancing up from his tea and his book.

'Is it?' Hard to whack? 'OK. I'll have a lentil soup, thanks.'

'And a cup of coffee.'

'Yes, thanks.'

'No problem. Espresso, macchiato, cappuccino, latte, or mochaccino?'

'Really? Gosh. Erm. Espresso?'

'We've not got espresso at the moment.'

'Right. Just a regular cup of coffee would be fine, then, thanks.'

'Filter coffee?'

'Yes.'

'Actually, the machine's not working.'

'OK.'

'Tea?'

'That'd be lovely.'

'Coming right up. You just relax there and soak up the atmosphere.'

Israel sat in silence and tried to soak up the atmosphere. Unfortunately, someone else seemed to have soaked it all up before him. Everyone in Zelda's looked as though they were between a trip to the Post Office and their lunch-time nap, having blown all their pension money on scones, and the only decoration in the place were giant plastic yuccas in giant plastic terracotta-style pots, and plastic vines trailing from the ceiling, and in a corner a large computer was perched on a table, with a printer, and a laminated sign haphazardly Blu-Tacked to the wall above it announcing INTERNET: £2 HALF HOUR. EUROS ACCEPTED.

Another waitress approached Israel. She was about the same age as the first woman, but shorter and fatter, and she resembled more what Israel believed an elderly lady should look like: she wore a tartan skirt and a brown cardigan. Her hair was permed and short, and uniformly grey. Her fingernails were not green.

'You getting, love?'

'Sorry?'

'You getting?'

'Er ...'

'You're not from round here, pet, are ye?'

'No. I'm not.'

'Och,' she said, as if this were a terrible misfortune. 'I'm Minnie.'

'Pleased to meet you, Minnie,' said Israel. 'I'm Israel Armstrong.'

This announcement caused a considerable and audible indrawing of breath from Minnie, who now looked at Israel with great attention.

'Och! Really?' she said, peering at him intently. 'I thought it might be you. It is you then, is it?'

'Yes. It is. At least I think so.'

'Zelda!' called Minnie. 'Zelda! Come on here!' The lady in the suit with the green fingernails and the high hair came over to the table. 'Zelda. This is him.'

'Who?'

'The librarian.'

'Is it?' said the fingernail lady, disappointed. 'We've been expecting you.'

'You have?'

'Of course we have,' said Minnie. 'We all have. You've been all over the paper.'

'Have I?'

'Och, aye. You're over from London, aren't you?'

'Yes,' said Israel.

'Twelve GCSEs!' said Minnie, marvelling.

'I thought it was thirteen?' said Zelda.

'Well, it depends if you count General Studies,' said Minnie.

'No, you don't count that,' said Zelda.

'Hang on,' said Israel. 'How did you know that?'

'It was in the paper,' said Minnie. 'Now tell me this: d'you really no' have hobbies and interests apart from the reading? You must have some, eh, young fella like yourself?'

'What?'

'It was all in the paper.'

'What, my whole CV?'

'Yes. Of course,' said Minnie. 'People have the right to know about their new librarian. It's like public office. You were definitely the best candidate, wasn't he, Zelda?'

Zelda was looking Israel up and down in a manner that clearly indicated that she did not believe him to be the best at anything.

'Head an' shoulders,' continued Minnie.

'They published my CV in the local paper?' said Israel.

'Not just yours.'

'Don't flatter yourself, my dear,' said Zelda.

'Oh yes. They had all the seaviews in the paper. Sure they were gaunches, weren't they, Z, half of them?'

'Hmm,' said Zelda, in a tone that suggested that Israel, too, might have been a gaunch, which he might well have been: he had no idea what a gaunch was.

'Sure, it's been desperate here without you,' said Minnie. 'Since they shut the library.'

'Hmm,' added Zelda.

'Anyway, look, what happened to your eye, pet?'

'That? Oh. It was an—'

'And is that a wee bump on your head?'

'Fightin', eh,' said the old man next to Israel, not raising his head from his book.

'Sshh, Thompson,' said Minnie. 'We're talking here.'

'It's very busy today,' said Israel, changing the subject.

'Bunged, isn't it!' said Minnie. 'We're an Internet café as well you see, these days.' She nodded towards the computer in the corner, which no one was using. 'They love it. So, what can I get you?'

'Well. I've already—'

'I've got it,' said Zelda, hurrying away.

'Good,' said Minnie. Well, very nice to meet you.'

'Erm. Minnie?' said Israel, as she was about to go.

'Yes?'

'Minnie. I wonder if you could help me? I really need to get hold of a map.'

'A map?'

'Yes. Of the town.'

'Of here?'

'Yes. You've not got one, have you?'

'A map? Of here? What for?'

'For getting around.'

'Why? D'you not know where you are?'

'No. I'm not from round here, so it's difficult, you know, to find places. I keep getting lost.' It was the thought of Ballygullable.

'Oh, right.'

'And I need to start planning my route, for the mobile library.'

'Oh good. You all set to get her going then?'

'No. Not exactly. Not quite.'

'No? Och well, never mind.'

'So, a map? You don't have one, or know where I could get one?'

'Well, I don't think so. I can see if Zelda has one out back here.'

'Well, if you did have one I'd be eternally grateful.'

Minnie bustled away and Israel went over his gathering evidence in his mind and on a napkin, where he jotted down his ideas about his leads in the case of the missing books. He wrote Norman's name down first, and then Ted, and he decided to try giving them points out of ten, with a maximum ten points for motive, and another maximum ten points for opportunity, and another ten for general bonkersness, and so on: unfortunately they both got maximum points. He was maybe going to have to work a bit on his system. He'd have to check to see what Hercule Poirot did in order to eliminate his suspects; something to do with exercising ze little grey cells as far as he could remember from Peter Ustinov in the film version of *Death on the Nile*.

Minnie brought the lentil soup, and the scone: that might help his little grey cells.

'There we are now. That'll put some colour in your cheeks,' she said.

'Right,' agreed Israel. 'That's great. And any luck with the map?'

'The what?'

'The map? So I can plan my routes?'

'Och, yes. Silly me. No, there doesn't seem to be anything there.'

'Oh well.'

Israel took up a spoon.

'Och, well. You'll just have to use your initiative,' said Minnie.

'Initiative?'

'To find places. My late husband, he could tell whatever time of day it was just by looking at the sun.'

'Could he?' said Israel. 'Right. Was he a ... a sailor or something?'

'Ach. No. He was a window-cleaner, but. He used to love getting out with the dog though.'

'Good. Well. You don't know anyone who might have a map of the area, do you?'

'Och, no, son. It's not really the sort of thing people have around the home, is it?'

'No, I suppose.'

'You'd have to be an outsider to have one really.'

'Quite.'

'So – och, I know! Silly me! You should try the Reverend Roberts.'

'Reverend Roberts?'

'He's the minister at the First Presbyterian? He's not from round here. He maybe has one.'

'OK. Thanks, Minnie.'

'Now, but never mind your auld map, what about this soup?'

Israel tried the soup. 'Mmm,' he said. 'Beautiful.' It was: thick, velvety and full of flavour.

'Och,' said Minnie, blushing. 'I bet you say that to all the girls. Speaking of which, how are you finding that niece of mine?'

'Niece of yours?'

'George.'

'George, as in George at the farm George?' said Israel.

'That's her,' said Minnie.

'I didn't realise she was your niece.'

'Of course she's my niece. You know, in fact, thinking about it, you're similar ages. You'd make a lovely couple ...'

Israel sprayed hot lentil soup from his mouth.

The man next to him in the Soviet republic flat cap and sports casual wear and reading Andy McNab was not amused.

'Hey!'

'Sorry!'

The man started fussing, wiping the spray of soup from his clothes.

'Och, Thompson, don't be so soft. It's just a wee drop of soup.'

'Aye, it's maybe a wee drop of soup to you, Minnie and to the young fella here, but this is my best suit,' said Thompson, indicating his polyester tracksuit.

'Sshh now. It'll wash. Drop of Daz.'

'I am so sorry,' said Israel, wiping soup from his glasses.

Thompson grumbled under his breath.

'Thompson, sshh. Now, Israel ...'

Thompson continued to grumble.

'Thompson!'

'I'd take another wee drop of your soup, Minnie, in lieu of the laundry bill, like.'

'All right, all right.'

'And maybe another cheese scone?'

'Och, don't be pushing your luck now.'

'I'll be having to have this dry-cleaned, sure.'

'Catch yerself on, Thompson. No more now. I'll attend to you in a moment. Israel. So what do you think, of George?'

'Erm ... She's very ... unusual.'

'Ah. I knew you'd get on. That fella she's with is no good for her at all. She's turning into an auld string of misery. I think he's a wee bit half-and-between ...'

'He's what?'

'You know. Funny.'

'What do you mean, funny?'

'Och, funny, you know.'

'No.'

'Man his age, never married.'

'Oh, right. I see. But that doesn't necessarily make him—'

'Aye, but the frost'll try the rhubarb.'

'What?'

'You're not funny, are you?' asked Minnie.

'No! Of course I'm not funny! Although, I mean, it's fine if pcoplc arc funny ...'

Thompson edged away slightly from Israel on the bench.

'Good. I'll have a wee word with her, then, see if I can't fix you up with a date,' said Minnie.

'No!' spluttered Israel, being careful to cover his mouth this time. 'Minnie! No!'

'Bit of initiative!' said Minnie, winking.

'What? No, Minnie, no!'

But it was too late: Minnie had glided swiftly away, bearing scraps of scone.

Once he'd finished his lunch Israel went to pay, which proved to be a problem, because he had no money.

'Ah. Erm. Minnie,' he said. 'I'm so sorry. I forgot, I've got a problem with my cash card and I've not—'

'Och, never worry,' said Minnie. 'It's not as if you're going to just disappear is it? We all know where you live, eh?'

'Yes,' said Israel. Unfortunately.

'We'll put it on the slate.'

'Right, thanks. And about you having a word with George—'

'Consider it done!' said Minnie.

'No!' said Israel.

But Minnie had moved away to serve another table.

It was as he made for the door then that Israel noticed that the computer in the corner was on, and seemed to be working – and there was an elderly grey-haired woman in a wheelchair with a rug over her knees squirling around with the mouse.

Israel went and stood beside her.

'Just surfing,' she said.

'Right,' said Israel. 'Could I ... Would you mind, when you're done?' he asked. 'I've just ...'

'Of course,' she said, wheeling herself away, backwards, and at some speed. 'Work away there, sure. I was just checking out the chat-rooms.'

'Right.'

'Some of them, honestly ...'

'Yes.'

And he sat himself down and paused for a moment, staring at the screen, his fingers poised over the keyboard, suddenly excited – checking his e-mails! He could hardly believe it. His first contact with the real world since he'd arrived here. He fired up Hotmail, typed in his user name and his password, hit return, and took a long, deep, anticipatorily satisfied breath.

No one had e-mailed him. Or at least no one he knew. His in-box was of course stuffed full with messages from people offering to extend his credit-card limits, and the size of his ... But no one else. Not even Gloria. Since coming here not only had he become lost: he seemed completely to have disappeared. He sent Gloria a rather self-pitying message with the subject line, 'Remember me?'

It had been Gloria's idea that he took the job in the first place. He was always complaining about his sad, wasted life at the discount bookshop, and the lack of opportunities with which he was faced, as a potential genius, and so when he was offered the job in Tumdrum it was Gloria who had convinced him that this was his opportunity, and that although they'd have to live apart for a while she would of course be over at weekends to visit him, and that it would only bring them closer in the long term, and that once he'd done his time in Tumdrum offers of other library jobs would be raining down upon him: he'd be fielding calls from the Bibliothèque Nationale in Paris, and the Vatican, and Harvard's Widener Library; and librarian head-hunters from all over would be tracking him down, waving big fat vellum hand-inked librarian contracts, written in Latin, stipulating twenty weeks' paid reading time per year; and before he knew it he'd be padding along foot-worn marble corridors into the unimaginable glories of the world's great stacks and depositories. So far things weren't turning out quite like he'd expected.

As he was about to sign out of the site it suddenly occurred to Israel where he might be able to buy a map of Tumdrum.

For years, Israel had been unable to afford to buy new books – which is why he worked in a bookshop, and one of the reasons he'd trained as a librarian in the first place: the prospect of free, or at least free access to books.

First of all he tried www.abebooks.com.

Nothing, and anyway he'd have to wait too long for the shipping from America.

Then he thought he'd try amazon.co.uk, the marketplace: lots more individuals selling books. He found what he was looking for straight away.

Ordnance Survey. One-Inch Tourist Map.
Good, some edge repair. Soft cover.
National grid seventh series, 1959. Printed on paper.
Covers good. Ex-library.

It was a little more expensive than he'd been planning to pay, but it all went on the credit card anyway and he needed the map, so he hit 'Buy with 1-Click' and the map was his.

Now, if he said it himself, *that* was showing initiative.

10

The chicken coop was beginning to feel suspiciously like home. There were books everywhere; and unwashed dirty mugs from the farmhouse littered every surface; and clothes piled on the bed; and a slightly chickeny, not entirely unpleasant smell of sweat and damp, as if a little pot of stock were simmering on some not too far distant stove.

Israel splashed some cold water on his face from the wash-jug and bowl and poured himself a large glass of whiskey and lay down to contemplate another day's successful amateur sleuthing. He had a growing list of suspects. He had a map on the way. And he was starting to find the whiskey almost as effective as a couple of Nurofen.

And then there was a knock on the door.

He got up, took a fortifying sip of his drink, and went and opened the door, expecting Brownie.

It was not Brownie.

It was a woman, around about his age, and, Israel had to admit, she looked more like his kind of person than a lot of the people he'd been meeting recently: she was wearing clothes that had definitely crossed the border from practical to stylish, and she looked intelligent, and thrusting, as though she was maybe on the way to drinks *after* work, rather than, say, as though drinking *was* her work. Her hair was dark; her lipstick was red; her overcoat was unbuttoned; and she looked like she meant business. She could easily have passed in north London.

'Mmm,' she said, taking a last quick draw on a cigarette and stubbing it out underfoot; and Israel reckoned he was probably the most politically correct person in about a hundred-mile radius at this very moment but even he couldn't help noticing her legs.

'Hello?' he said shyly.

'Mr Armstrong?'

'Yes.'

'Hi. I'm Veronica Byrd,' said Veronica Byrd, straightening up underneath her tailored overcoat and putting on a wide smile and forming the words carefully in her mouth.

'Hello, Veronica Byrd,' said Israel, his brow furrowing.

'I'm from the *Impartial Recorder*.'

'I see,' said Israel, in a way that suggested that he didn't see at all.

'We're the local newspaper.'

'Oh, right. I, er, I'm more of a *Guardian* sort of person myself.'

'Uh-huh. Good. Well, I was hoping' – she paused momentarily – 'I could ask you a few questions?'

She was straining slightly forwards now, standing up

on tiptoe, looking over Israel's shoulder into the room.

'Look,' said Israel, manoeuvring himself to block her view, 'if it's about the school gateposts, it was an accident, and no one was hurt.'

'The school gateposts?' said Veronica, still trying to look round him.

'It's not about the school gateposts?'

'No. I don't think so,' said Veronica Byrd disinterestedly. 'Although it sounds fascinating. Maybe you want to tell me all about it?'

'No. Thanks.'

Veronica looked at him and raised an eyebrow. 'Sure?'

'Yes. Thanks. Right. Well.'

Veronica continued staring at him. 'Have you been in a fight?'

'No. Why?'

'It's just, your eye.'

'Accident.'

'Oh. So.'

Veronica's gaze did not waver.

'Do you want to come in?' asked Israel, finally giving way, although really there was no need; Veronica was already across the threshold.

'Well well,' said Veronica, staring round, clearly unimpressed, 'this is home?'

Despite his attempts at home improvements – the scattering of clothes and books, the strategic placement of empty mugs – the place still looked exactly like what in fact it was: a home for chickens, with perhaps an untidy weekend guest who'd overstayed his welcome. A chicken coop, after all, is a chicken coop, no matter how many books and old clothes you leave scattered around. And Israel himself of course by this stage in his stay looked like a hobo who'd been riding trains: his corduroy jacket suit the only thing of his own remaining in an outfit in which he increasingly resembled the Unabomber. He needed some new trousers. And shirts. And shoes.

'It's temporary. Sorry,' he said, embarrassed, 'I can't offer you a seat or anything.'

'It's OK.' Veronica perched herself on the edge of the bed, pushing aside Israel's pile of books to make more room for herself. 'You like reading, huh? Isn't that a bit clichéd for a librarian?'

'Well,' said Israel, flushing. 'You could say that. Isn't it a bit clichéd for a journalist to barge in and be asking so many questions?'

'Touché!' said Veronica.

No one had said anything like 'Touché!' to Israel for quite a while. He liked it.

Veronica was sitting just inches away from Israel's bedside bottle of Bushmills and was now looking at him expectantly.

'Sorry. Can I get you a ...?' Israel said, indicating the bottle.

'Sure.'

'Erm ...' Israel searched around for another glass but there was no other glass, so he poured his own whiskey into a mug, and wiped out the glass with one of Brownie's spare T-shirts – The Thrills. Then he topped up the clean glass with whiskey and gave that to Veronica.

'You certainly know how to treat a girl, Mr Armstrong.'

'Ha, ha,' laughed Israel nervously, hovering at the side of the bed. 'So. How can I help you?'

'It's all right, you can sit down,' said Veronica, patting the bed beside her. 'I don't bite.'

'Right. Ha, ha.' Israel perched himself on the edge of the bed, as far away as possible.

'Actually,' said Veronica, removing a reporter's spiral-bound notepad and a pencil from her handbag, 'it's about the missing books.'

Israel coughed nervously. How did she know about the missing books?

'The missing books?'

'Yes. The library books? Is it true that over ten thousand books have gone missing from—'

'Fifteen thousand, actually.'

'Really?'

'No! No. That's just the stock, of the library. I believe. Look. Sorry. I really don't think I'm the best person to help you with this. I'm only—'

'The librarian?'

'Yes. But, I've only just—'

At that moment there was another knock at the door, thank goodness, and Israel was about to get up and answer it when the door flew open. It was George.

'George!' said Israel, leaping up from the bed, his voice slightly hoarse with relief and fear and excitement. 'Lovely to—'

'Armstrong,' said George, taking in the scene.

'Come in,' said Israel, taking off his glasses, and then putting them back on again. 'I was just—'

'No. Thank you. I didn't realise you were entertaining.'

'Ha, ha!' laughed Israel, blushing. 'I'm not entertaining. This is Veronica Byrd, from the local paper. She's just popped in to—'

'Georgina,' said Veronica.

'Veronica,' nodded George.

'Do you two know each other?'

'Yes,' said Veronica.

'From a long time ago,' added George. 'I'll leave you two to it then.'

'George, no, it's fine ...'

But George had already gone, shutting the door loudly behind her.

'So,' said Israel, embarrassed, turning towards Veronica, who was taking a long sip of her whiskey.

'So?'

'Erm. How do you two ...?'

'Oh, Georgina?' said Veronica, smoothing down her skirt. 'She was head girl when I was at school.'

'Really?'

'And I was deputy head girl.'

'Uh-huh.'

'We were sworn enemies, actually. Competed over everything: you know, homework, netball, swimming, boyfriends,' said Veronica, with some bitterness. 'She was an all-rounder. Straight As in her exams. She was going to go to university.'

'Really?'

'Yes.'

'But?' said Israel.

'But?'

'I detected a *but* there?'

'Oh you did, did you?'

'Yes.'

'You'd make a very good journalist, Mr Armstrong.'

Israel blushed. And Veronica moved a little closer towards him on the bed.

'It's all the Beckett and Pinter,' said Israel nervously.

'Sorry?'

'Samuel Beckett? Harold Pinter? Lot of pregnant pauses, silences, stuff like that. You know.'

'Oh.'

'I did them at university.'

'OK. Good. Well done.'

'So your "but"?' persisted Israel.

'My butt, Mr Armstrong?' said Veronica, shifting ever so slightly closer.

'Yes, your, er, not your ... ahem. Your ...'

'Oh yes, my "but",' said Veronica, laughing. '*But* – as I was saying – then George's parents died.'

'Oh dear.'

'It was the toy-shop bomb.'

'The what?'

'In 1986 they put a bomb in the litter bin outside the toy shop on Main Street.'

'Who? The IRA?'

'Of course.'

'In Tumdrum?'

'Yes. Her parents were going to buy a christening present for her little brother.'

'Brownie?'

'Is that his name? I don't remember his name.'

'Yes. Brian his proper name is, but people call him Brownie.'

'Ah, right, yes, that's him.'

'God.'

'He survived, anyway. His pram was blown across the road by the blast. Both parents killed instantly.'

'That's terrible.'

'Yes. It was. But that was a long time ago. Things like that don't happen here now.'

'Right,' said Israel, sounding unconvinced.

Veronica took another long sip of her drink.

'So what happened to George?' asked Israel.

'She left school and came to look after the farm with her grandfather, and to bring up her little brother.'

'I see.'

'Is he still around, Brian, the brother?' asked Veronica.

'Brownie? Yes. Yes, he is.'

'He must be, what ...?'

'He's probably late teens, early twenties. He's at university.'

'Inherited the brains then. And what about the grandfather?'

'Yes. He's still around too.'

'Huh,' said Veronica. 'So, how are you finding it, being stuck out here with them? Would it not put you in mind of the Addams family or something?'

'Well, it's—'

'Or the Simpsons?'

'It's not so bad.'

'Or *Psycho*.'

'Yes, well, thanks.'

Veronica finished her drink.

'Anyway,' she said, patting the bed, 'let's get back to the subject in hand, shall we?'

'Which,' gulped Israel, 'was?'

'The missing library books?'

'Ah, well. Yes, I really can't say anything about that. You'll have to ask Linda Wei.'

'Linda?' laughed Veronica, reaching into her handbag and taking out a pack of cigarettes and a lighter.

'Yes.'

'What about if you spoke to me, strictly' – and she leaned a little closer to Israel here, as she lit the cigarette – 'off the record,' and she spoke the words 'strictly off the record' as if they already were strictly off the record and slipping between silk sheets.

She exhaled.

Israel coughed.

'No. I...' Israel wriggled away towards the end of the bed, where a brass knob prevented him from going any further. 'Would you mind if you didn't ...'

'What?'

'Erm. Smoke?'

Veronica laughed. 'Why?'

'I'm a bit, er ...' He coughed again. 'And it's very bad for you, you know.'

'You're very funny, d'you know that?' said Veronica.

'Am I?'

'I think you know you are.'

Israel blushed. 'Yes. Well, I'm sure Linda will be able to help you out. And ...'

Israel went to open the door.

'Lovely to have met you,' he said. 'I need to...'

'Help muck out the pigs?'

'Something like that.'

'Well, I can take a hint, Mr Armstrong. It's a shame. I thought we were going to get along so well.'

'Thank you.'

'Here's my card. In case you decide you want to ... talk.'

Now, Israel could not deny that Veronica Byrd was a woman of considerable persuasive charms, and the pleasure was really all his, but all he could think about was that Linda Wei was going to kill him if she found out that the local paper knew about the missing library books: she'd blame him, without a doubt. The only people who knew about the missing books, apart from him and Linda, were Ted and Norman Canning, neither of whom was likely to have gone to the paper if they were guilty of stealing the books.

Israel could not work out at all how Veronica had found out about the missing books. He certainly hadn't told anyone else about them, except of course for George, and Brownie and Mr Devine ...

Oh, no.

He thought he could have trusted them. Surely he could have trusted them. He didn't have anyone else to trust.

He hurried to the farmhouse, looking for George. There was no one there, but then coming out he spotted her in a field – it was a late winter's afternoon and the sun was shining, and he could see her from way off, her red hair – and he trudged and trudged and trudged his way up to her in the mud, his brown brogues squelching beneath him, calling her name.

'George! George!'

George ignored him. She was holding a wooden post in one hand and a mallet in another, and she was scowling.

'George!'

'How's your lady friend?'

'What?'

'Your lady friend?'

'She's not my lady friend.'

'She looked pretty friendly to me.' George stood up straight, brushed her red hair out of her eyes and fixed Israel with a stare.

'Well, it was ... Business. Anyway, I've got a—'

'That's what you call it on the mainland, is it? Business?'

'No, it is not. Listen, I've got a bone to pick with you.'

'Aye, right, well.' George looked away. 'Sure, it's your business anyway, whatever it is. Now while you're here, you can make yourself useful.'

'No, hang on.'

'We need to strain these wires.'

'What? Why? No. I need to talk to you about—'

'Fine, you can talk and work, can you? Or that beyond you?'

'No. Of course it's not beyond me.'

'Good. Because we're stock-proofing the field.'

'What?'

'Stock-proofing. Stop the pigs getting away. We had a turshie out last week.'

'Right. What?'

'Never mind.'

'Wasn't it stock-proofed before?'

'It was. But we're having to sell off parts.'

'Of the field?'

'Aye.'

'Why?'

'Why d'you think we're selling the field?'

'I don't know. For money?'

'Aye, well done: it's certainly not for the sake of my health, is it?'

'No.'

'Same reason we took you in,' she said, looking at him disdainfully. 'We're not doing it out of goodwill.'

'No. Clearly.'

She handed Israel a wooden post. 'Here. Hold this. Have you sorted out anywhere else to stay yet?'

'No, I've not had the chance.'

'Unfortunately,' said George.

'Yes. Well. My feelings exactly. Anyway, George, I—'

'You just let me know when you do.'

'Believe me, you'll be the first to know. But—'

'Good. Hold it. There. *There*.' She placed her hands firmly on his, steadying them.

'What are you—'

'Just hold it straight. I need to mallet it in. I need it straight.'

'OK.'

'Straight! Holy Jinkers! What are you, stupit? Straight!' She pounded the mallet onto the post, Israel gripping tight all the while, his whole body shuddering.

The post stayed upright.

'Right. Is that it?'

'I need to box 'em.'

'Box them?'

'Box anchor.'

'Right. Well, first, let me—'

'I've already got the rocks in. I need the Number 8 wire from the box there. There.' She pointed to the box with a long fine finger. 'Can you get it?'

'The what?'

'The Number 8 wire!'

All wire looked the same to Israel.

'Is this it?'

'No! The Number 8!'

'This?'

'Aye, that's it.'

'George?'

George started tying and straining the wire.

'George?' repeated Israel, raising his voice.

'What? What?'

'Listen, I think I'm in trouble, because—'

'Oh, this is the bone you want to pick with me, is it?'

'Yes, it is, actually. If you would just let me explain.'

'Fine. Go on then.'

'Well. It's ... You or Brownie haven't mentioned the missing books to anyone, have you?'

'What?'

'The missing books from the library.' Israel looked around to make sure no one could hear him. They couldn't: he was in the middle of a vast silent field. 'You haven't mentioned it to anyone? It's just, we really didn't want rumours getting around.'

'And who's "we" then?'

'The Department of Entertainment, Leisure and Community Services.'

'Oh, right, you're speaking on their behalf now, are you?'

'Well. Yes. I am supposed to be the librarian.'

'Supposed to be. Aye.'

'Right. Anyway, it's just, you know, it wouldn't look good if people knew the library books were missing.'

'We said we wouldn't mention it to anyone.'

'Yes, that's right.'

'So we haven't mentioned it.'

'Not just accidentally maybe, or—'

'We *said* we wouldn't mention it.'

'But—'

'Is that it? Here, hold this.' She gave Israel the end of a piece of wire. 'Hold it tight!'

He held it tighter. 'So you haven't spoken to anyone at the paper or anything?'

'The *Impartial Recorder*?'

'Yes. You've not spoken to them—'

'If we said we wouldn't, we haven't. Do you understand that? Unlike some people I could mention, we do have standards in this family, Armstrong.'

'What? What's that supposed to mean?'

'Nothing.'

'I have standards!'

'Aye, right enough: snuggling up like with your lady journalist friend in your love nest, sipping on whiskey at half past four in the afternoon while other people are out working, earning an honest day's wages: that's your standards, is it?'

'What? My love nest! That … place!'

'Coop.'

'Exactly! And I told you, she's not my lady friend. I've only just met her.'

'Aye, well, that makes it all right then.'

'What? No! And anyway, what about you snuggling up with your man friend in the back of the taxi the other night?'

'That's different.'

'Is it? Why?'

'Because. It is.' George stared at him again, hands on hips, eyes blazing. 'Because it's my business.'

'I see. Fine. Right.'

'And I'd be grateful if you kept your nose out of it.'

'I will. And maybe you can do the same.'

Israel turned away as if about to go.

'Hey, Armstrong! Don't you just walk away from me. *I*'ve a bone to pick with *you*, before you go flouncing off.'

'I am not flouncing off.'

'Well, you can call it what you like. I had my aunt on the phone this afternoon.'

'Right?'

'Minnie. At the café? Have *you* been talking to her?'

'Well, I— '

'Well, don't. Her and that other woman are …'

'What?'

'We don't really have anything to do with them.'

'Why?'

'Because. They're almost as much trouble as you. And I don't want to hear from her or from you about how I should lead my life.'

'Fine.'

'And, just to make it clear, in case it's not, in your twisted little English mind, wild horses would not drag me out on a … date with you.' She spat out the word 'date' as if it were a stone or a pip.

'What? You don't think it was me that suggested that, do you?'

'Well, wasn't it?'

'Of course it was not!'

'Aye.'

'What do you mean, "Aye"?'

'Ach, sure you've your hands full anyway, with your lady friend.'

'She is *not* my lady friend!' shouted Israel.

George proceeded to tie wire round the fence posts. 'Hold this,' she instructed Israel, and they worked together in silence for some time.

'She told me about your parents,' said Israel, eventually breaking the silence.

'Who did?'

'Veronica. The reporter.'

'What about them?'

'You know. The …'

'What?'

'The way they ... How they died.'

George was silent again. Israel could see her bite her bottom lip.

'I just wanted to say how—'

'Listen, Armstrong,' she said, with barely contained rage. 'I am tolerating you around here, and that's all – *tolerating* just. D'you understand?'

Israel remained silent.

'And I have had *just about enough* of listening to your nonsense today – do you hear me? – and I would like to be left in peace and quiet, if that's all right? Some of us do have work to do, *if* you don't mind.'

'Right. It's just ... I just wanted to say ...'

'Listen! Listen!' She looked at him with something close to hate. '*I* don't need *you* saying anything. All right? Do you understand? Everything's already been said long ago. Do. You. Understand?'

'Yes. OK. All right. All right. Don't—'

'I don't need your interfering. I don't need your pity. I don't need *you*, or anyone else for that matter. What I do need is to get this field stock-proofed.'

'Fine!'

'Good! The sooner you learn to leave things you don't understand around here well alone, the better for everyone.'

'I'm sure.'

'You can go.' She turned her back on him.

'What?'

'I *said*, you can go.'

'I thought I was helping you to stock-proof the field.'

'I'll do it myself.'

'But— '

'Go. What are ye, stupit? Can you not see when you're not welcome?'

He could, actually. It was a feeling with which he was becoming increasingly familiar.

11

Israel was not exactly feeling welcome anywhere – not at the farm, not in Tumdrum, not in fact on the whole of the island of Ireland generally, which had not turned out to be the place he had imagined it might be, and if his father had been alive, he'd have called him and told him so. As it was, he'd called his mother a few times, but he didn't like to tell her exactly how he was getting on, in case she said, 'I told you so.' He kept on calling Gloria, but she was always too busy to talk:

'Hello?' he'd say.

'___.'

'It's me.'

'___.'

'Israel.'

'___.'

'Yeah, sure. I'll call you later.'

'___.'

'Yeah. Fine.'

'___.'

'No, that's fine. Yeah. OK. Bye. Bye.'

He missed her. She didn't seem to be missing him.

He was feeling pretty alone, then, in this godforsaken wasteland, and he most certainly did not expect to find himself feeling welcome in church of all places, but it was strange, he didn't have a problem being here now, in Tumdrum First Presbyterian; there was a Second, also, apparently, according to Mr Devine, and a Third and a Fourth, and if they were all like this then Israel felt he could maybe reconsider his position on the Christian Church, if not indeed on Christianity as a whole. Presbyterians might as well have been theosophists as far as Israel was aware, and they may have practised child sacrifice and believed in every kind of impossible thing, but he liked their style.

The big double church doors had been wide open when he arrived in town and wedged the mobile library in the nearest on-street parking space, just nudging the kerb, and there may have been a slight bump with the car behind, but nothing major, no lasting damage, and nobody seemed to notice so nobody needed to know.

And then he checked in his wing mirrors and leapt out of the van and ran inside the church, really sprinted – which was quite a feat, given the state of his old brown brogues and those pinchy combat trousers of Brownie's, and the amount of potatoes he'd been having to eat recently to make up for the lack of any alternative vegetables of any kind or any non-meat protein. He ran as fast as he could, under the circumstances; the last thing he needed was people stopping him and trying to borrow library books; anyone might have thought he was a librarian.

There'd been no sign of the map of Tumdrum in the post from Amazon.co.uk, or indeed of any post arriving for him at the Devines' whatsoever and he'd decided that before setting out on any more wild-goose chases to Ballygullable – Ballygullable, God – or anywhere else, he'd try the Reverend Roberts at First Presbyterian, who Minnie believed might have a map and who might be able to help him out.

Inside, Tumdrum First Presybterian was a root-bare kind of a church which looked as though the Reformation had just happened, about half an hour ago, and people had just been in with their lime and whitewash and stripped and scraped out all the craven images and left the place looking sparkling clean and not unlike a fresh-painted gallery waiting to be hung with one or two tastefully abstract paintings; a nice Rothko, maybe, or something done with a roller and a tin of matt emulsion, nothing too challenging or religious. It was a bit like the soft-seating area in a corporate reception: in fact, the church reminded Israel of the reform synagogue he'd sometimes attended with his mother as a child, which was more like a doctor's waiting room than a place of worship; all it would have taken would have been a few dog-eared copies of the *National Geographic* and the place could have been in business as a kind of giant, open-plan orthodontist's.

'Yes?' said an elderly, black-suited man, with a face like a gargoyle and a little floral pinny around his waist, who popped up suddenly from behind the large, oak lectern as Israel wandered down the aisle.

'Bloody hell!' said Israel.

'Mind your tongue now,' said the man.

'Sorry. I ... Erm. You gave me a hell of a fright there.'

'Aye,' said the man, who was holding a large multi-coloured duster-on-a-stick, which he was now absent-mindedly flicking around the lectern. 'But this is a house of God.'

'Yes. Sorry.'

'And what would you be wanting exactly?'

'Erm. Well. You're not the Reverend Roberts by any chance, are you?'

'That I am not.'

'Right. Sorry. I was hoping to see the, er, minister.'

'The Reverend Roberts?'

'Yes. If that's him.'

'Aye, it is, surely.'

'OK. Well, I wonder if I might be able to see him?'

'Aye. Mebbe.'

'Is he around?'

'Well, he's in, but he's out.'

Oh, God, another comedian. These people gave him a headache.

'OK,' said Israel pleasantly.

'Would you be having an appointment at all?' asked the man.

'No. No, I don't, I'm afraid. Do I need an appointment?'

'Generally those that don't, do, and those that do, don't.'

'Erm. Well, I can always come back later if now is not convenient.'

'Mebbe.'

'Right. OK. So, where does that—'

'Would it be a matter of personal and spiritual urgency?'

'Er. No, not really. It's more sort of business, actually.'

'Are you selling something?'

'No. No, I'm not.'

'Are you sure?'

'Yes. I'm the new mobile librarian.'

'You don't have the look of a librarian.'

Israel was currently sporting a Green Day T-shirt ('AMERICAN IDIOT'), the combat trousers, and his brown brogues and corduroy jacket, most of the rest of his own clothes having now gone mouldy hanging to dry – after he'd washed off all the chicken shit – in the Devines' stinking damp scullery back at the farm. Also he had had to apply another layer of masking tape on the bridge of his glasses to hold them together, so he looked like a down-on-his-luck Second World War fighter pilot, someone who'd perhaps lost both their legs coming down over France and who was now reduced to begging for a living.

'No. Sorry. It's just, I needed a very quick word with the, er, reverend.'

'Aye. Right,' said the old gargoyle man. 'Well, take a pew. We'll see what we can do.'

The man then disappeared somewhere behind the organ.

Israel sat down in the front pew and stared up at the creamy-white walls and the big grey organ pipes, like some grim industrial machinery: maybe the place could have done with some decoration after all.

The dark-suited man reappeared.

'Reverend Roberts is on the phone at the moment. If you come into the robing room, he'll be with you shortly.'

The man led Israel to the robing room in silence, through a door and down a little corridor and ushered Israel in, and said goodbye.

'I've just tidied in here,' he said, as his parting shot. 'So don't touch anything.'

'Right. OK. No, I won't,' promised Israel. 'Definitely not.'

There was nothing much to touch: the windowless room was as cold and bare as the church, like a cell, in fact, except for a table set in the middle of the room piled high with hymn books, and long low bookshelves all around, and portraits of unsmiling ministers in black and white up on the walls, and a long black gown which hung on the back of the door, which presently opened, and in walked the Reverend Roberts.

Who was a black man.

For a moment it was all Israel could see, and he was amazed, flabbergasted: it was like someone had fixed an aerial on the telly, and the world had suddenly gone into colour. He realised he hadn't seen a single person who was not a pure pasty white since he'd arrived, and he felt like going up to this man, this fine example of colour and contrast, and shaking him warmly by the hand just to say thanks. But then he thought better of it: when he was at university and he told people his name, they'd sometimes say to him, 'Some of my best friends are Jewish,' which as a welcome and introduction he'd always felt was rather less than warm, and very possibly a threat, in fact – the implication usually being, 'And therefore this justifies me being a raging anti-Semite.' So he just smiled.

'Hello,' said the reverend, who towered above Israel, and who had a booming voice born of years of sermonising and stating the sublime and the startlingly obvious, a voice of great echoey depths.

'Hello,' said Israel, 'you must be the Reverend Roberts?'

'Ah, it's the dog-collar that always gives me away, isn't it?' said the Reverend Roberts, booming.

'Right,' said Israel.

'But please, call me England.'

'Sorry?' said Israel, hesitating. He could feel a headache coming on. 'Say again? You lost me there. Call you England?'

'Yes.'

'Erm ...'

'That's my name.'

'England?'

'Yes. I'm from South Africa, as you may be able to tell.'

And here England boomed a laugh, a 'Ho! Ho! Ho!' as deep and as echoing and as resonant as Paul Robeson doing Santa somewhere in a grotto deep underground, and it was the sweetest, the richest and the most welcomingly ironic sound that Israel had heard since arriving in Ireland.

'My mother,' he continued, 'was a great admirer of your Queen. And indeed of the whole of your United Kingdom! I have a brother called Scotland, and another called Wales.'

'You're joking me?'

'No! Most certainly not. She always wanted us to travel:

she thought the names would give us a good start.'

'You didn't have a brother called Northern Ireland?'

'Yes. I did, of course, although my mother called him Ireland. Her grasp of post-partition politics was not strong. Ho, ho, ho! But I'm afraid he died shortly after he was born.'

'Oh, God, I'm sorry.'

'That's OK. He was unwell: God is merciful. Anyway. It's very nice to meet you, sir. You are ...?'

'Sorry, yes, I'm Israel Armstrong. I'm the new librarian.'

'Ah, of course. Welcome, sir, welcome! Your reputation precedes you. Everyone has been looking forward to meeting you. Including myself.'

'Right.'

'You were in the local paper.'

'Yes, so I believe. Unfortunately.'

'Ho, ho, ho. Yes! When I first arrived my photograph was in the paper every week for almost a year. You'll get used to it.'

'I will?'

'Of course. The novelty will wear off. How are you settling in so far?'

'Well,' said Israel, 'it is taking a *little* getting used to.'

'Ah yes. But you'll become accustomed to our strange ways. Ho, ho, ho! It took me about three years to get in the swing of things. But now, Israel – can I call you Israel?'

'Yes. Sure.'

'The promised land. You don't have brothers named Egypt and Canaan?'

'No, no. I don't.'

'Ho, ho, ho! Never mind. Well, I think it took me three

years to get used to things, but now I really love it here.'

'I doubt I'll be here for three years.'

'Ah, that's what I thought. I thought I'd be back home by now in South Africa, married and with little children running around, but instead here I am, all alone here among the mad Irish heathen! Ho, ho, ho! God moves in mysterious ways.'

'Yes, I suppose he does. I guess it must be much more difficult for you, actually,' began Israel, thinking aloud and then immediately regretting he'd set out on this train of thought.

'What? Being the only black man?' said England generously. 'Ho, ho! Of course, it can be a problem at first ...' He hesitated, as though he wanted to say more, but changed his mind. 'But enough about me, sir,' he continued. 'What can I do for you?'

'Well, I'm trying to put the library back together, rounding up overdue books and what have you, for the mobile library service – you know the main branch library's been shut?'

'Yes, of course.'

'But what I'm really after is a map of the area, that might help me get around, you see. And Minnie, down at Zelda's, the, er, café, she said she thought you might have something, you know, having been a stranger here yourself.'

'Oh yes, very much so. A stranger in a strange land, isn't it. Ho, ho, ho! Indeed. A map though. Hmm. Now I did used to have something, years ago, but it's all in my head now – worse luck! Ho, ho, ho! Actually, I think perhaps I borrowed the map from the library.'

'Ah. Oh well.'

'But!' boomed England. 'I'm sure I can help you with some overdue books, if that's a help to you?'

'Oh really?'

'Yes, of course. I can ask in the notices for the congregation to return their overdue books to me.'

'That'd be great, if you could.'

'No problem! But first, let's start with my own little hoard, shall we?'

England Roberts then indicated the long, low bookcases that lined the room. Israel glanced at some of the titles: it seemed to be all books about the Bible and devotional works, but then the Reverend Roberts went over to a small gathering, a group of books at the bottom row and far end of one of the bookcases, and all of them had the tell-tale purple mark of the Tumdrum and District Library along the spine. Israel bent down to look at the titles: Elmore Leonard; Carl Hiaasen; American crime, mostly, and true crime, plus a few books about serial killers and the occult.

'Phew. That's pretty racy reading for a minister.'

'Ah, well. I suppose as Christians we have a very well-developed sense of sin, ho, ho, ho!' laughed England, who was now heaping the books onto the table in the middle of the room: as well as the fiction there was also the Chartered Management Institute's *Guide to Building a Brand*, *The Hypnotic World of Paul McKenna*, and Stephen R. Covey's *The Seven Habits of Successful People*.

'There we are now. That's a start for you, I hope.'

'Yes. Thank you.'

'So have you gathered many in yet?'

'Well, a few dozen so far.'

'That's very good.'

'Actually, it's not,' said Israel miserably. 'There are thousands missing.'

'Thousands? Oh dear.'

'I'm a bit stuck, to be honest, trying to find them all.'

'These are all overdue books that people have at home?'

'Well ...' Israel glanced around, conspiratorially. 'If I tell you this in the strictest confidence?'

'Yes, of course,' said England, leaning slightly towards Israel. 'Anything you tell me is strictly between me, you and the gatepost – I mean the Lord, of course. Ho, ho, ho!'

'Right,' said Israel. 'Well, I think there's a possibility they've been stolen.'

'My goodness! Stolen? How many?'

'All of them.'

'All the library books?'

'Yes. But we've not told anyone.'

'I see. But what about the police?'

'Well, it doesn't look good for the library service.'

'Hmm.'

'So, you can't mention that to anyone ...'

'No. Absolutely. You have my word, as a man of God.'

'Thank you.'

Israel looked totally defeated.

'So, Israel,' said the Reverend Roberts, his voice dropping even deeper, unfeasibly deeper and warmer. 'It's all down to you then?'

'I'm afraid so. It's my job to find out who stole them.'

'To find the perp?' said the reverend, perking up.

'Sorry?' said Israel.

'The perpetrator: that's what they're called, in the books.'

'Is it? Right? Yes, I suppose.'

'Have you got many leads?'

'Er ... Well, a few.'

'Yes. You're going to need juice on the inside.'

'What?'

'Juice. On the inside.'

'Sorry, you've lost me.'

'You need a snitch, or a nark – isn't that what they're called? Someone with their ear to the ground, who'll tell you the word on the street.'

'The word on the street? Right.'

'Oh yes, that's essential. Have you tried at the market?'

'No.'

'Oh, well. That'd be the place for you to start, wouldn't it? You're bound to find people there who've heard about any missing books – you know what market traders are like.'

'Right. No, I don't actually.'

'Slags, mostly. Ho, ho, ho!'

'Sorry?'

'"Slags?" It means part of the criminal fraternity, I believe. Come, come, Israel, do you never read any crime fiction or watch television?'

'No. I don't watch a lot of TV.' Gloria didn't agree with TV. She was always busy working. 'I've read the classics, you know, Dashiell Hammett and what have you. And I read *The Name of the Rose* a few years ago ...'

'*NYPD Blue* though? *Murder One*? *CSI*? *LA Law*? *The Sopranos*? *The Bill* even?'

Israel shook his head.

'I used to love them. Can only get a lot of them on satellite and cable now, alas. You don't have satellite or cable, do you?'

'No. I don't, I'm afraid.'

'It doesn't look good for a minister, you see, to have a satellite dish.'

'I see.'

'Never mind. *CSI* is on terrestrial again at the moment. That's very good. And there's a new *24* coming up, apparently. Gives one something to look forward to.'

'Yes. Good.'

'Apart from the Second Coming, of course. Ho, ho, ho! But anyway. What we need to do is get you a grass or something.'

'Some juice on the inside?'

'Exactly! See – very good! – you're picking up the lingo already. Come on, the market's today: we can take a walk down there, if you like. I can introduce you to some people.'

'See what's the word on the street.'

'Yes. Ho, ho, ho!'

'And the slags?'

'That's it!'

The reverend made for the door.

'And also, Israel, can you remind me – let's see – while we're at the market I need some potatoes, a new scrubbing brush, and some out-of-date biscuits ...'

'Sure.'

The Reverend Roberts waved Israel through into the corridor.

'Now, just before we go, though,' said the reverend, lowering his voice ominously.

'Yes?' said Israel.

'How about a cup of coffee?' The reverend was virtually whispering now.

'Er.' Israel's experience of coffee in Tumdrum so far had not been good.

'Would you like an espresso?'

'Erm.' He'd been caught out with that one before also.

'I have my own machine in the kitchen,' explained the mighty reverend. 'My little luxury.' He looked around suspiciously. 'Don't tell the congregation, though: I keep it locked up. They'd think the money would be better spent on poor black children in Africa, you know. Ho, ho, ho!'

'Right,' said Israel, following the reverend's huge silent strides.

'It's my only vice,' he explained. 'I roast my own beans also: I have them sent from Scotland.'

'From Scotland? Really? Is it known for its—'

'No, no, no! My brother Scotland, in London.'

'Oh, right.'

'You can't underestimate the importance of a good cup of coffee, can you?'

'Absolutely. No. You can't.'

'And yet you can't describe it either,' said the reverend reverently, ushering Israel through a door. 'Which is a little bit like God, isn't it?' he mused. They were up behind the lectern.

'Yes. I suppose ...' agreed Israel.

'Now. Here.'

Glancing around, England Roberts knelt down and

extracted a large bag of coffee beans tucked behind one of the organ pipes.

'Keeps them cool,' he explained, grinning. 'Perfect temperature.' He then rustled around again. 'And ... To go with that ... My other vice ...' He pulled out a large box wrapped in brown paper. Israel suspected for a moment that ... 'Chocolates!' boomed England.

'Reverend?' said the dark-suited man in the floral pinny, who popped his head round the door.

'Ah!' said England, flustered.

'Keep the noise down.'

12

Israel and England spoke to a lot of traders down at the market – most of them slags, touts, sleeks and millies, according to England, who was nonetheless on first-name terms with them all and who greeted all the women with hugs and all the men with high fives and a complimentary booming 'Ho, ho, ho,' not a typical Presbyterian kind of a greeting, Israel guessed, judging by the fact that a lot of the various slags, touts, sleeks and millies tried to hide behind their stalls at England's approach. And anyway the word on the street down at the market was pretty much what the word on the street always is everywhere: that the price of petrol was getting ridiculous; that the traffic-calming measures on the one-way system were a joke; and that something should be done about the state of the public toilets, which were a disgrace.

But there was more: there was also word on the street that the closure of Tumdrum and District branch library was a huge cover-up, and that if books had gone missing, then it was the council themselves who were to blame.

If what he was being told was true, and he had no reason to doubt it, given his dealings with the council, then at the very least Israel had a new suspect to add to his list, and, at the very best, he was close to solving the mystery of the missing library books and pretty soon he was going to be packing up his old brown suitcase and on his way back home: he could almost smell that Brick Lane twenty-four-hour bagel bakery.

He rushed back to the farmhouse for lunch.

'Brownie, Brownie, Brownie,' he said, bursting into the farmhouse kitchen.

'Israel, Israel, Israel.' Brownie had books piled around him on the kitchen table, working on another essay.

'The word on the street is that the council stole the books themselves so that they could close the mobile library and—'

'What's he blethering about now?' said Mr Devine, pouring himself some tea from the never-ending kettle on the Rayburn. 'I don't know, young people today ...'

'The council did it. The council stole the library books.'

'The council?'

'That's what people are saying. That's the word on the street.'

'The word on the street?'

'That's what people are saying.'

'Paisley's not going to last much longer,' said Mr Devine. 'That's what people are saying.'

'No, not that,' said Israel. 'People are saying that the council themselves have stolen the books!'

'Hang on, Israel,' said Brownie. 'The council stole the books?'

'Yes, that's right. Linda Wei and everybody, in it right up to their necks.'

'Sure, I could have told you that,' said Mr Devine. 'They're quare and close up there.'

George was silently eating a sandwich up at the end of the table, resplendent as usual in dungarees and work boots.

'Armstrong,' she said, between mouthfuls, graciously acknowledging Israel's presence.

'George,' nodded Israel.

'And who exactly have you been talking to?' George asked, with a certain tone, a tone that carried a clear but unvoiced clause at the end of the sentence, a persistent, silent clause, it seemed to Israel, and which rang out clear and quiet at the end of most statements and sentences in the north of Ireland and which said, if you listened to it very carefully with English ears, 'you idiot'.

'Some people at the market,' he replied.

'Ha,' said George, with the same firm, quiet tone.

'"Ha?" What's that supposed to mean?' said Israel, who was after all a Highly Sensitive Person and who had studied English and American Studies at one of the best former polytechnics turned universities in the country, and who was not therefore unaware of certain tonal ambiguities in speech and writing.

'Ha?' said George. '"Ha" means "Ha" over here, Armstrong. Why? What does it mean where you're from?'

'Well ...'

'Who exactly have you been talking to?'

'A lot of different people.'

'Who?'

'I don't know their names. There's a chap who sells dog food and stuff for pets.'

'Who's that?' asked Brownie.

'Trevor is his name?' said Israel.

'Trevor?' said George.

'The fella Cormican?' asked old Mr Devine.

'Aye,' said Brownie. 'Kool For Kats.'

'Little fella,' said old Mr Devine.

'Wears a baseball cap,' said George.

'Yes, that's him, yes,' said Israel excitedly. 'Trevor told me—'

'Aye. Trevor,' said George, with her tone.

'So, he said…' started Israel again.

George put down the remains of her sandwich and looked pityingly at Israel. 'D'you know how Trevor ended up selling dog food at the market, Armstrong?'

'No. I don't, no.'

'Have you ever thought though that someone might not set out with selling dog food at the market as their career goal?'

'Well. I don't know …'

'Well then, let me tell you how he ended up down there, shall I? Your friend Trevor was involved in an insurance scam – wasn't it, Brownie?'

'Aye.'

'Yes. Selling non-existent insurance policies to people, particularly old and vulnerable people. He was put away for that.'

'Ah. Yes. But—' began Israel.

'How long was it for, Granda?' asked George.

'Three years I think it was,' said Mr Devine.

'Extortion with menaces, wasn't it?' said Brownie.

'Something like that,' said George.

'Bad packet altogether,' said Mr Devine.

'And you're taking what he says as gospel?' said George to Israel.

'No, I'm not saying it's gospel. It's just—'

'A conspiracy theory,' said George.

'Well,' said Israel. 'What if it is?'

'A huge conspiracy involving the council, here, in Tumdrum?'

'Well, why not?'

'Because this is the real world, Armstrong, and not a John Grisham novel.'

'Yeah, right, but ...'

'I prefer Tom Clancy,' said Mr Devine. 'I can't follow them others.'

'Look, look, think about it though,' said Israel. 'The council want to close all their library services, right? They get away with shutting the branch library, but by law they have to offer some library service, so they say they'll get the mobile library service back up and running. But at the moment at which the mobile library is about to be launched, they say they've lost all the books. Then they can close it simply on financial grounds, and they're not to blame.'

The collected Devines were not convinced.

'Aye,' said George.

'You've lost me, Israel, actually,' said Brownie.

'Hmm,' said old Mr Devine. 'Did you ever read *The Day of the Jackal*? That was a good book. Who was that by?'

'Right, let's work it out,' said Israel.

'OK,' said George.

'They made a film of it,' said Mr Devine.

'By a process of logical deduction,' said Israel.

'This'll be good,' said George.

'Where would you hide something, if you didn't want someone to find it?' Israel asked.

'Where someone couldn't find it?' said Brownie, quick off the mark.

'Exactly! And where wouldn't they be able to find it?'

'Somewhere they hadn't looked for it?'

'Yes! Yes! And where wouldn't they have looked for it?'

'Somewhere they didn't think it was?' said Brownie.

'Yes!'

'So that's it? That's the answer?'

Even Brownie had trouble following Israel's logic here.

'Aye, right, that's nice and clear,' said George.

'Look,' said Israel. 'Mr Devine, if you had a pair of socks you wanted to hide, where would you hide them?'

'Er.'

'Where do you usually find your missing socks?'

'In my sock drawer?'

'Exactly.'

'So?'

'So, the chances are, if you wanted to find some hidden books you'd look in ...'

'My sock drawer?'

'No! A library!' said Israel.

'Hang on,' said Brownie, burrowing in among the

pile of books on the table and producing a copy of Wittgenstein's *Remarks on Colour*.

'Look!' he said. 'Look!'

'Wittgenstein's *Remarks on Colour*?' said Israel.

'What is it, a colouring book?' asked Mr Devine.

'Look, here, on the spine,' said Brownie, pointing to the purple sticker.

'The purple sticker,' said Israel.

'Tumdrum and District Library,' said Brownie.

'Where d'you get it from?' said Israel.

'From Rathkeltair Central Library,' said Brownie.

'Even though it's got the Tumdrum mark on it?'

'Yep.'

'Aha!' said Israel, who couldn't believe his luck.

'Aha?' said George.

'Yes, "Aha!"' repeated Israel breathlessly. 'Aha! Aha! Aha! And I'll tell you what,' he said, brandishing the book. 'If this isn't prima ...'

'Facie?'

'Exactly! ... evidence, I don't know what it is. Oh yes! Mystery solved! We're done! I am out of here, people. Can I use your phone?'

The Devines looked at each other in sympathy and confusion as Israel left the table and took off again in the mobile library to see Linda Wei at the Department of Entertainment, Leisure and Community Services.

Linda was at her desk, with her back to Israel when he entered. She swivelled around on her plush imitation-leather seat, a vast red paper serviette in one hand, and an enormous scone in the other, her mouth full to bursting.

'Linda,' said Israel, with all the confidence of someone

about to reveal a major conspiracy at the heart of government, albeit only local government, and albeit only the Department of Entertainment, Leisure and Community Services within the heart of local government, and even then only the Information Resources Steering Committee within that, but still.

'Mmm.' Linda chewed and swallowed rapidly, waving to Israel to sit down, which he did, while she wrapped the serviette carefully around what remained of the scone and took a swig of coffee from a vast mug which proclaimed her, in big balloon letters, WORLD'S NO.1 MUM.

'Israel!' she said, coughing, crumbs catching in her throat. 'Cinnamon scone?'

'Right.'

'Would you like some?'

'No, thanks.'

'Missed lunch, you see.'

'Right.'

'It's from the canteen.'

'I see.'

'They have a scone of the day – every day.'

'Good.'

'Thursdays it's usually cinnamon.'

'Right.'

'So what can I do you for today?'

'Well, I wanted to ask you a few questions.'

'Oh. Really?' Linda tapped her greasy fingers on her desk.

'Yes,' said Israel seriously. 'It's about the library books.'

'Right. Sshh. Close the door, would you?'

Israel got up and closed the door.

'Walls have ears,' said Linda, flapping her ears in demonstration. 'So, how's the hunt going then?'

'Well,' began Israel.

'Uurgh,' belched Linda, patting her more than pattable chest. 'Sorry. Indigestion – it's the scones. Very fresh. Sorry. The book hunt?'

'Linda, where would you hide library books, if you had to hide them?'

'Oh, is this an interrogation?' giggled Linda.

'No, Linda, I'm just asking a question.' He'd decided to take the Socratic route.

'It's like Castlereagh,' said Linda. 'Er. I don't know. If I wanted to hide library books?'

'Yes.'

'Good question. In boxes?'

'Possibly.'

'Wrong answer?' said Linda.

'It's not the answer I'm looking for.'

'OK. Oh, I do like this. It's like Twenty Questions. Erm. Where would I hide library books if I wanted to hide them? In a shed?'

'No.'

'Some sort of underground bunker or something?'

'No.'

'Oh, I don't know, Israel. You'll have to tell me.'

'No. You were supposed to be telling me.'

'Oh, was I? Er ...'

'Oh, never mind,' said Israel. The Socratic route might take a while. 'How about in a library?'

'In a library?'

'Yes.'

'Oh, yes,' said Linda, 'that's very good. Because ...'

'No one would think of looking there.'

'Right. Oh yes. That's very good. That's brilliant. That'd be the perfect hiding place for some missing library books.'

'Exactly.'

'So?'

'So. Linda.' Israel paused here for dramatic effect. 'I have found the missing library books.'

'Oh good,' said Linda, without really registering the necessary shock and surprise, in Israel's opinion, but never mind. 'Where?'

'In Rathkeltair Central Library.'

Linda shifted in her seat – rather suspiciously, thought Israel, although it may have been because she had wind.

'Have you, really?' Linda looked rather nervous.

'Look.' With a flourish Israel produced from his bag Wittgenstein's *Remarks on Colour*.

'It's a book.'

'Yep.'

'This is it?'

'Look.' Israel indicated the purple sticker. 'See. It's from Tumdrum. But it's issued out of Rathkeltair.'

'So?'

'So, the old Tumdrum books are in Rathkeltair.'

It was because she had wind. Linda waved her hand to waft away the smell.

'OK,' said Linda. 'Sorry. Excuse me. Just run that by me again.'

'This book proves that the missing Tumdrum Library

books are now in Rathkeltair Central Library.'

'But this is only one book,' said Linda, readjusting herself on her chair.

'Yes.'

'I thought you meant you'd found them all?'

'Not yet, no.'

'Have you found any others in fact?'

'Not so far, no, but, I have deduced—'

'All right, Sherlock Holmes. Have you actually been to Rathkeltair Library?'

'Not as such at the moment, no, but—'

'Right,' said Linda, pushing back in her mock-leather seat. 'Well, Mr Armstrong. An entire stock of books in another library might be a discovery, but one book in another library is what we in the business call an inter-library loan.'

'Ah, but it's not.'

'Not an inter-library loan?'

'No. I've already spoken to the librarian at Rathkeltair on the phone: he says it's an acquisition.'

'Ah.' Linda looked a little sweaty now, Israel thought. But then she always looked a little sweaty. 'Well, yes, I suppose that does complicate matters a little.'

'Someone,' said Israel, with a hint of accusation in his voice, 'is distributing the Tumdrum Library books to other libraries.'

So, this was it. This was his big moment, his *J'accuse*. This was where Israel revealed the solution to the crime, wrapped things up, and collected his plane ticket out of here. This was where he could do his Hercule Poirot bit. He tried to look Hercule Poirotish.

'Are you all right, Israel?' said Linda.

'Yes, thanks.'

'It's just, you're ... It looks as though you're sort of pouting a bit there.'

'Sorry.' It wasn't a pout: it was supposed to be Israel looking pensive. 'Anyway, Linda, I believe I have solved the mystery of the missing library books. I believe, Linda,' he said, prodding his glasses and puffing out his chest slightly in his Eminem T-shirt, 'that it is the *council* themselves who have stolen the books. I believe,' he said, warming to his theme, standing tall in his too-tight combats and his old brown brogues, 'that the council closed Tumdrum Library and had no intention of ever reopening it. And' – he even raised a finger – 'that it is the council who have stolen or hidden the missing library books, which they are now selling or redistributing to other libraries, including Rathkeltair.'

'Israel,' said Linda, with more pity than anger, 'who have you been talking to?'

'I have conducted a number of enquiries.'

'People down at the market?'

'Well. Yes. How did you—'

'Ach, Israel, they're a bunch of hoods down there. Everybody knows that.'

'Yes, but—'

'Was it Trevor?'

'Er.'

'Ach, honestly, Israel. He'd have the cross off a donkey.'

'What?'

'He's always complaining about something. So this is all your evidence?'

'Well. At the moment.'

'Israel ...'

'What?'

'Last week you thought it was Ted who'd stolen the library books?'

'Yes. I did. But I was wrong about that. I was just affirming the consequent.'

'You were what?'

'It doesn't matter, it's a technical term.'

'Aye, well, right,' said Linda huffily, 'whatever it is, you can go and affirm your consequent elsewhere. Because frankly your suggestion that we at the Department of Entertainment, Leisure and Community Services are in any way complicit with the theft of the library books is preposterous, ludicrous and, I might add, quite offensive to me personally, as someone who has worked hard to ensure that the mobile library operates successfully, not to mention who has worked hard to have you appointed and remain here as librarian.'

'But—'

'One rogue library book turning up does not solve the mystery of fifteen thousand missing library books, Mr Armstrong.'

'Well ...'

'Does it?'

'No. Maybe not, but—'

'So may I perhaps suggest that if you spent more time looking for the books and less time listening to malicious gossip generated by people with nothing better to do than putting pure bad in other people's heads, you might be getting somewhere.'

Linda got up from her seat, gathered up some papers, and made to leave the office.

'But, Linda …' Israel had rather lost the advantage now. He had a headache coming on.

'But nothing, Mr Armstrong. I would be grateful if you wouldn't waste my time in future with your mad conspiracy theories. Now, I trust I shall be seeing you later this evening?'

'Sorry?'

'I had rather thought that's why you'd come here and interrupted me this afternoon – to discuss the reception for the launch of the new mobile library service?'

'The what?'

'You hadn't forgotten?'

'Erm.'

'All the details were in your welcome pack and guide.'

'Ah, right. I'm afraid … actually I lost all that stuff, I'm afraid. I … It was on the Rayburn at the farm, you see, and I …'

Linda was clearly losing interest in Israel's explanation.

'And all my money,' he continued, 'and all my cards and …'

Oh, God. Now he thought about it he wasn't going anywhere anytime soon. He was going to be condemned to living here for all eternity.

'Your personal misfortunes are no concern of mine, I'm afraid, Mr Armstrong. I do expect you however to attend tonight's reception. It's very important. The lady mayoress is going to be there.'

'But we can't launch the new mobile library service when we haven't got any books!'

'Well, whose fault is it we haven't got any books?'

'Yours?' said Israel.

'Yours,' said Linda, holding up a little fat finger. 'But we shall have to agree to disagree on that particular issue. In the meantime we can't alter the date of the launch. So if you could perhaps get yourself smartened up – I don't want you letting us down. And not a word to anyone, please, about the missing books? And certainly not a word about your pathetic theories? I don't want you embarrassing yourself and us.'

Israel remained silent.

'Mr Armstrong?'

'All right. All right, all right, yes.'

'Good. You'll be expected to say a few words of course.'

'What?'

'Just the usual: what a pleasure and privilege it is, blah, blah, blah. The mobile library is a fantastic community resource, blah, blah, blah. I don't know, whatever it is librarians say. "I love books," you know, something like that.'

'But we haven't got any books.'

'Yes, well, but no one needs to know that, do they?'

'I can't lie.'

'I'm not asking you to lie, Mr Armstrong.'

'Are you not?'

'Ach, no, silly. Just do what other people do at these things.'

'What's that?'

'Pretend.'

13

The grand civic reception to mark the opening of the new mobile library service was held at the Tumdrum and District Community Halls, which were thronged with flush-faced middle-aged men in suits and made-up women in heels. The peanuts, and the sausage rolls, and the Thai chicken-satay sticks, the Shloer and the warm white wine were flowing thick and fast. If not exactly bacchanalian, the atmosphere in the halls that night was at the very least convivial.

'Most convivial,' Israel was saying to everyone he met, unable to think of anything else to say to the endless parade of men in dark suits and the women in heels, whose names he didn't catch and couldn't remember.

'Most convivial. Lovely. Wonderful. Thank you. Thank you. Yes. Thank you. Lovely to meet you too.'

Once everyone had loaded up their paper plates and finished off a glass or two of the warm white wine there were a few kind words about the new mobile library service from the Tumdrum and District mayoress, the magnificently one-eyed Councillor Maureen Minty, who stood up at the front of the hall, beneath a portrait of the Queen, on a makeshift podium constructed from three thick gym mats.

Mayoress Minty spoke eloquently, from notes, with her black velvet eyepatch set at a jaunty angle, about her own personal love of reading, and about Shakespeare, 'The Bard', as she called him, and about Catherine Cookson, her own personal favourite, and about the importance of the library service in general and about large-print and audio books in particular, and she ended by reading a poem she had composed specially for the occasion, unmemorable except for the ingenious and uniquely Northern Irish rhyme, to Israel's ears, of 'librarian' with 'non-sectarian'.

And then there was the handing over of the mobile library keys to Israel.

He was hauled up to the front and introduced to the many gathered guests and dignitaries as the new Outreach Support Officer. There was a rousing round of applause and he stared out at the sea of round and wine-lipped faces.

He could have said anything. He could have told the people of Tumdrum exactly what he thought of them – not much. He could have revealed the scandal of the missing library books; he could have revealed his hunches and explained his theories. He could have spoken passionately about the cause of vegetarianism or pleaded for peace and reconciliation among the people of the island of Ireland and in the Middle East. He could have delivered an oration worthy of the end of a Hollywood movie, something stirring and profound that would have been right up there with the likes of Al Pacino and Ralph Waldo Emerson, but instead, under the fierce monitoring gaze of Mayoress Minty and the Queen on the wall and Linda Wei at the back of the hall he just mumbled a few words of thanks – words consisting mostly of 'Most congenial', 'Lovely', 'Wonderful', 'Pleasure and a privilege' – and shuffled off the gym mats.

He wanted to go home. Instead he found himself instantly plucked and pushed and ushered and introduced to yet more women in heels and more men in suits, including the local MP, a tall and sweaty fat man, a Mr Peter Easton, a man who looked and sounded as though he had devoted a lifetime to sucking on lemons and riding uncomfortable hobby-horses. Israel gulped down some wine and some Nurofen to steady his nerves.

'Ah, yes. I've always taken a very close interest in the arts,' said Peter Easton, MP, as though somehow blaming Israel for this unfortunate state of affairs.

'Have you?' said Israel, who had taken an instant and huge and not, he felt, entirely irrational dislike to the man, who was wearing some sort of sickly, thick after-shave and whose pin-stripes on his pin-stripe suit seemed suspiciously far apart, and the knot of whose tie was too perfectly plump, and his hair too smooth and too silky, making him look like a comedy or imitation MP, a huge, weird, life-sized, hand-operated puppet of Mr Peter Easton, MP, and not the thing itself.

'Stalin,' said Israel.

'Sorry?' said Mr Easton, MP, leaning down over Israel.

'Stalin – you know, Soviet leader. Big moustache. He took a very keen interest in the arts.'

'Really?' said Mr Peter Easton, MP, who was already gazing around, his pin-stripes wriggling, his tie and hair stock-still, ready to move on and press more flesh.

'Yes. Used to phone Pasternak to ask him about Mandelstam.'

'Hmm. Fascinating.'

'And then he had him executed.'

'Well,' said Mr Peter Easton, MP, smiling. 'Let's hope that won't be necessary in your case, Mr Armstrong. Pleasure.' And he shook Israel's hand and was gone.

Israel wiped his hand of MP sweat and cologne on his trousers and went to help himself to some more crisps, and a couple of mushroom and mayonnaise vol-au-vents – actually, the plate was nearly done, so he took the lot – and another glass of wine, which was being dished out from big tin jugs set on a makeshift table constructed from the base of a vaulting horse and a flip-chart with its legs removed. Israel was feeling hot and uncomfortable and ever so slightly woozy, so he took a few mini-quiches also, just in case, to line his stomach: Jews, his mother always said, can hold their drink, as long as they're eating at the same time. It seemed to be working.

Then he spied Ted on the other side of the hall, done up in a suit and tie, looking as though he'd been trussed up and was ready for slaughter. He hurried over.

'Ted,' he said. 'Ted!' He'd pretty much ruled Ted out as a suspect and hoped he might be able to patch things up a bit. 'I ...' He could really have done with a hand with the hunt for the missing books.

'You,' said Ted.

'Yes, me!' said Israel.

'I've nothing to say to you, young man.'

'No, don't be like that, Ted.'

'You're still in my bad books.'

'Yes. Well. Sorry. Would you like a vol-au-vent though?' said Israel, attempting both apology and pathos at the same time, and offering the plate.

'Hmm.'

'They're nice.'

'Are they vegetenarian?'

'Yeah, but not so's you'd notice.'

'Ach, all right. But don't think a volley vont means I'm forgiving and forgetting now.'

'No, of course not,' said Israel.

'Mmm,' said Ted. 'Mushroom?'

'Yes. I think so.'

'Not bad. So, I s'pose you're going to tell me, how's the auld hunt going?' asked Ted, brushing flaky pastry from his chin.

'The hunt?'

'For the books, you eejit.'

'Oh, it's coming along.'

'Aye.'

'I've got a couple of very good leads. Actually, Ted, you wouldn't think about coming back and—'

'Who, me? The criminal mastermind?'

'I don't think you're the criminal mastermind, Ted.'

'Oh, not smart enough, eh.'

'No. Ted. It's not that. I've crossed you off my list of suspects.'

'Aye, right. That's nice of you, Kojak.'

Israel leant in close. 'I'm working on a major conspiracy theory at the moment,' he said.

Ted finished chewing his vol-au-vent. 'I'm sure: still not a titter of wit about ye then. What happened to the hubcaps?'

'What?' said Israel.

'Aye, you heard me. What happened to the hubcaps? Don't think I haven't noticed. I've seen yous driving about: there's no hubcaps on the van anymores.'

'Ah, yes, that was a little mishap.'

'And I see you've her bent up and twisted round the bonnet?'

'Ah, yes, that was another little mishap.'

'Aye, right. Well, I entrusted her to you,' said Ted. 'And I'll tell you what,' he continued, leaning over close to Israel as he spoke, with vol-au-venty intensity, 'you'd better start looking after her better than you're doing at the minute, boyo. Or I'll beat the blinkin' lard out of ye. D'you understand?'

'Yes,' squeaked Israel.

With which friendly threat Ted turned his back on Israel and walked away, just as Linda Wei approached him from the other direction, took him firmly by the arm and led him off to introduce him to the redoubtable Maureen Minty.

'Hmm. Excuse me. Hello!' said Israel. 'Lovely speech.'

'Thank you,' said the mayoress, staring at Israel with her one good eye from under her firm-set hair and through a thick pair of glasses, looking for all the world like a cross between Moshe Dayan and Golda Meier.

'And that's a lovely ... chain,' said Israel, trying to think of something to say to an elderly one-eyed lady mayoress he'd never met before, and pointing to her chain of office. 'Can I ... touch it?' And before he knew what he was doing he was reaching out towards the lady mayoress's ample bosom.

Maureen Minty slapped his hand.

'If I was forty years younger I'd be flattered, young man. As it is, I'm appalled by your bad manners.'

'Ouch,' said Israel. 'Sorry.'

Linda led the lady mayoress away, frowning at Israel, who raised his hands in his mother's traditional Jewish 'what-have-I-done' gesture.

'He's a bold 'un, isn't he,' murmured Maureen Minty.

'Aye,' said Linda, flashing a warning stare at Israel.

'You haven't lost the old charm then, I see.'

It was Veronica, the reporter from the *Impartial Recorder*, and the funny thing was Israel had known she was there, in the room, from the moment he'd first arrived, even though he hadn't been able to pick her out. She seemed to have a peculiarly vivid presence, seeming to announce herself from a distance, as if subtly lit, like in a film, or like she was emitting a high-frequency sound, like a minky whale perhaps, or something similar, and it was as if he had a sixth sense, attuned to her. He'd had this feeling before. He tried to remember when: it was when he'd first met Gloria.

'You're looking very ... natty,' said Veronica, with that characteristic hint of mischief and mockery in her voice.

'Natty?' said Israel. 'Natty? Gosh. No one's used the word natty since about 1950, have they?'

'Well, no one I know has worn a three-piece herring-bone suit since about 1950.'

'Ah. True,' said Israel. He was wearing one of Mr Devine's old suits. It was a little tight, but it certainly made a change from Brownie's combat trousers and T-shirts, and he thought it gave him a certain Cary Grant kind of a look, actually, or maybe a Sidney Greenstreet kind of a look, if he was being absolutely honest, but drink had been taken, so there was no need to be absolutely honest. He was looking pretty good.

'Will you have your photo taken with me?' asked Veronica.

'Me?'

'Come on.'

She pulled Israel over towards a man with a huge camera and a flashgun.

'Here we are now.'

'Israel, Michael – photographer at the paper. Michael, this is Israel, our esteemed librarian.'

'Outreach Support Officer,' said Israel jokingly, although neither Veronica nor Michael seemed to see the joke. 'My little joke,' he explained.

'He's a comedian as well, then,' said Michael.

'Oh yes,' said Veronica, winking at Israel, 'he's a terrible tease. He's English.'

'Aye.'

'OK then, by himself first I think.'

And before Israel knew it, it was flash and the picture had been taken.

'Great,' said Veronica. 'Now together,' and she squeezed up close to Israel, cheek to cheek. 'Do your worst.'

Another flash.

'One for the family album. Thanks, Michael.'

'OK, Veronica,' said Michael. 'That it?'

'I think that'll do us for tonight.'

'See you tomorrow.'

'Night. What's happened to your hair,' asked Veronica, turning to Israel, fishing around in her handbag. 'Do you mind?' she asked, going to light a cigarette.

'It's your funeral. I combed it.'

'Well, I think it suits you,' she said. 'You scrub up nicely.'

Israel blushed. 'Thank you ...'

'At which point' – Veronica leant closer towards him, touching his arm, blowing smoke in his direction – 'you're supposed to say, "And you're looking rather lovely too."'

'Ah, right, sorry. You're looking lovely too,' said Israel, which was true, actually; Veronica was wearing a long black clinging skirt and black leather boots and a tight, buttoned-up blouson, which made her look rather as if she'd just flown in specially for the evening, like flying-ace Amelia Eckhart.

'There's no smoking in here, love,' said a woman, tapping Veronica on the shoulder.

'Oh, really?' said Veronica, smiling. 'I had no idea. I'm so sorry. Shall we?' And she indicated the door to Israel, who followed her obediently outside.

'Ah,' said Veronica. 'That's better. God, I hate those things.'

'Me too,' said Israel.

They stood leaning up against the side of the graffitied wall of the community hall, staring up at the stars.

'No luck then yet in your great book hunt?'

'What great book hunt?'

'Now, now. You know I know.'

'That you know what?'

'About the missing library books?'

'Ah. Well, you'll have to talk to Linda about library provision. I'm just—'

'Doing your job?'

'That's it.'

'Well, I'm sure you're very good at it.'

'I hope so.'

'Well, let me ask you another question then, librarian.'

'Outreach Support Officer.'

'Whatever. Do you have a girlfriend?'

'Erm ...'

'I'll take that as a no then, shall I?'

He did not correct her.

Veronica had finished her cigarette.

'Shall we go somewhere we can get warmed up?'

The pub they went to was in a village several miles up the coast from Tumdrum, and it was just like an archetypal English pub, with beams and an open fire, and knick-knacks, which was all very nice but which did nothing to calm or reassure Israel, who was now devoutly wishing he hadn't come away with Veronica and had stayed instead with the middle-aged men in suits and women in heels at the gala reception for the new mobile library service. That would have been much safer. But it was too late now: a few glasses of cheap wine and a bellyful of vol-au-vents and here he was with an attractive lady reporter in a pub in the middle of nowhere and no good could come of it, he knew that from the moment he'd got into Veronica's

Renault Clio and she'd put on her Dido CD, and they were speeding along the coast road, laughing about leaving everyone behind at the community halls and enjoying a shared sense of adventure. Desire, boredom, guilt and being a long way from home can make a man do strange things. Israel had seen *Lost In Translation*. Several times. And he suddenly felt as though he was in some kind of parallel Bill Murray universe, where he made witty remarks to good-looking women who laughed at his jokes.

'OK, what can I get you?' he asked, as calmly and filmically as possible, when they entered the pub.

'A gin and tonic, please,' said Veronica, and they went together to the bar, but unfortunately, because Israel kept turning round to smile at Veronica nervously, he had some difficulty in attracting the attention of the bar staff, and eventually Veronica said, 'Shall I?' and Israel admitted defeat.

'Um, yeah, if you like.'

They sat down eventually, Veronica with her gin and tonic, Israel with his pint of Guinness and a packet of crisps.

'Cheers,' said Israel.

'Sláinte,' said Veronica.

And then there was a silence between them, and Israel looked at Veronica and Veronica looked at Israel, and Israel looked back at Veronica looking at Israel.

'Read anything good lately?' asked Israel, breaking his gaze.

And Veronica laughed and laughed.

'Oh, that's original, for a librarian.'

There was another long pause and Israel became

suddenly aware that he was desperately in need of some small talk in order to see his way out of things here; that was definitely what he needed at this point, just to calm things down and make things clear. He was currently down to about five conversations a week, maximum, and most of them were with George about animal husbandry and with Mr Devine about young people today, and so he was more than a little bit out of practice when it came to the old low-level chat, and when he did finally think of what to talk about all he could come up with was mostly asking Veronica about her job, and how had she ended up working for the *Impartial Recorder*, and what was it like, and unfortunately she told him all about it, all about her unhappy childhood and her time on local papers and her ambitions to make it big, and it turned into quite a heavy conversation really. Israel nonetheless thought it had steadied things between them, except that when Veronica got up from the table to go to the ladies, he suddenly realised how closely they had been leaning in towards each other as they spoke, and as Veronica brushed against him in order to get past he felt as though he'd been set on fire.

To calm himself Israel tucked into the crisps – cheese and onion, or, strictly speaking, Tayto Cheese and Onion, crisps unlike he had ever eaten in England, and much better than the average cheese and onion in fact, much stronger somehow, but not in an unpleasant cheesy or oniony kind of a way; they seemed somehow to embody the very essence of cheese and onion crisp, their cheesy yin in perfect harmony with the oniony yang. Israel knew he should probably save some of these absolutely perfect crisps for Veronica but because he was nervous and because generally he ate when he was nervous he finished the crisps in just a few swift mouthfuls, shaking out the final crumbs into the palm of his hand, throwing his head back, and swallowing, and then he cupped his hand and smelt his breath. His breath smelt very bad indeed.

'You're back, then,' said Israel, like an idiot. She had reapplied her make-up.

'Yes, of course I'm back,' said Veronica. 'What did you think I was going to do, climb out the window?'

'No, no,' said Israel.

'It's fine. Why don't you just relax.'

'Sorry I'm a bit tense, it's, you know, the new job and what have you.'

And Veronica reassured him that that was fine and she started asking him questions about his work, and as she lit another cigarette he noticed that she squinted her eyes, like people do, and the conversation took off again.

When they finished their drinks Israel got up to go to the gents and it was then that it happened, that finally he lost all perspective on where he was and what he was doing, in a single moment of madness, in a moment of musth, like a bull elephant during rutting season, when he stopped in front of the condom machine and had a look at the selection available, something he had *never* done before in his life and was unlikely to do ever again – Gloria had always taken care of that end of things – but the extreme and unusual circumstances in which he found himself seemed to have given him permission to do so. He just couldn't quite believe that he was here, in a pub, with a beautiful woman; it seemed so fantastic that almost anything could happen.

He prodded his glasses and stared at the machine, as if mesmerised, and then he made his decision.

Fortunately, though – for everyone concerned – he didn't have any change. He didn't have any money at all in fact, so that would have been that, except for the middle-aged man with slicked-back hair standing beside him by the machine.

'D'you know what, son?' said the slicked-back-hair man. 'In all my years of patronising these facilities, I have never once seen a soul use that machine.'

Israel didn't know what to say.

'Not once,' mused the man sadly, and Israel felt suddenly emboldened then, by the Guinness, and by the wine, and the vol-au-vents and the best cheese and onion crisps he'd ever tasted, and by this sad admission of a life half lived – never to have bought condoms from a machine in a pub because there was a fighting chance you might end up having to use them – and he asked the man if perhaps he had any change so that he could use the condom machine, in a tone that suggested that unlike this sad middle-aged man, he, Israel, purchased pub condoms all the time, because that was the kind of footloose, fancy-free James Bond existence he lived in his borrowed three-piece herringbone suit, but alas, no, the man did not have any change, and nor did the next man they asked either, who also claimed never to have seen anyone use the condom machine before, and Israel was beginning to wonder what sort of contraception people used around here. But eventually someone came through from the pub into the toilets who did have change and who was happy to see it put to good use, and a small crowd had formed now, waiting for Israel to insert the money in the slot and make his decision: whisky-flavoured, mint-chocolate, multicoloured, or ribbed? The choice was overwhelming. The crowd of onlookers by this time was spilling out of the door.

'Green for starboard, red for port,' shouted someone at the back of the crowd, and everybody laughed.

And at that moment, at the *very* moment that he was pulling out the little metal tray which dispensed his choice, to the sound of cheers and a small round of applause, Israel looked up.

And he saw Veronica. Who was sitting at their table directly opposite the door of the gents toilet, looking straight in.

Oh no.

He grinned at her like a moron, waved, pocketed the condoms, the crowd parted, and out he walked, absolutely mortified.

Veronica was gathering up her handbag as he made it to the table and he opened his mouth to start to apologise.

'I, I ...'

'Most convivial,' said Veronica.

The next day what Israel remembered most clearly about the rest of the evening was Veronica saying to him, after they'd kissed, 'Ugh! Never eat Tayto Cheese and Onion on a first date.'

And he also remembered her saying, 'Now, tell me all about the missing library books.'

And he also remembered her saying, 'My boyfriend'll be back soon. You need to leave.'

14

The *Impartial Recorder* carried the story two days later under the banner headline THE GREAT BOOK ROBBERY, easily trumping the competing front-page stories about a local sausage-maker, the improbably named Tommy Snorker, who'd won a prize for his speciality pork and cranberries (SNORKER'S PORKERS A CORKER), and a man who'd been fined £75 for disorderly behaviour, plus £150 for assault, for spitting at a bouncer after having been denied entrance to Rathkeltair's premier nite-spot, Meltdown, his defence solicitor having unsuccessfully pleaded with the judge that his client had simply had too much to drink and was only dribbling (HERE'S ONE IN YOUR EYE).

When Israel arrived at the farmhouse for dinner, Mr Devine handed him a note.

'This woman called.'

'Oh.'

'She says to phone her immediately.'

'OK.'

'You seen the paper?'

'No.'

'Here.'

Mr Devine handed him the newspaper. Under the headline there was a photograph of Israel, looking like a tried and guilty Fatty Arbuckle, glass of wine in hand, with the subtitle, 'Israel Armstrong, Tumdrum's new mobile librarian, carousing this week at the launch of the new mobile library service'.

'Carousing?'

'What?' said Mr Devine. 'Caruso?'

'No. No.'

'I like Pavarotti. He's good.'

Israel read the full story.

'Oh, God.'

'He's got awful fat though, hasn't he, the big grumphie.'

'What?'

'Are you all right there, Mr Armstrong?'

'Yes. Fine. I'm fine.'

'Aye, you seem a wee bit distracted, but.'

'Yes.'

'Trouble?'

'You could say that.'

'Cast your troubles upon the Lord.'

'Right. Thanks. I'll maybe give that a go.'

Israel arrived, as requested, at Linda Wei's office an hour later.

For the first time that Israel could remember Linda Wei wasn't actually eating when he saw her: instead, just for a change, she bit his head off.

'What,' she bellowed, 'is this?'

She waved the *Impartial Recorder* at him. She was wearing a banana-yellow trouser suit with padded shoulders. She looked like an exploding canary. She jabbed her finger on the front page.

'That? Is the front page of the—' began Israel.

'Don't you get smart with me! I have had just about enough of you and your London attitude, Mr Armstrong.'

'No, Linda, hold on, my *what*?'

'We've been bent over backwards trying to accommodate you ever since you've arrived.'

'No, now, I think you'll find that—'

Linda ignored him and began reading the first paragraph.

'"Local library services are in crisis. Speaking to a source close to the library service, the *Impartial Recorder* has learnt that all of Tumdrum and District Library's stock of books has gone missing, possibly stolen." So, what happened?'

'What happened with what?'

'*Who* did you tell about the missing books and the mobile library?'

'Mobile learning centre,' corrected Israel.

'Don't get funny with me, *Mister*!'

'Sorry.'

'So?'

'I didn't tell anyone.'

'Don't treat me like I'm stupit, Mr Armstrong.'

Israel prodded his glasses and fiddled nervously with the fraying cuff of his brown corduroy jacket.

'So, how did she suck the story out of you?'

'Sorry?' said Israel, rather startled by Linda's turn of phrase.

'You know what I'm talking about. Veronica Byrd.'

'Oh, Veronica. Erm. I don't know. I may have let slip in conversation that there were a few books missing.'

'Let slip? Let slip? I wasn't born yesterday, Mr Armstrong. We know all about the birds and the bees round here, thank you very much. She'll not die in her own bed, that woman.'

'What? Who?'

'The *Impartial Recorder*'s own little Mata Hari. I saw you sneakin' off like a pair of teenagers.'

'Well ...'

'Honest, are you soft in the head, man?'

'No,' said Israel, sounding soft in the head. 'I am not soft in the head.'

'Aye, well. They say where there's a Jock there's a Jinny.'

'I'm sorry, Linda, I have no idea what you're talking about.'

'Obviously. D'you have any idea how much trouble you've caused here? You're lucky we don't just send you back to where you come from.'

'Well, that would be unfortunate, but—'

'Oh no,' said Linda, wagging her finger. 'Oh no, no, no. It wouldn't, would it? That'd be just what you wanted, wouldn't it? In fact, I wouldn't be surprised if you hadn't deliberately leaked this to the paper in order to be sacked from your job, Mr Armstrong. I certainly wouldn't put that past you.'

If only he'd thought of that.

'No,' he said truthfully, 'I— '

'So, bearing that in mind, we've decided we're going to let you cool in the skin you het up in.'

'What?'

'We're not going to sack you, Mr Armstrong.'

'Well, I'm—'

'We're going to extend your contract.'

'What?'

'Extend your contract.'

'You can't do that!'

'I think, Mr Armstrong, if you ever bothered to check the small print you'd find that you are expected to fulfil all the duties required of you as Tumdrum's new Outreach Support Officer and that if you don't certain disciplinary procedures and penalties will come into effect, which— '

'You can't do that!' repeated Israel.

'We have done it. And you've signed it.' Linda dangled the contract before him.

Israel's headache had appeared earlier on the horizon of his mind – at exactly the point at which he had entered Linda's office, in fact – and it was now gathering full speed towards him.

'Actually, I've had enough of this,' he said, getting up to leave. 'I'm going.'

'Well, of course, you're free to leave.'

'Good. Thank *you*.'

'But I'm assuming you have no means of leaving. I think you'll find you haven't received your first month's salary.'

'No, but I've...' He patted his pockets. And he remembered that he hadn't yet replaced his crinkled credit card. Or his debit card. And that he had no money. And that all he currently possessed were the clothes he stood up in, a few books, his black eye and a bump on the head. He quickly tried to draw up a list in his mind of all the people in Tumdrum who might be prepared to sub him the money for his trip back to London. There was no one on the list.

'Er.'

'Now. Sit down then, please.'

Israel sat down.

'Clearly we need to discuss how we can move forwards from here, Mr Armstrong. So, given all of your conspiracy theories—'

'They're not conspiracy theories,' protested Israel weakly. 'They're … hypotheses.'

'Aye, well, given all these weird and wonderful *hypotheses* of yours, how many books have you *actually* managed to recover so far?'

'Well, we are still missing … a few,' said Israel.

'How many?' said Linda.

'Er …'

'How many are still missing?'

'I reckon … probably around about fourteen and a half thousand.'

'So you've hardly got any in fact?'

'Well …'

'I strongly suggest then, sir, that you rapidly revise your so-called hypotheses, in the light of the evidence that you're making a sad hash of the whole thing. Or you're going to find yourself with us here forever.'

Israel's headache had now arrived, scooped him up on its back and was thundering away at full gallop.

'Look,' he said, trying a different tack. 'I can't do this on my own, Linda. I need help.' Even Sherlock Holmes had help. Everybody needs help.

'Well, we would of course love to help you, Mr Armstrong,' said Linda, flapping her canary arms, 'but *actually*, in case you hadn't noticed, *you* are the person who is supposed to be helping *us* find the missing library books.'

'But can't we just go to the police now it's all out in the open?'

'I think you'd agree, Mr Armstrong, that would only make matters worse at this stage. And also I have issued a statement to the paper this morning denying that the books are missing—'

'What?'

'And guaranteeing that the mobile library will be up and running by the end of the year.'

'But Linda that's only, what, a couple of weeks away?'

'Indeed.'

'I can't find the books by then.'

'You have to find the books by then, *if* you want to be going home any time soon. And you're going to look pretty foolish, aren't you, driving around with no books in the back of the van?'

'I can't. No. Sorry. I can't do that. I can't do it on my own, Linda.'

'Well, you could ask Ted to come back and help you out, unless he's still on your Most Wanted list.'

'No, I've eliminated Ted from my ... my, er, enquiries.'

'Good, well,' said Linda, 'maybe you should ask Ted then. He's not an unreasonable man.'

'Ted is a very unreasonable man, Linda.'

'Well, given that you probably don't have that many friends around Tumdrum, I suggest you try and cultivate what few contacts you do have.'

'Right, thanks a lot.'

Linda glanced at the clock and got up to leave.

'That'll be all then, Mr Armstrong. Unless you have anything else useful to add to our conversation?'

'No,' said Israel, defeated. 'Fine. OK. Right. Where does Ted live?'

'Ted? Up on the coast, isn't it? You'd be best looking for him at the First and Last, I would have thought, though he's off the drink but, these days.'

'Right,' sighed Israel. 'And where is it, the First and Last?'

'On the main Ballymuckery road as you're coming into town.'

'Right. I don't suppose you have a map, do you?'

'A map?'

'Of the town.'

'Och no, of course I don't. What would I want a map for?'

'It doesn't matter.'

'Is that all?'

'Yes.'

'Well, I do have to say,' concluded Linda, making for the door, 'I'm really very disappointed in you, Mr Armstrong. I had expected much better of someone of your obvious talents.'

'Right.'

'It'll no doubt be better news the next time we speak though,' said Linda, leaving her office.

'No doubt,' said Israel, full of doubt, giving her a two-fingered salute behind her back.

'I saw that,' shouted Linda, retreating down the corridor. 'I'm watching you.'

15

The First and Last was so called because depending on whether you were entering or leaving Tumdrum, it was either the first pub you came to, or the last, a distinction which one would have thought was hardly worth the boast since there were at least another dozen pubs to choose from in town, most of which had more to recommend them than merely their convenient location for thirsty or fleeing travellers. But the First and Last had acquired its name not merely because it lay on the edge of town, but also because Elder Agnew, who had established the business back in the 1950s, was a member of the Plymouth Brethren and a strict teetotaller who believed strongly in the Bible, and in the Lord which is, which was, and which is to come, and who felt that just as Christ had consorted with thieves and prostitutes, so too it was his calling to offer comfort and consolation to the destitute and the wretched of the earth and in particular to the many heavy drinkers of Tumdrum and district, and to all those who sought refuge from the trials and tribulations of this world, and from their wives, at the bottom of a pint glass. Elder's calling and ministry had eventually led to his expulsion from the Brethren, and to his joining the Church of Ireland, which had a rather more relaxed attitude towards evangelism and to the various natural products of fermentation. Elder served up strong drink to his customers on Scripture beer-mats and surrounded them with posters and samplers and big etched mirrors which bore warnings and exhortations about the vanities and miseries and disappointments of this life, which most of his customers were more than fully aware of already and who probably wouldn't have been in the First and Last if they weren't, and which certainly did not dissuade them from their evening's drinking.

Times had changed, though, of course, and under the guidance of Elder's son, the confusingly named Elder, the First and Last had in recent years begun to relax its unwritten men-only and only men in caps rules, and to serve women, and to offer live televised sports on a giant screen, but it still remained a pub like no other in Tumdrum: it still had its huge Greek letters painted above the door, for example, which gave it the look of a masonic temple; and it still had the words, 'I Am Alpha And Omega, The Beginning And The End', painted around its doorposts and on the lintel, which made it look like the homes of the children of Israel as the angel of death passed over; and its corrugated-aluminium walls and the cantilevered roof meant that it still looked like a cattle-shed. In addition, the crudely painted mural on the building's gable end showing a bearded man in robes treading the bodies of sinners in a huge wine press meant that the pub remained unmistakable to passers-by, and to all those entering or leaving the town. The First and Last was a north coast landmark.

Israel had finally caught the attention of the barman – Elder the Younger himself, no less, a man who was fully bearded, and who wore a novelty waistcoat featuring rambling red roses, and a permanent neck-brace, after an accident in which he had fallen into a vat of his own home-made liqueur, brewed out back, an accident which he had been lucky to survive but which some people claimed had affected his mind more than his body, a few minutes in a wooden vat of base spirit and herbs seeming to have done irreparable damage to his nervous system and to have irrevocably coloured his outlook on life. Like his father, Elder was a born-again, teetotal, evangelical Christian, but unlike his father he regarded his customers not so much as a gathered congregation as some unspeakable herd of the damned, and he was renowned for the rudeliest welcome in the whole of Tumdrum, if not in Christendom.

'Yes, son?'

'Erm. Just a mineral water, please.'

'And what do you want with that?'

'Just the mineral water, please.'

'No.'

'What?'

'I'll not be serving you just with th'water.'

'What?' said Israel. Elder started to move away. 'Hang on. This is a pub, isn't it?'

'Aye.'

'So, can I have a mineral water. Please?'

'No.'

'Why not?'

'D'you think I can make money out of people who come in here to drink on water?'

'Well...'

'Aye, well, you might as well be takin' money out of my till. You're nothin' better than a common thief. You're barred!' said Elder, moving on to another customer. 'Pint, Tommy?'

Israel suddenly remembered he had a headache, and had done since arriving in this bloody place.

'Ignore him,' said a dark-haired woman, who had appeared behind the bar.

'Barred!' shouted Elder, from the other end of the bar, wagging his finger at Israel.

'Ignore Elder,' said the barmaid, 'his bite's worse than his bark.'

'Right,' said Israel.

'You're not from round here?'

'No, no. I'm not actually ...'

'I like your accent.'

'Oh. Well. Thank you,' said Israel, who was blushing all the way down to the soles of his worn-out brogues: his Estuary English had never made much impression anywhere before; in fact, he hadn't even realised he had an accent; he thought it was all the other people who had the accents.

'So what it is you'll have?'

'A mineral water just?'

'Would you not try a First and Last? It's Elder's liqueur.

He makes it here, on the premises.'

'His own liqueur? What's it like?'

'It's ... unusual. A bit like Benedictine ...'

'Really?'

'And a little bit like mouthwash. Most people take it hot in the winter.'

'Hot?'

'Uh-huh. You know, like a punch-type thing.'

'I don't know.'

'Make a man of you,' said the barmaid, rather playfully. 'At least, that's what they tell me. I couldn't possibly comment.'

'Well, if you put it like that,' said Israel, lowering his voice a little and attempting an international playboy kind of a face, to match his exotic accent, 'maybe I'll try one.'

'Right you are. Jus' to pass yerself, eh? One First and Last coming up.'

She disappeared behind the bar and Israel took in the sights: the traditional Irish TV on the traditional Irish high shelf in the corner; the traditional Irish worn and cracked lino floor; and the traditional filthy Irish bar faced with the traditional Irish red Formica, and a sign above the row of optics which read: SHOW PROPER RESPECT TO EVERYONE, LOVE THE BROTHERHOOD, FEAR GOD, AND HONOUR THE KING.

'She's a fair pup, isn't she?' said the man sitting next to Israel at the bar, as the barmaid reappeared with a tumbler of dark steaming liquid.

'Er. Yes. Indeed. Quite a ... pup,' agreed Israel.

'You wouldn't say no, would you?' said the man, who smelt strongly of drink and Tayto cheese and onion crisps.

'Erm. No. I mean yes. Well …'

'There you are now,' said the barmaid. 'Yes to what?'

'Nothing,' said Israel, blushing. 'Just chatting to my, er, friend here.'

'Go on then,' said the barmaid, 'pang it into ye.'

'What?' said Israel.

'Try it – the First and Last.'

It went down smoothly at first – not unlike a hot toddy, though more fragrant and flavoursome, and perhaps a little thicker. Israel could taste cloves, and aniseed, and vanilla, caramel, a hint of toothpaste perhaps: it was pretty good. But then he felt his mouth begin to burn and his throat become enflamed and swollen, as if someone had grabbed him, attacking him from behind by the neck, and was threatening him with his life.

'Good grief!' he gasped.

'It's good, isn't it.'

'It's …'

'Some people prefer it with a pint. Would you like a Guinness with it?'

Israel was speechless.

'Give him a Guinness with it, Rosie, for goodness sake,' said Israel's cheese-and-onion-smelling companion. Israel was clearly in some discomfort. 'Ach, Jesus, here, drink this,' said the man, pushing his half-drunk pint over towards Israel, who drank it down in great gulps.

'Thanks,' said Israel, recovering his powers of speech.

'It's all right,' said the drinker. 'I'll take a pint.'

'Right,' gasped Israel, 'pint, please, for my friend here.'

'Right you are. What d'you reckon?' asked the barmaid.

'Erm,' said Israel, 'it's … unusual.'

'I'll tell Elder you liked it. He'll be delighted. Some people can't stand the stuff. Elder!' she shouted. 'Elder! Look, look! He liked it! Sean, I'll get you your pint.'

Elder gave a thumbs-up sign from the other end of the bar.

Israel excused himself for a moment to use the toilet, and to splash water on his face – the mirror above the hand-basin was helpfully etched with the words, CHRIST DIED FOR THE UNGODLY, just in case anyone had forgotten – and when he returned the barmaid was setting up another First and Last for him.

'There you go. Drinks on the house.'

'No, really, thanks. It's fine. I'm not here to drink as such. I'm just, er, just waiting to see Ted – Ted Carson? – if he comes in tonight.'

'Och, Ted? He'll not be in for ages.'

'Oh, right. Well, I'd rather have a mineral water while I wait, if that's OK.'

'This one's from Elder,' she whispered. 'I don't think you want to upset him.'

Elder waved at Israel from the far end of the bar, pointing his finger at him, and mimicking drinking, and then rubbing his tummy with glee.

'No. Well. Thanks.'

'And a pint,' she said, setting a pint of Guinness before him.

'But I didn't - '

'That's from Sean here.'

'My round,' said Sean, who'd managed to finish a pint in the time it had taken Israel to go to the loo.

'Oh. Really, there's no need ...' said Israel.

'You saying my money's not good enough for ye?' said Sean, scowling, breathing out his fierce cheese and onion fumes.

'No,' said Israel, laughing slightly hysterically. 'Of course not. Very kind of you. Thanks.'

'Only joking!' said Sean, patting Israel hard on the back.

'Cheers,' said Sean.

'Cheers.'

The drinks stood on the bar staring at Israel accusingly, like miserable little orphaned children waiting to be taken home, and the raven-haired barmaid and Elder and Sean were looking at him too, and Israel reckoned he'd probably toned up pretty well recently on all the whiskey he was drinking back at the farm, and so he smiled manfully at them all and steadied himself on the bar-stool and tipped back his head, and drank down the First and Last in one gulp – hoping to avoid the throat-scorching – and it worked, his throat was unscathed, and the on-lookers turned away to get on with their business ... until suddenly the drink hit his stomach and Israel wished he'd sipped because it felt like something had ruptured or exploded down there, causing havoc, the fumes and the fall-out quickly working its way back up his throat, and once again robbing him of the powers of speech. The second Guinness was a great blessing though, and the third, and by the time Ted arrived Israel was four sheets to the wind, and was treating everyone at the bar to his favourite Jewish jokes.

'No, this is the best bit,' he was concluding. 'You're going to love this!' he guaranteed, barely able to contain his own mirth, 'So she said: "But the chicken was delicious!"' There were gales of laughter. 'Ted!' called Israel. 'Ted! Ted! Ted! Come here, Ted. What'll you have?'

'Ach, Israel, what are you doing in here?'

'Now. Ted.' Israel put a beery arm around Ted's shoulder. 'I'm not ashamed to say this, Ted. I'm just ... I just. I wanted to say ... I really ... Ted ... I wouldn't want ...'

'All right, Israel.'

'No. Let me finish. Let me finish. Let me finish. I wouldn't want what's been ... said. To. Come ... And ... A beautiful friendship.'

'Has he been drinking?'

The barmaid nodded her head. 'First and Lasts.'

'Ach, Rosie.'

'He seemed all right with them.'

'He's a vegetanarian, Rosie, for goodness sake. He's hardly going to be able to manage a First and Last.'

'No stomach lining,' agreed Sean, sniffing.

'He'd struggle with a pot of hot tea and a fry.'

'Sorry, Ted. I thought ...'

'Ted,' said Israel. 'Ted! Ted!!'

'Yes, Israel.'

'I can't do it without you, Ted. I'm like a ... rudderless ... Ted. Ted! I am a ... lonesome ... fugitive.'

'All right, Israel,' said Ted.

'No. No. Let me finish. I'm ... Feeling. Please. Ted. I need you, Ted. I need ...' He put an arm on Ted's shoulder. 'Please, Ted, say you'll. Come back to me ... Come! Come! To the mobile library, Ted. Ted? Ted?'

'All right, all right,' said Ted, 'take it easy, Israel.'

Ted had faced enough drunks in his time in the back of

his cab to know exactly how to deal with them: you just agreed.

'Ted, Ted, Ted, Ted,' persisted Israel. 'Come back to me, Ted. I'm never going to … I can't … Without you, Ted.'

'Aye, all right, no problem,' said Ted. 'I'll come back and help you.'

'Mmm!' groaned Israel. 'Hey!' he shouted, to everyone and no one in particular, throwing his arms up in the air. 'Hey, hey, hey! Did you hear that? Ted! Is going to help me … On the mobile … Learning Centre!'

At which point he went to put his arms around Ted, missed, and fell off his stool.

'You're barred,' said Elder, from the other end of the bar. 'Barred!'

16

'Here,' said Ted, taking a hand off the wheel and fetching into his pocket.

'What?' said Israel.

'Take these.'

'What are they?'

'What do you think they are? Boiled potatoes? They're headache tablets.'

'Ugh. Thanks. Have you got any water?'

'I'm not your mother. And don't make a habit of it, all right,' warned Ted. 'Sets a bad example.'

Israel took the tablets dry.

'Yeeuch.'

'And remember, I'm only back because of the van,' said Ted. 'Not because of you.'

'Eerrgh.'

'You made such an auld mess of the van, I can't believe it. I shouldn't have let you out on the streets alone in the first place.'

The morning after the night before had not got off to a good start. Back at the farm, George and Brownie had been less than sympathetic towards Israel's hangover, and the permanently aproned Mr Devine had offered up last night's leftover grilled fish and onions for breakfast, the mere thought of which had delayed Israel's departure when Ted had arrived to collect him.

'How's he doing then, the king of comedy?' Ted had asked Brownie, while he waited for Israel to compose himself.

'Israel? Oh, he seems to be settling right in,' said Brownie, as Israel scuttled back and forth, whey-faced, to the toilet. 'Wee touch of the skitters just.'

By the time Israel was steady enough on his feet, Ted had finished off a pot of tea, two plates of grilled fish and onions, and had successfully set the world to rights with the elderly Mr Devine, who agreed absolutely with Ted about young people today, and that another war might not be such a bad thing and lock 'em all up and throw away the key.

'Here,' said Ted, in the van, fetching into his pocket again.

'What's this?'

'It's a tie.'

'I know it's a tie, Ted.' Israel was having to take deep breaths to prevent himself from ... 'I mean what's it for.'

'Ach. What do you think it's for? You got a dog with no lead?'

'No. Is it a hangover cure?'

'Of course it's not a hangover cure – unless your hangover's that bad you're thinking of doing away with yerself.'

'I don't … wear ties,' said Israel weakly. And he certainly didn't wear this tie – which was fat, and purple, and nylon, and shiny.

'You're a librarian, aren't you?' said Ted.

'Yes.'

'And this is not a disco, is it?'

'No.'

'So?'

'I'm not wearing a tie.'

Ted slowed the van as they approached some lights.

'Sorry, Ted!'

'Aye?'

'Could you just …' Israel gestured for Ted to pull over, which he did, and Israel almost fell out of the van as he went to be sick at the side of the road.

All done, he clambered back in, ashen-faced.

'Well, look at it like this, son,' said Ted, as if nothing had happened, 'if you're not wearing a tie, I mightn't be pulling over at your convenience.'

Given Israel's track record of working without Ted, this did not appeal to him as a pleasing prospect.

'We're doing things my way now,' continued Ted, who was warming to his theme, 'since you've made such an outstanding success of things on your own. Do I make myself clear?'

'Yes, Ted.'

'Which means wearing the tie.'

'I'm wearing a T-shirt though, Ted.'

'I don't care if you're wearing nothing but a vest and pants, if you're out with me in the library, you wear a tie.'

'All right, I'll wear the tie.' Israel laid the long thick

purple tie in his lap. He felt as though someone had hoovered out his stomach lining.

There was a pause at the lights and in the conversation, as Ted waited for the green and for Israel to put on the tie, and Israel attempted to overcome his feelings of nausea.

'It's not really my colour though.'

'Aye, well, next time bring your own tie. If you're out in the mobile library with me, you're representing the library, which represents the council ... which represents the ...' Ted was struggling a little with his extended metaphor here, but he ploughed on. 'Government ... which represents the ...'

'People?' offered Israel.

'That's it,' said Ted. 'So put on the tie.'

Israel slowly and carefully knotted the tie round his neck and looked at himself in the wing mirror. If he said so himself, he was looking pretty bloody rough.

'And you'll need to get a haircut,' said Ted.

'Ted, I'm not feeling well.'

'D'you want me to stop again?'

'No.'

'I don't want you bokin' in here.'

'No. I'm not going to.'

'Sure?'

'Yep.'

'Good. So, what's that supposed to be, your hair?'

'It's my hair.'

'Aye, right. It looks like a bird's nest.'

'Thanks.'

'If it touches the ears it's too long. You're a librarian, you know, not a pop star.'

'Yeah.'

'There's a place in town.'

'All right. I'll get it cut. OK?'

'Good.'

Ted was picking up speed now on the outskirts of Tumdrum.

'So, where are we heading exactly?'

'Listen. I'm telling you. We're doing a service run. We're doing it all methodo … Methododo …'

'Methodically?'

'That's it.'

'OK.'

'So we're collecting in all the books that are overdue first, to try and establish exactly how many are missing.'

'Right.'

'Rather than just running around accusing people willy-nilly and at the drop of a hat. You've got to be disciplined with this sort of thing. You've got to think …'

'Methodically?'

'Logically.'

'Of course.'

'You can add up, can you?' said Ted.

'Yes. Of course I can.'

'Aye, right. Because you're keeping the tally. As far as I can work it out, currently we're missing … See that notebook there, on the dash? Open her up. What's the figure there on the first page, where I've written it?'

'Fifteen thousand.'

'Aye.'

'But I've found some already.'

'Aye. How many?'

'Not many.'

'Well, let's say fifteen thousand, then. That's our starting figure, give or take a few. Let's go round 'em up.'

The further they drove out of town the more exotic the housing became – the whole landscape becoming freer, and wider, and looser, taller, stretching itself out and slipping off the grey render and the pebble-dash and stripping down and relaxing until you might actually have been driving through southern Spain, there were so many fine, bright, hacienda-style bungalows, with spreading palm trees standing tall against the pale sea. If it wasn't for the cloud and the drizzle and the signposts for places like Brablagh and Ballycleagh and Doomore you might have thought you were gazing at time-shares along the Mediterranean.

Out on a stretch of road with no one coming and nothing around Ted slowed the van and pulled over.

'Are we stopping?'

'We're stopping.'

'Here?' Israel looked around.

There was nothing around: just road and hedge and cliff and sea.

'Aye.'

'Are you all right?' said Israel. 'Is there something wrong with the van?'

'The van's fine. It's a pick-up,' explained Ted. 'This is a service point. You know what I told you about service points?'

'Erm. What? The stops? The places where the mobile library stops?'

'There you have it.'

'What? This is one?'

'Aye. You're a fast learner.'

'The side of a road?'

'That'd be it. Second furze on the left afore the bridge there.'

'But I thought a service point was a timetabled stopping point where members of the public can safely gather to meet the mobile library.'

'Strictly speaking. But some service points are by private arrangement.'

'I see.'

'So, by the bridge, second furze on the left.'

'People are meeting us there?'

'No, you eejit. Someyin's left their books there.'

'What? Someone's left their books by the side of the road?'

'Yes! For pity's sake, man.'

Israel looked outside nervously: hedges, sea, nothing, Irish skies.

'Is it safe?'

'What are you talking about, is it safe?'

'I don't know. I mean, you know, safe.'

'There's no book-rustlers out here, as far as I'm aware.'

'What about ... I don't know. The IRA?'

'The IRA?'

'The IRA.'

'The IRA?'

'Yes, the IRA! You know, like booby-traps or something?'

Ted took a deep breath. 'D'you get the news over there on the mainland, do you?'

'Yes.'

'So you'll be knowing there's a ceasefire on.'

'I know, but ...'

'Since 1994. And there's no longer a British Empire. You're up to date with all that, are you?'

'Yes. Of course I am.'

'Good, well, I wouldn't worry too much about it then, if I was you. I don't think the Tumdrum and District mobile library is currently a prime target for dissident republicans.'

'No. I didn't mean that.'

'Aye, right. I don't know why we bother, to be honest.'

'Who?'

'We, us, the loyal people of Ulster. I think we should maybe set up our own republic or something.'

'Well, I'm sure—'

'Aye, right. That'd suit you, wouldn't it? Get rid of us all.'

'Erm. I've got a terrible headache actually, Ted, and I would love to discuss the ...'

'Aye.'

'Shall we just get back to the books?'

'You brought the subject up.'

'Right. Well, why have they left their books there, at the side of the road?'

'Who? The IRA?'

'No. Whoever's left their books there.'

'Mr Onions.'

'Mr Onions?'

'That's right.'

'Is that his real name?'

'What do you think?'

'I would, er, I'd guess not, no.'

'Aye, well, all that education didn't go to waste then, did it. He's a farmer.'

'And he grows onions?'

'No, he grows mangoes and oranges.'

'Right.' Israel caught himself on. 'No … Hang on … Well, why's he left his books here?'

'When he's too busy on the farm he leaves them. I pick 'em up, and then leave him some more. It's a private sort of arrangement. It's traditional.'

'Right.'

'Go on then.'

'What?'

'Go and get 'em.'

'But it's raining.'

'Aye, hardly but. It'll not melt you.'

'I'm still feeling a bit—'

'Well, you've only yourself to blame there, haven't ye. Go on.'

Israel got out of the van, turning up the hood on his old brown duffle coat.

'And Israel,' called Ted.

'What?'

'Mind the land-mines.'

Israel went over to the bridge. It was another harsh, wet winter's morning: the trees were bare, shivering in the wind; and the stream was flowing fast; and Israel's head felt like it was splitting in two, and the fresh air hit him so hard in the face he felt even more sick than he'd been feeling in the van. He didn't know where he was supposed to be looking. He turned around and gestured to Ted. Ted wound down the window.

'The furze!' he shouted. 'The gorse! The second furze!'

Israel wasn't entirely sure he knew what a furze was but he started rootling around under a couple of likely looking bushes, ripping his hands on their yellowy spiny branches.

'Ouch!' he cried.

Ted ignored him.

'Ouch!' he cried again, louder.

Ted still ignored him, and eventually Israel found a couple of old feed sacks, tightly tied with cord, stuffed with something, and tucked under a bush, and he brought them to the van.

'This them?' he said to Ted, offering up the bags.

'Jesus Christ, no, that's a bomb!' said Ted, covering his face with his hands.

'What!' screamed Israel, flinging open the door to throw out the bags.

'Of course it's them,' said Ted, laughing through his fingers. 'Were you born yesterday?!'

Israel's hair was plastered to his head, and steam was rising off him, he was panting, and his hands were cut.

'That's not funny,' he said.

'No, you're right,' said Ted, wiping tears from his eyes, and starting up the engine and pulling off. 'That's not funny. You're absolutely right. That's not funny at all. I'll tell you what that is: *that* is hilarious. You're a geg, d'you know that? That is precious, so it is ...'

Israel opened up the bags, which contained some slightly damp books, and a small bag of potatoes.

'There's potatoes in here as well, Ted.'

'Aye.'

'For us?'

'I'd warrant.'

'That's very kind of Mr Onions.'

'Aye, that it is.'

'Ted,' said Israel.

'Hmm.'

'I hope these are not gifts or services in kind.'

Ted remained silent.

'Ted? Are these gifts or services in kind?'

'Of course they're not. They're potatoes.'

'But you know you're not allowed to receive goods or services in kind?'

'Ach, give over.'

'I'm serious.'

'I'm serious. Now, be quiet, boy, will you, and keep your head down, or the snipers'll see you.'

Israel flinched, and Ted roared with laughter.

'Ha! Got you! Oh yes, that's good!'

'Ted, I've got a headache.'

'Aye, me too. Listening to your auld nonsense.'

'We're never going to find all the books like this, Ted.'

'Ach, Israel, quiet, will you. You're like an auld woman.'

A couple more miles down the coast road and they came to the Myowne mobile home park. It looked like an open prison, actually: it had an air of miserable solitude about it, an air of unwelcome and rebuke, like a barracks, a place that had turned its back upon the world not through choice but through necessity, and which had grown sad and bitter as a consequence, appalled by its own exile and isolation. There were whitewashed boulders flanking the entrance, and rows of bollards linked together by rusty chains, and floodlights set upon tall posts. Signs indicated that it was an RAC-approved campsite, but it would have done equally as well as a detention centre for asylum seekers.

'I don't think I'd fancy spending my holiday here much,' said Israel.

Ted ignored him and turned off the road and drove in under the big metal arching sign which announced MYOWNE: PRIVATE, HOMES TO BUY AND RENT and they pulled up into the clearly signposted Visitors' Car Park and then went into the reception, a long, low building all flaky with paint and with faded inflatable toys hanging in its windows, and out-of-date posters advertising summer bingo nights in the communal hall, and an evening of Country Gospel with a singer called Bobbie Dylan, and a children's Bible holiday club.

'God. Holiday from hell,' joked Israel.

Ted continued to ignore him.

Inside the reception there were more pathetic inflatables hanging from the ceiling, and a rack of postcards, and shelves with nothing on them, and two trestle tables set up in front of an old wooden counter which had set out upon it newspapers and bread and milk, and a man was sat behind the counter, smoking a fragrant pipe and flicking through a newspaper, the *Irish News*. He was wearing a boiler suit and had a fat alsatian lying at his feet.

'Ted,' said the man, nodding to Ted.

'Jimmy,' said Ted, nodding back.

'Hello,' said Israel, extending his hand, his purple tie glistening against his brown corduroy jacket under the lights. The man named Jimmy in the boiler suit just looked at him – at the tie, at the T-shirt, at the brown corduroy jacket – and looked back down at his paper. 'My name's Israel Armstrong,' said Israel. 'I'm the new mobile librarian.'

'Aye.'

'And—' began Israel.

'Anything strange or startlin', Jimmy?' said Ted.

Jimmy shook his head.

'Rosie?'

'Aye,' said Jimmy, nodding, not breaking stride with his reading of the paper or his smoking, and Ted walked off, through a door at the back of the reception, outside and along a paved path and through a picket gate in the direction of the rows of caravans.

'Hold on, Ted,' said Israel, catching him up.

'He'd talk a dog to death, Jimmy.'

'Yes,' agreed Israel. 'Where are we going?'

'We're going to see Rosie. Collect some books off her. She looks after the library books on site for everyone. Unofficial librarian, like.'

'Right.'

'You know Rosie.'

'Do I?'

'You do.'

'I don't think so.'

'Aye, you do,' said Ted knowingly. 'She runs a little childminding business.'

'What? Here? In a caravan?'

'They're not caravans, they're mobile homes,' said Ted.

'Right,' laughed Israel, mistaking Ted's statement for a joke. 'And so what's the difference exactly between a caravan and a mobile home? Is there a difference?'

'People live in mobile homes, Israel,' said Ted. 'This isn't a holiday for them. This is their life.'

Israel looked shamefaced, as they tramped over scrubland and grey gravel paths, towards sand-dunes in the distance: it was like approaching the edge of the world.

Rosie's home was one of the last on the site, at the very edge of the dunes – a long, creamy-brown, flat-roofed mobile home which had not been maintained to the highest of standards. There was a rusted barbecue outside, and rusted children's bicycles, rusted chairs, a washing-line and a rusted bin: the sand and wind and the sea air seemed to be gnawing everything down to stumps and bare bones. Ted knocked on the twisted aluminium door. A woman opened, with a beaming smile.

'Ach, Ted!' she said. 'There you are now! Come on in! Isn't that desperate weather altogether?'

Rosie Hart, it turned out, was the barmaid at the First and Last, the woman who had served Israel enough drink the night before to knock him down and lay him out flat. Today her dark black hair was tied back, and she was barefoot and she was wearing the kind of happy, slightly Scandinavian-looking clothes that one might at one time have associated with hippies, before hippy clothes became sanitised boho chic, and which Rosie seemed now to be successfully reclaiming for genuine dirty hippiness, and she ushered them into her caravan – her mobile home, rather – where four fat babies were rolling around on a play mat. In the background there was the unmistakable sound of Enya.

'This is Israel, Rosie,' said Ted. 'He's the new mobile librarian.'

'We've met,' she said teasingly. 'Last night.'

'Yes,' said Israel, ashamed.

'Of course,' said Ted, gloating. 'I almost forgot.'

'How are you feeling then?'

'OK,' said Israel, not feeling well at all.

'Good,' said Rosie. 'Now, you must have known I'd had the kettle on, Ted – it's only just boiled. What'll you have, fellas, tea or coffee?'

Israel looked at Ted, looking for a cue.

'Tea, please,' said Ted, who then got down on his stomach on the floor and started playing with the babies. 'OK, you wee rascals, who's for sparring?'

'Israel?' asked Rosie.

'Erm. I'll have a cup of coffee, thanks, if that's OK.'

'Who have we got here?' asked Ted.

'That's Liam with the hair. And Joel there with the cheeky grin. Charlotte in pink there. And Charlie with the bogeys – he's a wee dote, isn't he?'

'Aye,' said Ted.

'Sorry, Israel, what was it you wanted?'

'Coffee?'

'Now it's only instant, I'm afraid,' said Rosie, going down towards the kitchen area, Israel following.

'That's fine.'

'And it's mugs.'

'Fine.'

'Probably not what you're used to, though, eh?'

'Well ...'

'Roasted coffee beans where you're from, I'll bet.' She took a few mugs from a mug-stand. 'And nice white china?'

'Well, I don't know about that exactly ...'

'So?' she said, turning to Israel, hands on hips, having set out the mugs and put the kettle on to reboil, and fixing him with a quizzical gaze. 'How have you found it here so far?'

'It's been ...'

Rosie crossed her arms and raised an eyebrow.

'It's been ...' continued Israel, embarrassed.

'Och, I know, pet, don't worry. It's a dump, isn't it?' said Rosie, waving a hand in dismissal. 'It's all right. You can be honest.'

'Well ... I don't know if I'd ...'

'Not like what you're used to, I bet.'

'No, not exactly.'

'London, isn't it, you're from?'

'Yes.'

'You know, I'd love to live in London. Or New York. I've got a cousin in Hackensack.'

Israel had never heard of it.

'He went to Fairleigh Dickinson University?'

'Right. I'm afraid I'm not ...'

'And one of my aunts lives in Greenford.'

'Really? In America?'

'Och, no. Greenford, in London. D'you not know it?'

'No. I'm afraid not.'

'Well. I've never been to visit her even.'

'That's a shame.'

'I'd love to live over there,' said Rosie, quietly and thoughtfully, pausing as she poured boiling water into the mugs.

'Well, why don't you?' asked Israel.

Rosie laughed, stirring tea bag and granules.

'This is where I live,' she said, gesturing at the four walls of the mobile home.

It was one room, with a stained and sagging red sofa dividing the living area from the kitchen, and the kitchen units were chipped and scratched and the brown carpet was worn and there were damp patches on the walls, but you didn't really notice any of that, or only for a moment, you didn't notice what was inside, because on three sides of the room were these huge windows, looking directly out to sea, which was all breaking waves under a slate-grey sky, headlands either side.

'That's quite a view you've got.'

'Aye,' said Rosie. 'The strand. Three miles, isn't it, Ted? Joel, don't do that.' Joel was punching Ted on the nose.

'He's all right,' said Ted.

'You sit here and it feels like being on a ship,' said Rosie. 'I could sit here all day, you know, just looking out, dreaming and that.'

In one corner of the room, under a window, by the television, was a table with a Star Wars chess set. 'Do you play chess?' asked Israel.

'No. That's my son. Conor!' she shouted. 'He loves chess.'

'Great game.'

'Is it?' said Rosie. 'God. I can't stand it myself. Conor!'

Ted was still wrestling with children on the floor. Rosie brought him his mug of tea.

'Thanks, Rosie,' said Ted. 'We've come about the books actually,' he continued, holding a baby up in the air. 'Lagalagalagalaa! Snaggleaggleuppaluss!'

'Oh, I'm sorry, Ted. I haven't collected them all in yet. I've only got ours.'

'It's all right,' said Ted. 'Weeee!' he called.

'We'll take whatever you've got,' said Israel.

'OK,' said Rosie. 'Conor!' she said. 'Conor! I'll go and get him. Are you all right with the wee ones there, Ted?'

'Aye. We'll manage. Here's one for you, Armstrong,' said Ted, trying to hand Israel a child.

'Erm. No, I'm all right thanks, Ted,' said Israel, clutching his mug of coffee tighter and backing away: he wasn't what you'd call a natural with children.

The baby started crying.

Rosie returned. 'Conor's there in his room – he's a wee bit shy of strangers, you know. I'd better deal with this one.' She picked up the crying baby and smelt its bottom. 'No, all right down that end. Let's get you something then, little man. Just pop your head round the door there, Israel, he'll let you in. Tell him I sent you. All the books are in there with him.'

Israel went to knock on the plyboard door at the end of the room. There was no answer.

'Hello?' said Israel, and he pushed open the door.

There was a boy sitting upright on his bed. He was about eight years old – but he had the face of an old man. The room was in most respects a typical boy's room – posters Blu-Tacked to the walls, clothes and toys everywhere. But it was also full, from floor to ceiling, with books. Towers and towers of books. A miniature New York skyline of books.

'Wow!' said Israel, taken aback at what must have been at the very least the entire children's non-fiction section of Tumdrum Library. 'Hello? Conor? I'm Israel. Your mum said I could come in. I'm a librarian.'

The boy stared at Israel in silence.

'You've got a few books here, mate.'

'You've got a few books here, mate!' repeated Conor, mimicking Israel.

'Conor!' said Rosie, appearing next to Israel, sensing trouble, the now pacified baby in her arms chewing a biscuit. 'Behave!'

'Sorry, Mum,' said Conor. 'That's not fair, he's a biscuit!'

'Conor!'

'Erm. Are these all library books?' asked Israel politely.

'I'm afraid so,' said Rosie.

'How did you ...?'

'He loves reading, you see. And so, they ...'

Israel sensed that Rosie was searching for an explanation.

'They?'

'They ... the old librarian.'

'Norman?'

'Yes, yes, that's right. He ... Er. He let Conor take them all out.'

'All these books?'

'Yes, that's right!'

Having met Norman Canning, Israel doubted that very much.

'Conor?' said Israel.

Conor remained silent and looked at the floor.

'Well, we'll have to return all these to the library, I'm afraid.'

'But we'll not be fined, will we?' said Rosie. 'I mean, we couldn't possibly afford to pay the fines on all these.'

'No. We're having a fines amnesty.'

'What's an amnesty?' asked Conor.

'Amnesty?' said Israel. 'Good question. An amnesty is when there's a sort of pardon for some crime or—'

'Like in a war,' explained Rosie. 'When you decide to forgive the other side.'

'Couldn't you and Dad have an amnesty, Mum?'

'Conor!'

'Right,' said Israel, embarrassed. 'Perhaps if we could just gather these up and we'll be out of your hair?'

'Aye, right, of course. I'll get you some bags and Conor can help you.'

'Mum!'

'Conor!'

Rosie went to get some bags.

'Do you like reading, Conor?' asked Israel, with Rosie out of the room.

Conor didn't answer.

'Did you get these books from the library, Conor?'

'"Did you get these books from the library, Conor?"' repeated Conor, speaking with his tongue in his bottom lip, like a monkey.

Israel didn't seem to be getting very far with his line of questioning, but then he remembered the chess.

'Do you play chess, mate?'

'"Do you play chess, mate?"'

'Do you though? And without the funny voices, eh. The novelty sort of wears off, you know, and I've got a terrible headache.'

'Are you drunk?'

'No, I'm not drunk.'

'Are you hung over then?'

'No.'

'Are you an alcoholic?'

'No.'

'You look like an alcoholic.'

'Do you play chess with your mum, Conor?'

'She's rubbish.'

'I'm sure she's not rubbish. I like chess.'

'Are you any good?'

'I'm not bad.'

'I bet I could beat you.'

'Well, I'll tell you what. I'll give you a game if you tell me where you got the books.'

'Here we are, now,' said Rosie, reappearing with bin bags. 'Come on, Conor, you give Israel a hand here, please.'

'I'm going out to play,' said Conor, leaping out of bed and running out of the bedroom.

'Conor!'

There was the sound of the slamming of the front door.

'He's certainly a ... boisterous little chap,' said Israel.

'Yes,' agreed Rosie.

'You must be very ... proud.'

'Well. Would you mind just collecting them up yourself?'

'Sure.'

Rosie went outside.

'Ted,' she called, 'can you watch those wee ones for me a minute, OK?'

'Sure,' said Ted.

Israel could hear her shouting.

'Conor!' she called. 'Come here, this minute!'

Which left Israel to pack a couple of hundred books into plastic bin bags.

He did half a dozen trips to and from Rosie's home and through the mobile home park and to the Visitors' Car Park and the van, the plastic carrier bags sometimes spilling and splitting, and in the end Ted joined him and they said goodbye to Rosie – although there was still no sign of Conor.

'Where d'you think he got the books, Ted?'

'He's a great reader, the wee fella.'

'He's got enough books to keep him going until he's at university, though.'

'Aye, Rosie'd love him to go to university.'

'I'm sure she would, but the books, Ted – Rosie said Norman had let him have them all from the library?'

'Aye.'

'Well, you know Norman, Ted.'

'I do.'

'And he's not likely to have given an eight-year-old boy unrestricted borrowing rights, is he?'

'I don't rightly know, Israel.'

'Maybe he stole them?'

'Ach, give over, Israel. Wasn't it last week I was your criminal mastermind?'

'Yes, but—'

'And then this week it's a big conspiracy involving the council and the Shinners and the Orange Order and the Ancient Order of Hibernians?'

'No, Ted.'

'Aye, well, the wee fella's probably behind it all, isn't he, I would have thought. He's your Mr Big? D'you want to try a citizen's arrest?'

As they trudged along the grey gravel path towards the reception a man approached them, running steadily, in running shorts and windcheater.

'John!' called Ted to the runner. 'John! Hey! Over here!'

The man stopped in his tracks.

'John, it's me, Ted.'

'Ach, what about ye, Ted?'

'This is Israel, John, the new mobile librarian. Israel, John Boyd.'

'Hello, Israel,' said John, 'pleased to meet you. People call me Feely.'

'Right, well, hello, erm, Feely,' said Israel, who was about to ask the man why people called him Feely as he went to shake his hand, and found his hand engulfed by a massive muscular shake: John was over six foot tall, had a shaven head, and was built like a boxer. He looked like a younger, fitter version of Ted: the only real difference was, John was completely blind.

'What brings you out here then, Ted?'

'We're getting the mobile library up and running. Israel here's rounding up all the overdue books.'

'Right.'

'Have you any, John?'

John hesitated.

'There's a fines amnesty, but, so you're all right.'

'Great, Ted,' said John with relief. 'They were months overdue. Would have cost me a fortune returning them.'

'That's all right,' said Israel magnanimously. 'Happens all the time.'

'I've got audio books mostly.'

'That's OK. An audio book's still a book, in my book,' said Israel jocularly.

'Right.'

'Don't mind him, John,' said Ted. 'He's from England.'

'Oh, aye.'

John led them to his mobile home.

From outside it looked exactly the same as Rosie's, but inside it was done out entirely as a gym: where Rosie had her sofa and her coffee table and the Star Wars chess set, John had a rowing machine, a running machine, racks of free weights, a weights station and a huge contraption like a gibbet hung with punch bags.

'This new, John?' said Ted, patting the big metal contraption.

'The UBS?' said John.

'The what?'

'Universal Boxing System.'

'Aye.'

'Yeah.'

'Speed bag, heavy bag, and double-end striking bag all in one, eh,' said Ted, walking round, admiring the kit.

'Nice, isn't she.'

Ted took a boxing stance and threw a succession of punches into the centre of a heavy bag. There was a lovely soft sound of *oofs*.

'I've got spare gloves and wraps if you want them, Ted.'

'No,' said Ted, laughing, throwing another couple of punches at the bag. 'I'm too old for that game – beaten docket, me. It's not canvas then?'

'No, it's all this plastic these days.'

'I wish we'd had these little double-end bags when I was younger,' said Ted, moving round to another small bag, suspended between two plastic cords. He threw a punch at it and it sprang back and forwards as he leant his body to the side, ducking and bobbing.

'Good for coordination,' said John.

'Aye.'

'Cost a few pound, eh?'

'Well, got it on eBay.'

'Oh, right.'

'Got my medicine ball as well,' said John.

'God, I haven't seen one of them in a few years,' said Ted, going over and picking up a big black leather ball.

'Great for the old abdominals,' said John.

'Aye,' said Ted, and then, 'Here, Israel, catch!' and threw the ball to Israel.

Israel saw the ball coming towards him as if in slow motion, and he had a flashback, of gym at school, of being unable to climb ropes, of panicking in the swimming pool, of getting pounded in rugby, and collapsing in cross-country, flailing in tennis, as the medicine ball hit him in the stomach.

'Steady, Ted,' said John.

'Ach, get him in shape,' said Ted. 'Look at him, he's a belly like a drowned pup.'

'Aaggh.'

'Anyway,' said Ted, turning to John. 'It was about the books we came.'

'Yes.'

'What have you got?'

'Here we go,' said John, going over to a state-of-the-art sound system, which had CDs and tape cassettes piled around.

'Israel?' said Ted. Israel remained doubled over. 'Ach, come on. Stop clowning about. What have we got here then, John? *The Odyssey*, read by Ian McKellen. Any good?'

'Not bad.'

'Have you heard that one of him doing *Les Misérables* though?'

'No. I must get that out.'

Israel had staggered over. 'God, you've got most of the history of English literature on tape here,' he said.

'Aye. Well, makes a break during training: I need to cool off actually, now. Do my stretching. D'you mind?'

'No, go ahead.'

Ted and Israel left John Boyd's caravan with a bag full of audio books and John doing some hamstring stretches.

'Was he blind since birth?' asked Israel, as they piled the books into the van.

'No. He was caught in a bomb blast, up in Belfast.'

'That's terrible.'

'Yeah, it was. His wife died.'

'God.'

'Don't take the Lord's name in vain.'

'Sorry.'

'Thank you. Now you get in the back there,' said Ted, pointing to the dark interior of the van.

'What?'

'To count the books.'

'Oh.'

Israel counted, all the way back to Tumdrum, and with some allowance for bumps in the road he made a total of 284 books and 75 audio books.

'Well?' said Ted, as they pulled up outside Tumdrum Library.

'What's seventy-five plus two hundred and eighty-four?' said Israel. 'Three hundred and fifty-nine?'

'I don't know.'

'Anyway, so what's fifteen thousand take away three hundred and fifty-nine?'

'Ach, Israel,' said Ted, 'my mental arithmetic's not what it was.'

'Fourteen thousand, six hundred and forty-one?'

'Sounds about right,' said Ted.

'So that's it: we've got approximately fourteen thousand, six hundred and forty-one books left to find.'

'Not bad then.'

'That's terrible,' said Israel. 'It'll take us years.'

'You know what they say?' said Ted.

'No.'

'Patience and perseverance would take a snail to Jerusalem.'

'What?'

'We'll have this all rightened out before Christmas.'

'Hanukkah.'

'Bless you.'

17

They were on the road together for the best part of a week, Ted and Israel, starting off from Tumdrum around eight every morning and not getting back until much before seven, day in, day out, rounding up books from outlying farms, and from schools and hospices, and old people's homes, and big houses and flats, and a few places down almost as far as Ballymena and up almost to Coleraine, past the Giant's Causeway, and the strain was beginning to tell. Israel had drunk enough tea to drown himself and eaten enough wee buns to weigh him down while he was drowning, and everyone they met and everywhere they went was slowly becoming a murky blur, a giant milky-tea-and-biscuit-tray of Achesons and Agnews and Begleys and Buchanans, all handing back their Jilly Coopers and their Catherine Cooksons and talking so fast and in accents so impenetrable that Israel just nodded, sipped tea and ate more buns, and let Ted do all the talking. A few faces and a few places stood out: he remembered the ancient and improbable vegetarian Mrs Roulston, for example, who'd done them a nice vegetable stew for lunch one day, and who lived all by herself in a painfully neat flat above her son's butcher's shop somewhere down near Ballygodknowswhere, and who had somehow ended up with all sixty-one volumes of the library's collected St Aquinas, which she'd been working through and testing by the yardstick of the Holy Bible and her own strong Presbyterian faith; and it turned out that he had the wrong end of the stick, apparently, Aquinas. Israel also remembered a Mr H. R. Whoriskey, a big fleshy man with Brylcreemed hair, who had the library's complete set of 1970s lavishly illustrated volumes on amateur photography, featuring bikini-clad beauties and women with perms in see-through blouses, and a disturbing number of books about Hitler and the Third Reich. Also, he had dogs.

Ted and Israel had rounded up audio books, and tape cassettes, and fiction and non-fiction, and children's books, and reference works that should never have left the library in the first place, and they had a haul so big now it could have filled at least a few shelves in the mobile library, although, as it was, they were in carrier bags in the back of the van.

'What's the tally, Mr Tallyman?' asked Ted.

'Erm.' Israel consulted the tally book while Ted started singing.

'Come, Mr Tallyman, tally me bananas!'

'Ted! Ted!'

'What?'

'You're giving me a headache, Ted.'

'Aye. Right. Well. And the vice versa.'

'Anyway, the total for this week,' announced Israel wearily, reading from the tally book. 'Is four hundred and thirty-seven books, comprising fiction, non-fiction and children's titles; one hundred and twenty-two audio books; forty-two tape cassettes; five CD-ROMs; fourteen videos; an unbound set of last year's *National Geographic* magazine, and the *Sopranos* first series on DVD. God.'

'Aye, right, mind your language,' said Ted. 'How many's that leave us?'

'Erm. Hang on. Let me work it out.' Israel took a Biro and had a quick go at the sums.

'Come, Mr Tallyman ...'

'Ted!'

'What?'

'Nothing. I think we're still missing about fourteen thousand.'

'It's a start,' said Ted.

'Yeah, well. It's only a start. There's only so many over-due books out there, Ted. We're never going to get them all back like this.'

'Ach, your glass always half empty, is it?'

'Yes, it is actually.'

'Then you need to learn to graze where you're teth-ered, but.'

'What?'

'It's a saying.'

'Right. Meaning?'

'We're doing what we can, and we're doing it metho-do...'

'Methodically.'

'That's it.'

'It's not getting us very far, though, is it?'

'Ach, will you give over moaning? It's like throwing water over a dog.'

'What?'

'It's just a—'

'Saying, right. Well I'm just saying we're never going to get them all back like this. You know that and I know that. Someone's stolen the books. We need to find out who.'

'Aye, aye, right, but it's the weekend now, so you'll have to get back to your mysteryfying on Monday, Inspector Clouseau.'

'But—'

Ted turned up a lane.

'We just need to take a wee skite in here,' said Ted, ignoring Israel, as usual, 'see Dennis about the shelves, get her measured up, and then I'm away home. Friday's my night with the BB.'

'The who B?'

'Boys' Brigade.'

'Right. Sorry, I have absolutely no idea what that is, Ted – what is it, like an army or something?'

'Ach, where are you from, boy? It's like the Scouts, but, except more…'

'What? Gay?'

'Protestant.'

'Jesus.'

'Israel!'

'Sorry, Ted.'

'So anyway, you'll be doing the last call yerself. It's up by the Devines' there – if I drop you off you can walk down the wee rodden when you're done, sure. Bring you out by the big red barn.'

'Which big red barn?'

There were quite a lot to choose from round and about.

'The Devines' big red barn. "Awake To Righteousness Not Sin".'

'Oh, right, that big red barn, yes.'

Israel had quickly become accustomed to seeing walls and barns and signs painted with light-hearted biblical texts and evangelical appeals, which he'd found shocking at first, the reminder that 'Brief Life Here Is Our Portion', or that 'And After This, The Judgement', but you can get used to anything, it seems. He now found something of a comfort in the thought that all this was temporary.

'Yeah, that's fine,' said Israel, who had also become accustomed to agreeing eventually to whatever Ted suggested.

'Good. Dennis's first then.'

They drove up the long lane to a tall red-brick building, taller than it was wide, and which must have commanded fantastic views from the top.

'What's this place?' said Israel.

'Dennis's? It's the old water tower.'

'It's amazing.'

'It's an old water tower.'

'Towers are very important, you know, to the Irish imagination. I read a book once—'

'Ah'm sure. Well, I'll tell you what's important to this Irish imagination. Getting these shelves sorted and getting home for my tea.'

Ted pulled up the van and honked the horn.

A man appeared at an upper window of the tower.

'Dennis,' shouted Ted, getting out of the van.

'Ted,' shouted the man at the window, who was bearded, and probably about the same age as Israel and probably half his weight. He reappeared at the bottom of the tower a few minutes later.

'Dennis, Israel,' said Ted. 'Israel, Dennis.'

'Hello.'

'Pleased to meet you,' said Israel. Dennis seemed to be splattered all over with paint.

'Shelves for the library then, is it?' said Dennis, in businesslike fashion.

'Aye.'

'I'll need to measure her up.'

'Help yourself. Israel, open her up there for Dennis, will you?'

Israel and Dennis climbed into the back of the van.

'Where d'you want them?' asked Dennis.

'Down the sides, I suppose. I can ask Ted.' Israel stuck his head out of the window. 'Ted, where do we want the shelves?'

'Where d'you think, Einstein? On the ceiling?'

'Yeah, along the side,' said Israel to Dennis.

'Fine. Hold this then.' He gave Israel the end of his tape measure.

'How long have you been in this old game?' asked Israel, which was the question he asked everyone he didn't know what to say to.

'What game?'

'This, er, game. You know, erm ...'

'I'm not.'

'What?'

'I just do it on the side, like. Bend down,' said Dennis. 'Lovely.'

Ted appeared at the front of the van, smoking.

'Garden's looking well for the time of year, Dennis.'

'Aye.'

'Leeks and potatoes, is it?'

'Aye.'

'What's your day job then?' asked Israel.

'I'm a painter.'

'Oh, that's handy. You can do the joinery then and the painting and decorating?'

'No,' said Dennis, unimpressed. 'I'm an actual painter.'

'He does portraits and everything,' explained Ted.

'Oh, gosh. Sorry,' said Israel.

'He's been to college and everything,' said Ted. 'Where was that place you went? He'll know. He's from England.'

'It's a big place, England,' said Israel, laughing. 'There's a lot of colleges.'

'The Royal Academy,' said Dennis.

'Oh. Right. Yes.'

'Other side then,' said Dennis, and they moved to the other side of the van to start measuring.

'You heard of that?' asked Ted.

'Yes. Yes. That's quite famous,' said Israel.

'Bend down.'

Israel, embarrassed, bent down.

'That'll do, then,' said Dennis. 'What do you want them in, Ted?'

'I don't know,' said Ted. 'You know the council. They're going to want the cheapest, aren't they?'

'MDF then?'

'Aye, I s'pose.'

'You'd be better with something a wee bit more sturdy, like,' said Dennis, 'Even for the look of it just.'

'Aye, I know, but.'

'D'you want to come in the workshop, have a look at what I've got? I've maybe something recyclable.'

Dennis's workshop was a red brick outbuilding behind the tower, stuffed to overflowing, *literally* stuffed to overflowing, stuff coming out of the doors and windows, like it was making an escape for the wild across the gravelly yard: old broken-down bits of furniture, and tables, and chairs, and picture frames, and window frames, and doors, and planks, anything wooden, like something out of Walt Disney's *Fantasia*. Inside there was an overpowering smell of polish and sawdust.

'This is like an Aladdin's cave,' said Israel, noticing cartwheels and a rocking horse, and a couple of old shop display cabinets.

'Everybody says that.'

'Oh, sorry.'

'It's all right. It is like Aladdin's cave. I just get used to it, I suppose.'

'What's it all for? Do you collect it?'

'Ach, no. I do a bit of conservation, like. Restoration. You know.'

'Right,' said Israel.

'D'you have any waney-edge?' asked Ted, who was poking around in a pile of logs. 'Just, I'm thinking of putting up a wee bit of fencing, for the dog.'

'Maybe somewhere, Ted. I'll have to look around.'

'Right enough.'

'Here's the planks but,' said Dennis, pointing to a row of old and seasoned timber stacked against the wall.

'That oak?' said Ted, pointing to a beautiful big golden plank with silvery flashes.

'Aye,' said Dennis. 'That was off of a trawler I think, down County Down.'

'Lovely that, isn't it, Israel?' said Ted.

Israel did his best to show enthusiasm for the old plank. 'Mmm,' he said. 'Yes. That's lovely.'

'We've got more oak here,' said Dennis, moving along the row of planks, running his hand across the wood. 'More oak. Elm. Mahogany. Teak. Walnut. Ash. There's cupping on some, but, so you wouldn't get the full length.'

'Cupping?' said Israel.

'A wee bit bowed, just,' said Dennis. 'Well?'

'What do you think?' Israel asked Ted.

'You're the boss,' said Ted. 'But in my opinion – I'm biased, mind – the old girl deserves the best.'

In the end, with Dennis's guidance and Ted's encouragement, Israel chose some old beech which had apparently originally graced the floor of a dance hall down in Belfast that Ted had once been to: it certainly had a beautiful grain. And it was considerably more expensive than the MDF.

'You'll square that with Linda then, will you, Israel?' said Ted.

'Oh yes,' said Israel. 'I think I can handle Linda.'

'Aye,' said Ted. 'Ah'm sure.'

Before they left, Dennis fetched a carrier bag full of books from the tower.

'Blimey,' said Ted when Dennis handed them over. 'What have you got in there?'

'It's art monographs, mainly,' said Dennis. 'And I threw in a few spares in case. Exhibition catalogues and what have you.'

'Great,' said Israel. 'That's brilliant.'

'Have those shelves for you beginning of next week, Ted,' said Dennis.

'Aye. Right enough,' said Ted. 'Bye then.'

'This is you then. I'll set you down here,' said Ted, about ten minutes after they'd left Dennis. 'Last call. You're doing it yerself, remember? I've to get on to the BB. I'll drop the van in to the farm later.'

'Oh, yes. Sure.'

Israel went to get out of the van.

'It's just up yonder there. And when you're done, look, it's back down here and left down the rodden there, and you'll be back at the farm in ten minutes.'

'Right. OK. Whose house is this then?'

'Pearce Pyper, he's called. You'll like him. He's more your sort.'

'What's that supposed to mean?'

'Well, you know, he's a bit ...'

'What?'

'Ach, Israel, I don't know. Nyiffy-nyaffy.'

'What? What does that mean?'

'It's a—'

'Saying?'

'Right. Bye! See you Monday.' And Ted leant over, pulled the door shut, and drove off.

Approaching Pearce Pyper's house up the long gravel

drive in the dusk, Israel was immediately struck by what appeared to be examples of very, very bad decommissioned public art: large chunks of painted concrete lined the driveway, like giant discarded baubles, and there were also driftwood sculptures, resembling large, soft, melted Greek statues, and then closer towards the house were what appeared to be wonky totem poles set at intervals along the driveway, their wings and arms outstretched in welcome and benediction, bulbous, beastly heads nodding at the visitor's approach. It was like walking into a Native American reservation, except the totem poles seemed to have been crafted out of old railway sleepers rather than giant native sequoias, and fixed together with carriage bolts, and screws and nails, and painted with thick exterior gloss. The trees that flanked these curious, echt sculptures had been variously pleached, espaliered and cordoned, giving them the appearance of having been shaped out of old scraps of tanalised timber rather than having actually grown up naturally from the earth.

If the approach to the house was a little unusual, the house itself, when Israel finally reached it, was in comparison a welcome reassurance and really only in the mildest degree eccentric: an example of the late nineteenth-century baronial extended and renovated by someone with an interest in thirteenth-century Moorish palaces, and the Arts and Crafts movement, and Le Corbusier, and fretwork DIY. There was much use of rusted metal and carved oak, and palm trees, and concrete-rendered empty space. What was amazing was that it worked, after a fashion. It was a house that seemed to reflect the inner workings of a human mind, and the gardens surrounding the house did the same: there was black bamboo growing out of huge concrete boulders; and giant carved heads set with gaping mouths, half human, and half Wotan, spitting out ivy; and dozens of topiaried shrubs, perfect little nymphs and huntsmen and hares cavorting along the tops of hedges and the lawn in a shrubby kind of dance; and huge mosaic containers shaped like women bearing mosaic containers shaped like women bearing mosaic containers; and a pond shaped like a DNA double helix, its surface brilliant with algae. There was richness of colour and variety everywhere you looked, and over-sized, frivolous, brilliant plants, and for all the apparent chaos Israel had to admit it was one of the most beautiful, composed gardens he had ever seen: it was a pure act of human wilfulness and exuberance; it was the work of an artist.

Israel pulled at the big chain doorbell at the front door, which rang ominously. The big oak door was open, and there were cardboard boxes piled up inside the hall. But no one came. So Israel called out.

'Hello? Hello? Anybody in?'

He didn't like this at all: calling unannounced at people's houses with Ted he'd found difficult enough; it seemed like bad manners. Back in London, if you wanted to see someone you texted or rang at least a week in advance and left a message on their mobile. Turning up at people's houses on spec in a beaten-up old van with Ted to collect library books was not what he'd imagined he'd be doing when he took on the job in Tumdrum: he felt like a book-vigilante, which is exactly how they'd been treated on some calls. Some places they'd gone to collect the books, children had been sent to answer the door.

'My mum's not in,' the little children would say, although you could clearly see their mums hiding in the kitchen, or in the front room, watching the telly.

'Tell your mum I'm no' the tick man or the coal man,' Ted would say. 'I'm from the library.'

It didn't look as though that approach was going to work on this occasion though, because there was no one around at all. The only sign of recent human activity seemed to be the cardboard boxes in the hall, and a Volvo estate parked outside the house.

Israel stepped cautiously across the threshold and cleared his throat.

'Hello?' he said, sticking his head forward, his voice growing weaker in the quiet. 'Excuse me? Anybody about?'

His voice echoed and the house remained silent, completely deserted apart from all the fine furniture, and the paintings on the walls, and the vast rugs on the terracotta floors, and ornaments and objets d'art stuffed in cabinets and on plinths and in recesses and cubby-holes.

A black retriever and a white Persian cat appeared in the hallway from behind the cardboard boxes, regarded Israel slowly and with animal disinterest, and then walked on by, out of the front door and down into the garden.

'Hello? Hello?'

Now he'd entered the house he figured he might as well keep going, and so he slowly made his way through the hall and down a corridor, past doors and double doors, calling as he went, and eventually he came through to a vast kitchen painted an electric yellow, with black and white chequerboard tiles, and there, outside the kitchen window, with views out across a small orchard, he saw a motionless human figure, silhouetted against the darkening sky.

'Hello?' called Israel, extremely faintly now, his heart beating like a little bird's. 'Hello?' The figure did not respond. Israel gulped and began to walk across the kitchen, his brown brogues clicking accusingly across the floor, through the utility room full of wellington boots and Barbours, and outside.

It was a long terrace at the back of the house. The dark, motionless, stooped figure that Israel had seen inside turned out to be an elderly man standing at a long wooden workbench. He was wearing a trilby hat, and a boiler suit over a three-piece suit, and he was working very slowly and with deep concentration with what looked like a cooking spatula, shaping and moulding a concrete bust, like one of the huge heads Israel had seen in the garden.

'Hello?' said Israel uncertainly.

'Ah. Yes. Good,' said the old man, snapping out of his reverie, and turning round and smiling warmly, his bright blue eyes sparkling, as if he were expecting him. 'Good. Ah. You're not Bullimore?'

'No. Sorry.'

'I thought you were Bullimore.' The man waved the concrete-covered spatula at Israel.

'No, I'm not.' Israel had no idea who Bullimore was.

'You're not with Bullimore?'

'No.'

'So you are?'

'Israel Armstrong. I'm the new librarian.'

'Ah, the new librarian. Marvellous. Can't shake hands, I'm afraid. Covered in stuff.' He wiped his hands on his boiler suit. 'Chairman Mao was a librarian, did you know?'

'Yes.'

'Would have been better off sticking to it, really.'

'Yes.'

'Would have saved the world a lot of trouble.'

'Er.'

'And Hitler was an artist.'

'...'

'Not sure about Stalin. What was he?'

'Erm. I'm not sure.'

'Pipe-smoker, anyway. Never to be trusted. Don't smoke a pipe yourself?'

'No.'

'Good. Always worth asking. Now, I've heard a lot about you.'

'You have?'

'Oh yes. You know, small town. Word gets around. Great write-up you had in the paper.'

'Thank you.'

'You're settling in OK?'

'Yes.'

'Good. Excellent. Well, very nice of you to come out and see us.'

'That's all right. You are ...?'

'Sorry, forgive me. Awfully ill-mannered. I'm Pearce Pyper, widower of this parish.'

'Right.'

'Now, by your accent I detect that you're not from here, Israel, is that right?'

'Yes. I'm from London, actually.'

'Ah. Yes. That's right. I remember. It was in the paper. Us outsiders must stick together, you know. I'm a Cork man originally myself – long time ago, of course. Rebel Cork!'

'Right.'

'Lot of nonsense. Anyway, where exactly in London are you from? Big place, London, or at least it was the last time I was there.'

'Yes. North. North London. I don't know if you know it at all ...?'

'Yes. Of course. Not all of it, mind. Kensington and Chelsea I know very well. And my club, the Athenaeum. You're not a member?'

'No.'

'Ah, well. Name like Israel, I suppose you're Jewish, are you?'

'Er ..'

'I knew the Chief Rabbi once. You didn't know him?'

'No. I don't think so.'

'Not the current fella. The one before the one before that. Can't remember his name now. What was he called?'

'I'm sorry. I don't know. I'm not really—'

'Never mind. It'll come to me. My first wife was Jewish. Jabotinsky? Her family were in the fur trade? And little Irving Berlin I knew briefly. Wonderful parties. And Heifetz.'

'You knew Heifetz?'

'Yes. Well, through my wife. Could never see why people got so excited about the fella myself. Much preferred George Formby: great fun at a party.'

'Anyway, I've come about the, erm, the library books, Mr Pyper.'

'You can call me Pearce.'

'OK, Pearce. I'm collecting up all the old stock and overdue books.'

'Jolly good. Getting it all ship-shape and what have you. Come on then inside.'

They went back through the house, through rooms that no longer seemed inhabited, which seemed in fact merely like the shelter for the remnants of a grand inheritance – hunting trophies here and there, and cheetah skins on the floor – and finally they entered into what Israel assumed was the drawing room, looking out over the gardens. Israel had never seen a room quite like it – a room completely and utterly replete, perfectly satisfied with its ornaments and its fine furnishings, every inch of its panelled walls filled with family portraits. Israel thought miserably of his chicken coop.

'Now. Drink. What can I get you? Sherry OK?'

'It's a bit early for me actually.'

'Nonsense. By the time you get to my age you'll not bother with that sort of thing. Sweet or amontillado?'

'Er ...'

'I'll pour you the sweet. You come back round to it in old age. Now.' Pearce Pyper poured the drinks from cut glass into cut glass.

'Sláinte.'

'Cheers. This is quite a place you've got here.'

'Oh yes. We were very lucky with this place. My wife and I bought it in 1939. Post-partition, before the war. Happy days. Lot of work, mind.'

'Your wife, is she still ...'

'No, no. Four wives actually. First two died. Third one divorced me. Fourth one I divorced. Quits all round. Are you married?'

'No.'

'Wouldn't recommend it. Are you a homosexual?'

'No.'

'The companionship's always nice of course, but you can always get a dog. Have you got a dog?'

'Er ...'

'Cost me a fortune.'

'The dog?'

'No, the divorces. Had to get rid of a lot of the ormolu. My first wife, she was a terrible one for the Persian bowls, and the African tribal art: influence of Picasso, and the other fella. What was he called? God ... Weird little man. Obsessed with sex? Beard.'

'Erm.'

'Yes, yes, anyway, that was him. Used to collect Elizabethan crewel-work myself. Had to sell it all off, mind. The Art Deco I'm trying to hang on to: I've got a bit of a thing about the Art Deco. Had to let some of it go, of course. Like losing a child.'

'Oh dear.'

'To Bullimore actually. I thought you were with him.'

'No.'

Pearce Pyper dropped his voice. 'Dreadful man. Bumptious, to be honest, if you know what I mean. Buys the stuff, carts it off to his shop, or down south, wherever, I don't know. Bit of a shit, actually.'

'Oh.'

'But you know, upkeep of the house and everything. Beggars can't be choosers. Difficult keeping on top of it all.'

'I'm sure.'

'But we do our best. "Go muster thy servants; be captain thyself."'

'Right.'

'Another sherry?'

'No, I'm fine, thanks.'

'I shouldn't really, but I shall.'

Pearce poured himself another sherry and took Israel by the arm.

'Come on, let's get your books from the library. *Tenax propositi* and what have you.'

The library was adjacent to the drawing room, divided only by a set of heavy, ornate, satiny-white doors; thrown open, the two rooms might have once been a magnificent ballroom, but now separated they were like two halves, two varieties of exquisiteness. Leaving the densely furnished drawing room they now entered the ordered calm of the library. Simple mahogany shelves reached up high to the ceiling and at both ends of the room – which was at least forty or fifty feet long – were two beautiful desks, with carved legs showing rampant lions. Sofas and rugs and small occasional tables piled high with books were all around.

A man sat in the centre of this magnificent room, surrounded by boxes.

'Ah, Mr Bullimore, this is my young friend, Israel Armstrong.'

'How do you do?' said Israel.

'Mr Bullimore here is culling for me. Weeding, eh, Bullimore?'

P. J. Bullimore struggled to his feet. He looked uncomfortable and incongruous in the surroundings – a ruddy, stout-faced man with a huge, heaving stomach. He sported finger rings, and a chunky watch and wore the clothes of someone who looked like they'd just been practising their chip shots, and who had enjoyed a couple of gin and tonics, and who was warming up to tell you an amusing story that wouldn't be suitable for the ladies.

'Pleased to meet you,' he said, shaking Israel's hand.

The cardboard boxes all around Bullimore were packed with books and marked on the side either 'Poetry', or 'Philosophy', or 'History', or 'Religion'.

Pearce Pyper stood by the boxes.

'Now, what was it we agreed?'

P. J. Bullimore was silent.

'Mr Bullimore? Was it fifty pounds per box?'

Bullimore was looking silently ahead.

'That's pretty reasonable, isn't it, Israel? He's a librarian, you know,' Pearce said to Bullimore.

'Sounds very reasonable,' said Israel, assuming that Pearce Pyper's library might be similar in kind and in value to his own: a rainforestful of dampening paperbacks.

But then he took a book from the top of the box marked 'Poetry'.

'T. S. Eliot?' he said.

'Yes,' said Pearce. 'He was a cold fish. Friend of my first wife's. Used to send us all his books.'

'You knew Eliot?'

'Well. I wouldn't go that far. He was friendly with my sister as well. Little too friendly, actually. Bertrand Russell, he was the same.'

'But this is ...' – Israel opened up the book, *The Waste Land*, and looked at the flyleaf – 'signed by Eliot?'

'Is it? Yes. Probably.'

'Hmm.'

Israel then moved on to another box, which was marked 'Cookery'.

'The *Alice B. Toklas Cook Book*?'

'Ah yes. Too French for my tastes.'

Israel examined the flyleaf. 'Signed by Alice B. Toklas.'

'Yes. God, she was a handful, let me tell you. And the woman, what was the other woman ...?'

'Gertrude Stein?'

'Good God, yes. Like a bloody prize-fighter. Forearms the size of my thighs.'

Israel had moved on to 'Fiction' and had taken the first book off the top of that box.

'*The Great Gatsby*.'

'Lovely book. Nice man. Never liked his wife. Highly strung.'

'You know, Mr Pyper—'

'No, no. Call me Pearce.'

'Pearce, some of these books are ... they're priceless, you know.'

'Well, I don't know about that,' said Pearce Pyper modestly.

'I really think I should be the judge of that, Mr, what did you say your name was?' said Bullimore suspiciously.

'Armstrong.'

'Mr Armstrong. I don't know if you know much about the book trade.'

'I'm a librarian.'

'Ah. But the book trade? The *trade*?'

'A little.' Israel didn't mention that the little he knew about the book trade was from his experience working as a deputy store manager in the Bargain Bookstore in the Lakeside Shopping Centre in Thurrock in Essex.

'Yes. I'm sure,' said Bullimore. 'But you should really leave the valuation to us experts. Look,' he said, picking up another volume from the 'Fiction' box. 'For example. This probably looks fine to the untrained eye. But if you look closely you'll see that here there's some water damage.' He pointed to a brown fleck. 'And the covers are torn. And the binding is loose.'

'Right,' said Israel, taking the book from his hands and opening it up. 'But it's signed by James Joyce. It's a copy of *Ulysses*.'

'Yes, well, obviously, once I've gathered all the worth-while items together I was going to put the higher value items aside and price them separately.'

Israel doubted that very much.

'Anyway, Mr Pearce,' said Bullimore. 'I'm just about done for the day here. I'll leave you and your young friend and perhaps call back later next week to finish off?'

'Yes, of course. Finish things off. That'd be marvellous. Let me—'

'No. It's OK. I can see myself out.'

And he left, rather quickly.

'Mr Pyper?' said Israel, once Bullimore had left the library and closed the door behind him.

'Do call me Pearce.'

'Sorry. Pearce. I don't mean to speak out of turn or anything, but if I was you I think I'd be careful of him.'

'Who?' said Pearce Pyper, finishing his sherry.

'Bullimore, Mr Pyper.'

'Do call me Pearce. Sorry, what did you say?'

'Mr Bullimore. I think you should be very careful.'

'Really?'

'Yes. Really.'

'I've been dealing with him for years now. Furniture and what have you.'

'He was offering you a pittance for those books.'

'Well, they're no good to me now.'

'Some of those books are worth thousands.'

'Well, I'll talk to Bullimore about it. I'm sure we'll come to some agreement that is amenable to all parties. But now, we mustn't forget what you came for.'

They went to a small console table beside a velvet-upholstered chaise-longue, which had a tartan rug folded upon it, beneath one of the big windows.

'Very important to support your local library,' said Pearce.

'Yes.'

'Here we are then,' he said, grandly presenting Israel with half a dozen plastic dust-jacketed paperbacks, as out of place in Pearce's library as they belonged in the mobile. 'I always keep them separate.'

Israel glanced at the titles.

'Damon Runyon?'

'Oh yes. Dashiell Hammett. Raymond Chandler. I do like the American hard-boiled. Chandler was at school with one of my cousins. Lunatic, apparently.'

'Right,' said Israel, 'well, it's good to have them back. Thank you.'

'Not at all.'

'It's a wonderful garden you have there,' said Israel, nodding towards the view of sculptures and trees outside.

'Oh, I am glad you like it. It's a labour of love, I'm afraid, but there are worse ways to spend one's old age.'

'I like the sculptures and the ...' Israel couldn't think of word to describe the totem poles, and the moulded concrete flowerpot heads. '... And the other things.'

'Good! Some people are rather sniffy about them, I'm afraid.'

'Really?'

'Oh yes.'

'Do you make them yourself?'

'Absolutely. My means of self-expression I suppose you might say. You must come back for a proper tour one day.'

'That'd be lovely, thank you.'

'Sherry?'

'No. Thanks. I should really be going.'

'Yes, of course.'

Israel could see the red barn on the Devines' farm in the distance, beyond Pearce Pyper's gardens.

'Shall I go out this way?' he asked, indicating the French doors leading onto the rear terrace.

'No, no. You must go out the way you came in. Bad luck otherwise.'

'Is it?'

'Of course!'

Pearce Pyper led Israel back through the house.

'So, where are you for now?' asked Pearce Pyper.

'I'm staying with the Devines,' said Israel, pointing. 'Just past the big red barn there.'

'Ah, the Devines? Lovely family.'

'Yes.'

'Terrible business with the parents.'

'Yes.'

'Lovely girl, though, Georgina. Done them proud. Make some lucky man a wife one day, eh?'

'Yes, I'm sure.'

'Anyway, good luck to you.'

'Yes, thanks,' said Israel.

Pearce Pyper pointed down the driveway, and Israel set off, library books tucked under his arm.

It was getting dark. The lane was narrow. Overhead it was threatening rain. And as Israel walked he went back to trying to work out where the missing books had gone. Ted honestly seemed to believe that if they just kept rounding up overdue books they'd gather them all in eventually. But Israel knew this wasn't the case: the books had been stolen. He just still couldn't quite work out who might have had a motive for stealing fifteen thousand library books from Tumdrum and District Library – or fourteen thousand, or however many it was. Maybe they wanted to inflict harm upon the council, or upon the library, or upon librarians, so maybe it was someone with a grievance: thus, Norman Canning. Or it might be the council themselves, trying to cover up their plans to withdraw all library services. Then again, it was possible that someone simply wanted to sell the books and make some money. He therefore still had several lines of enquiry, none of which was so far working out.

He thought he heard something behind him: it sounded far off, at first, like a faint crunching. But the sound suddenly grew louder, and Israel turned around.

There was a vehicle approaching down the narrow grassy lane at high speed – in the dark he couldn't make out what it was. He dropped the library books and dived into the hedge, moments before the vehicle sped past him.

It was his head that hit the tree first.

18

His nose. He'd broken his bloody nose: in the impact of leaping out of the way of the oncoming vehicle and into the tree his nose had gone; it had popped. Israel had always been very attached to his nose.

When he finally made it back to the Devines', covered in blood, Mr Devine had fiddled around trying to straighten his nose up a bit and instead he seemed to have increased the spread, like too much jam on toast. When he looked in the mirror now Israel no longer saw a proud young north London librarian with all the future ahead of him: what he saw instead were the bruises, and the bumps and the nose of a bloated and washed-up old boxer.

The next morning Brownie had given him a lift into town and Israel gave a statement to the police, who said they'd look into the incident, although unfortunately Israel didn't have the registration number of the vehicle, nor could he identify it precisely – he said it was a long sort of car, at which the police officer, a Sergeant Friel, a man with the kind of moustache once touted by RAF pilots and a smart-arse attitude to match, had smiled and said, 'How long exactly?' and spread out his arms, 'This long?' and 'No,' Israel had said, 'Longer,' and 'Oh,' said Sergeant Friel, 'Well, well, well,' and he was sorry but in that case he was afraid there wasn't that much the police could do to help, there were an awful lot of long cars out there these days.

Israel spent the rest of his Saturday feeling profoundly sorry for himself and wishing he was back home in London, where of course all policemen are gentlemen and hit-and-run drivers leave their particulars at the scene of the crime. He was sitting in the kitchen by the Rayburn with his swelling nose, reading the paper, or trying to read the paper: the *Impartial Recorder* was not the *Guardian*, to be honest, and there were just only so many reports on the possible go-ahead of plans for new local renal units and photographs of Mayor Maureen Minty planting trees in the grounds of old people's homes that he could take. On Saturdays he and Gloria liked to get up late, read the papers, go and see an interesting independent film in an interesting independent cinema, and have something nice to eat in a young and happening person's kind of a restaurant. He rang Gloria to see what she was up to. She wasn't answering her mobile: she was too busy being young and happening, probably. Israel poured himself more tea from the never-ending teapot on the stove: he was slowly moving towards tea, actually, and away from coffee; and he couldn't help thinking that this was a very bad sign.

There were the usual comings and goings in the farmhouse: Mr Devine hauling coal and food around;

Brownie up and down with books; George in and out in her dungarees. Israel remained in the kitchen, dreaming fondly of his old life.

'Aye, right, you're there,' said Mr Devine, bringing in a bundle of small sticks, which he'd spent most of the afternoon chopping out in the yard: the distant echoing sound of axe on wood had given Israel a terrible headache. 'Parcel for you.'

'For me, really? Thanks.'

Mr Devine handed over the package.

The only post Israel had received since arriving in Tumdrum had been a few circulars that his mother had forwarded to him – credit card offers and requests for charity donations.

He prodded his glasses and looked at the package. It was a Jiffy bag. He recognised Gloria's writing on the package. He ripped it open.

There was no note from Gloria. Her PA had probably sent it.

Inside the Jiffy bag was another Jiffy bag: the inner Jiffy had been posted to their London address.

Israel tore it open.

Inside the inner Jiffy was the map of Tumdrum and District that he'd been waiting for from Amazon.co.uk, which he'd ordered what now seemed like a lifetime ago in Zelda's.

Well, frankly, it wasn't the most exciting item he'd ever been sent in the post – his GCSE results, they'd been pretty good, and there was that time Gloria had ordered something on the Internet from Agent Provocateur, which was pretty good also, but still, this was something, it was a package, it was better than nothing, and he glanced absentmindedly at the seller's invoice.

And then he checked the postmark.

And then he looked again at the map.

And he couldn't believe it: the invoice was from someone calling themselves North Coast Books. And the postmark was Tumdrum. And the map had the tell-tale purple sticker on it: it was the old Tumdrum Library copy. It took him a moment, but then it all fell into place, there was a clunk and a click and the Eagle had landed, and it was all he could do to stop himself from shouting Eureka!

Receiving the map in the post was as good as receiving a written statement or a letter containing a confession; it wrapped it all up and gave it all away. The mystery was as good as solved.

All he needed to do now was to explain to someone this amazing breakthrough in his admittedly rather ad-hoc investigation. Brownie had gone out, otherwise he'd have been good to talk to, and Israel knew better by now than to try to talk about anything to George or Mr Devine and there weren't that many other people he could talk to; it was getting on for teatime, after which time traditionally in Tumdrum everyone battened down the hatches and prepared to repel boarders, but because of the import of his discovery, because he believed that finally he'd cracked it, and because he had absolutely no one else he could share the news with, he decided to take the liberty of going to see Ted, not something he would usually have considered under any circumstances. Israel had not been in the habit of making social calls since he'd arrived in Tumdrum – he had no one to make social calls upon – and Ted would not have been his choice of confidant, but he didn't have time now for mere niceties and pussyfooting around: he was hot on the trail of his man, and his ticket out of here and home. All he needed was a little support and back-up.

Israel had passed Ted's house a few times on some of the service runs. It was a neat little bungalow on the coast, at the foot of a sheer cliff, and it would have had fantastic views across to the sea if the main coast road didn't run right in front of it, inches from the door, so the magnificent view was obscured by the constant stream of traffic, carrying people and goods and food and drink up and round and back again, to and from the north coast, and so Ted's view in fact consisted mostly of the word 'Guinness' flashing by, again and again, and of the shining silver and red of thousands of nearly new cars, with the appropriate and accompanying sound of BBC Radio Ulster faintly to be heard above the hum of slightly worn tyre on tarmac.

Israel pulled the van over onto the weed and gravel forecourt cut into the cliff, and got out, and knocked and rang at the door. There was the distinct sound of growling: Ted had a dog. He might have guessed.

Israel's usual approach with dogs, as with small children, was to ignore them in the sure and certain hope that they'd soon get bored and go away. Israel hadn't grown up with dogs, had never had a dog, and he did not like them. He was more of a cat person.

'Ted! Ted!' he called, ignoring the barking dog, as Ted opened up.

'Israel,' replied Ted. He was wearing a pinny covered with flour and had a rolling pin in his hand, and there was a little Jack Russell at his heels.

'Are you cooking?' said Israel.

'No, I'm creosoting my fences.'

'Ted, I've done it.'

'Sorry to hear that.'

'What?'

'You've crashed the van again?'

'No! No. No. I've found the books.'

'The library books?'

'Yes, the library books. Of course the library books.'

'Aye, well, congratulations.'

'So.'

'So?' said Ted, who was not as excited as Israel might have hoped.

'So, let me come in and I'll tell you all about it.'

'Right.' Ted folded his arms across his chest, blocking Israel's way into the house and getting flour all over his arms in the process.

'Ted?'

Ted frowned – and when Ted frowned the deep frown lines ran all the way from behind the top of one ear, multiplying as they went, and all the way across to the other. They weren't so much frowns in fact as the folds on a complex origami forehead.

'All right. But don't be making a habit of making house calls. OK? It's not good for the dog. It makes him nervous. It's all right, Muhammad, he's a friend.'

'Muhammad? Your dog's called Muhammad?'

'That's right.'

'Oh. OK. After the Prophet Muhammad?'

'No. After the boxer.'

Ted turned to go inside, and Muhammad the Jack

Russell terrier allowed Israel to enter.

The house was pretty much what you'd expect from a man of modest means in his sixties living by himself with a small Jack Russell called Muhammad on a windswept coast several miles from the nearest town: it was clean and it was practical and it made a good effort to appear cheerful, even though the overall and unintended effect was profoundly saddening, a consequence not only of the stench and scuffs of small dog but also of the clear and apparent lack of a woman's touch. There was a rich, thick, meaty smell, with just a hint of urine, coming from the kitchen, a smell that may have been mould, or it may have been food. There were old green oil cans containing peat by the front door, and a fire in the grate. The living room had its orangey 1950s sofa and a wood-effect Formica coffee table, and a plain pine dresser set with a few pieces of crockery. There was one door through to the bedroom and another straight out back into the spartan kitchen, which was empty save for an old sink, and a cupboard, and a narrow table, and a cream-coloured Rayburn. The dog basket with its vivid red blanket sat proud by the back door.

'Lovely house, Ted,' said Israel, standing awkwardly in the living room.

'All right, Israel, sit down if you're staying and get on with it. I'm cooking.'

'Thanks.' Israel noticed pastry draped over dishes in the kitchen. 'OK.'

'What's that with your nose?' said Ted.

'Ah yes, that's part of what I'm about to tell you.'

'You gone arse over heels agin?'

'No. Or yes. But anyway, I know where the books are.'

'Good. Where are they?'

'At P. J. Bullimore's.'

'Bullimore's?' Ted raised an eyebrow.

'Yes. Do you know him?'

'Course I know him. He's the big antiquey place round by the First and Last.'

'Yes! That's him!'

'And what, they're all there, are they, the books?'

'Yes, I think so.'

'You think so?'

'Yes.'

'You haven't actually seen them there then?'

'No. Not yet. But I know they're there.'

'Oh, aye. Because the wee fairies told you, or you have X-ray eyes, or you just have a feeling in your water?'

'No. Of course not. But I've got this.'

Israel took the padded envelope from his duffle coat pocket.

'Oh, that seals it then.'

'Yes! Ted, this is the smoking gun.'

Ted laughed, and started to move off towards the kitchen.

'Sorry, Israel. Time and pastry wait for no man. Lovely chatting to you. See you on Monday ...'

'Hold on. Look, let me explain.'

Israel followed Ted out into the kitchen.

And this was the source of the smells.

'Mmm,' said Israel. 'What are you making?'

'Pies.'

'How do you do that?'

'What?'

'How do you make pies?'

'You don't know how to make a pie?'

'No.'

'You just get your pastry and you—'

'How do you make the pastry though?'

'Ach, for flip's sake, Israel,' said Ted, rolling out a circle of pastry. 'Do you know nothing?'

'Well ... we eat out a lot in London.'

'Aye.'

'But my mum's a good cook.'

'Is she now?'

'Yes. She does a lovely vegetarian lasagne.'

'I'm sure.' Ted brushed the thin pastry.

'What are you doing there?'

'I'm brushing the pastry.'

'Ah, yes, I remember my mum doing that.'

'Good.' Ted then placed the thin pastry on top of a dish of steaming meat and took a knife, trimmed off the pastry from around the pie dish, and then took a fork and began sealing the edges. Israel was watching closely.

'There's a word for you, you know,' said Ted, washing his hands at the sink.

'Is there?'

'Yes. Bloody annoying.'

'That's two words.'

'Bloodyannoying,' said Ted.

Ted went into the living room and then returned.

'Here. Take this.'

'What is it?'

'What's it look like? It's a cookbook. That'll tell you how to make pastry.'

'Delia Smith's *How to Cook, Book One*?'

'You can borrow it.'

'Are you sure?'

'If it saves you asking me stupid questions about how to make pastry, I'm sure.'

'Well, thanks. Anyway. Ted, this is the key to the crime,' said Israel, brandishing the envelope.

'It's a key now, is it?'

'Metaphorically.'

'Aye, Ah'm sure.'

'It's the envelope in which I received the map—'

'That tells you where to find the buried treasure?'

'Yes. No! I'm serious. A map of the local area.'

'OK,' said Ted, carefully placing the pie inside the Rayburn. 'Someone sent you a map in the post? Why?'

'Because I needed to find my way around, for the service runs.'

'Right.'

'So I found one on the Internet.'

'Sure you could have got one out of the library.'

'But all the library books have been stolen!'

'Aye. True.'

'So I had to find one. So I sent off for it, and it was delivered to my home address in London. Forwarded to me here.'

'Fine.'

'And. Look ... at this.'

He showed Ted the postmark on the envelope. It was red, and thin and smudged, like a lipstick trace, but you could still read it.

'It's Tumdrum,' said Ted.

'Exactly.'

'So?'

'Well, look at this.'

Israel then produced from the envelope the map – a perfectly ordinary green and cream-coloured Ordnance Survey map. It had a small purple reference label in the top right-hand corner.

'It's the library copy.'

'Precisely!'

'So, what, the person who sent you this map had it from the library?'

'Right. They must have stolen it.'

'Not necessarily,' said Ted.

'Probably.'

'Aye, well, maybe.'

'And then they're selling the stolen books on the Internet.'

'Hmm,' said Ted.

'Which means if we find the person who sent me this we'll find the person who's stolen the books.'

'Right, well,' said Ted thoughtfully, 'fair play to you, big fella. It beats your other auld nonsense. D'you get an invoice or anything with your map?'

'Yes. Here. North Coast Books. But it doesn't say who they are or where they're based.'

'Nope.' Ted studied the invoice. 'So what makes you think it's Bullimore?'

'Well, it has to be him. He's the only person locally who trades in books, isn't he?'

'Aye, but. Just because he trades in books doesn't mean he trades in stolen books.'

'No. True. But last night he tried to run me down in his car.'

'What?'

'I'm serious.'

'Aye.'

'I am. He was trying to kill me.'

'Ach, Israel, wise up ...'

'He was! He's running a scam to get Pearce Pyper to part with all his books. When I was there yesterday, he was there, under-pricing all these priceless books of Pearce's – James Joyce, and Eliot and—'

'Aye, right, I get the picture.'

'And then when I pointed this out to him, he left, and then he tried to run me down, and I jumped into a tree ...'

'You what?'

'I fell into a tree, down the lane by the big red barn. And broke my nose.' Israel pointed at his nose. 'See?'

'Aye, I see your nose all right – wee bit wonky but. But I'm not sure I see how all the rest fits together.'

'It does, it does! It's a dead cert, Ted. Bullimore's our man. Trust me.'

Ted considered this last appeal with huge and intense wrinkling of his forehead.

'Aye. Well, if you're right – and I'm not saying you're right, mind – what are you going to do? Just go in there and say hello, you've stolen the library books, and I wonder if you couldn't hand them over please, thank you very much.'

'No. Of course not.'

'So. You're going to the police then?'

'No. We can't go to the police.'

'Because?'

'Because this is my case.'

'Oh, right. Jim Rockford you are now then, are ye?'

'We're going to break in.'

'Hold on. You said "we"?'

'Yes. We. Me and you, we'll break in and find the books.'

'No way, José.'

'Come on, Ted.'

'No.'

'Oh, come on, this is it. We get the books back, and then I'm out of here. I'm a free man again. I'm gone.'

'Aye, to prison.'

'No. I'm serious.'

'I'm serious. No can do.'

'Why?'

'Because you're talking about breaking in somewhere. It's wrong.'

'It's not wrong. It's the lesser of two evils.'

'Aye, it's wrong.'

'It's not wrong. We're breaking in for the greater good. Like you hid the mobile library.'

'That was different.'

'Why?'

'Because.'

'What?'

'We were protecting the mobile. It's not the same at all. And anyway, what if it's not him?'

'Well ... Then we would have made a mistake.'

'Quite a mistake.'

'Yes, but.'

'No, I'm sorry, you're on your own, Israel.'

'Oh no, Ted. Not again, Ted. Please.'

'No.'

'Please.'

'No. I said no, and I mean no. There is nothing on God's green earth that is going to persuade me to become engaged in any ne ...'

'Ne?' said Israel.

'Ne ...' Ted was struggling.

'Negative?' offered Israel.

'No!' said Ted. 'Ne ...'

'Farious?'

'Exactly. Nefarious business. I've kept my nose clean these past few years, I'm hardly going to start getting in trouble now.'

'Ted!'

'No!'

'Well, what am I supposed to do?'

'I don't know. That's up to you. I've got my pies here.'

'Ted.'

'No! I mean no! Muhammad'll see you out. Muhammad!'

The Jack Russell led Israel to the door.

'And you want to get a doctor to look at your nose,' shouted Ted from the kitchen. 'Get it straightened out proper.'

'Right,' said Israel. 'Thanks a lot.'

'Or yous'll end up like me,' said Ted, with a sigh.

19

P. J. Bullimore's was an old red-brick building on the edge of town which called itself the Antiques and Collectables Treasure Trove and which was surrounded by a high corrugated-iron fence and which did not look anything at all like an antiques and collectables treasure trove; it looked more like a high-security prison.

Now Israel would have been the first to admit that he didn't have that much experience in breaking and entering – he'd sometimes had trouble getting into a vacuum-sealed pack of Fair Trade coffee back home with Gloria, or splitting open a gaffer-taped box of books back at the discount bookshop at the Lakeside Shopping Centre off the M25 in Thurrock in Essex. But fortunately he just happened to have with him now, at his own personal disposal, a bit of kit that even the most hardened and experienced of professional house-breakers would have been happy to get their hands on: a red and cream liveried rust-bucket of a mobile library which seen in a certain light and under certain desperate circumstances made a pretty effective Trojan-horse-cum-battering-ram-cum-elevating platform. He pulled up this lethal public-service vehicle alongside the corrugated-iron fence around midnight, turned off the engine, took one of the Devines' kitchen chairs which he had wisely thought to bring along earlier and hoisted himself up through the skylight and onto the roof. He was level with the top of the security fence. Sometimes it felt good to be a librarian.

It was about a fifteen-foot drop the other side though; he hadn't got quite that far in his planning.

He prodded his glasses and looked down. The ground looked like dirt rather than concrete, but he couldn't be sure. And was that a mangle and an enamel bath and a few bits of old fireplace and tiles and cast-iron radiators and other architectural salvage-type items lying around down there?

He thought he could hear a car approaching in the distance. The car was coming closer. He looked down again. That was definitely a roll-top bath down there. He could see the headlights now. He didn't want to jump. But nor did he want anyone seeing him standing on the roof of a mobile library at midnight: it would take some explaining.

So he took a deep breath and he leapt.

Aaggh.

Bright security lights came on all around him. He lay still, face down in the dirt. No one came. Nothing happened.

So he picked himself up and dusted himself down – duffle coat, brown corduroy jacket, combats and brogues and all. He'd just missed being impaled on an ornate cast-iron balustrade (£500) and dashing his brains out on a pile of handmade bricks (£2 each, 25 for £40). He'd made it.

And then the dog came out of nowhere.

It was an Alsatian.

Oh, Jesus.

Fortunately though, Israel was prepared even for this, though he didn't know it: the dog leapt up towards him across a pile of mossy coping-stones and Israel may have been a vegetarian and everything but he had no intention of being bitten and he instinctively thrust his hand into his duffle coat pocket and pulled out the first thing he found there and thrust it forwards into the dog's slavering maw – a fine use for a copy of Yann Martel's *Life of Pi* if Israel said so himself.

The dog was whimpering and thrashing about to try and dislodge the Booker Prize-winning fable about the relationship between man and beasts from his mouth, so Israel didn't have much time.

He ran across the yard to the front of the shop, dodging the mill-stones, and old slate hearths, and nymph-type statuettes and antique garden furniture as he went.

Unfortunately he had no idea how to break into a building, but he did have a couple of other books stuffed into his pocket, including a pre-remaindered copy of *Harry Potter and the Half-Blood Prince*, which they'd given to him as a leaving gift back at the discount bookshop in Thurrock in Essex – because he hated J. K. Rowling, obviously – and he hadn't read it, but right now, at this moment, a work of thick, dense, self-indulgent children's fantasy seemed to him just about the best book published this century; perfect in form, fit to purpose and just what he needed. He took the book firmly in his hand, thrust his arm forward and smashed it through the glass in the top half of the shop's stable door, reached in, fiddled with a few bolts, lifted the top of the door off its hinges, and walked inside. This was probably not what Matthew Arnold had meant when he argued that literature can save you, but it did the trick.

The security lights illuminated the scene inside like something from film noir: dark furniture looming up from the shadows, an armoire here, a little pie-crust-edged table there, studded wooden doors to the right of him, bureaux to the left of him. Some quite nice clocks.

He could hear the dog howling outside. He didn't have long. He started moving quickly through the warren of rooms, rushing past bedsteads and chaise-longues and stuffed birds and desks and tables and cabinets.

But no books. There was absolutely no sign of the bloody books! The only books he could find were tooled leather volumes sitting on a little mahogany book carrel; a snip at £300. But no Hayes car manuals. No Dorling Kindersleys. No Catherine Cooksons. No little purple stickers and the Dewey number. No sign of the Tumdrum and District Library books.

He thought he heard a noise – someone approaching. Oh, shit. Shit, shit, shit, shit, shit.

His breathing was heavy – his blood seemed to be pumping round his body at twice its normal speed. He was shaking. His broken nose throbbed. He opened up the nearest door to him and climbed through and wedged himself inside a nice double pine wardrobe: it would have done him and Gloria actually, the wardrobe. He could hear his heart echoing round the wooden space. For a moment he thought his heart might explode. The footsteps approached nearer and nearer.

As the sound of footsteps passed the wardrobe Israel took courage, pushed open the doors and leapt out, shouting and slinging a punch.

The dark figure in front of him turned as Israel swung, blocked the blow, struck him under the chin, hit him in the face, and kneed him in the groin. Israel fell to the floor.

'Aaggh.'

'Get up.'

'Aaggh,' continued Israel.

'Get up, you eejit.'

It was Ted.

'Ted? Ted, what are you doing here?' groaned Israel.

'I couldn't let you come here on your own, you bloody fool.'

'Right. Aaggh. I think you've broken my jaw, but – aaggh – thanks anyway.'

'Don't thank me. I haven't broke your jaw. We're getting you out of here.'

'Right. Yeah,' said Israel, raising himself up to his feet.

'You never go anywhere without back-up. D'you find them though?'

'What?'

'The books, boy!'

'No.'

'Ach, Israel.'

'Ah, but I haven't quite finished my search yet.'

There was a sudden flash of light – like the director of Israel's little film noir had suddenly called 'Cut!' and thrown the switch. It was P. J. Bullimore standing in front of them with a huge torch and dressed in pyjamas, a nasty pink golfing jumper and monogrammed slippers.

'I think your search is over, gents.'

'Ah,' said Israel – in a tone that conveyed all at once anger, surprise, and complete and utter despair.

'Where are the books, Bullimore?' said Ted, rather more evenly.

'Ted. I might have guessed you'd be involved,' said Bullimore.

'The books, Bullimore?'

'The books? I'm sorry, I don't know what you're talking about.'

'The missing library books?'

Bullimore laughed. 'I think the police might have something to say about this,' he said. 'In the meantime ... '

And then he grabbed a shade-less standard lamp and started advancing towards them.

'Steady!' said Ted.

'Reasonable force,' said Bullimore, moving slowly towards them, enraged, his face flushed, 'in the protection of myself and my property.'

At which point big blind John Feely Boyd came blundering out of the dark towards them.

'Ted!' he called. 'Ted!'

'John!' called Ted. 'Look out!'

Bullimore turned with the standard lamp, wielding it in front of him like a sword, but because John couldn't see he just kept coming forward, which unnerved

Bullimore, who hesitated in his thrust and John quickly disarmed him, grabbed him and got him in a head-lock.

'That's the relief o' Derry, John, I tell you,' said Ted.

'Come on! Let's go,' said Israel, adrenaline pumping. 'Before the police get here.'

'Wise up,' said Ted.

'We called the police,' said John.

'Oh,' said Israel.

'You're going to have some explaining to do, boyo,' said Ted.

20

People afterwards liked to talk about what really happened, but no one really knows apart from those who were there, and those who were involved.

It was the farewell dinner at Zelda's. Linda Wei was there in her middle-management evening wear of trouser suit and character scarf. Ted was there in a black suit and a black shirt and a black tie, and he seemed also to have shaved his head specially, which doubled the usual menace: classic henchman chic. Minnie was there, in a sparkly cardigan. And George, with her red hair down; Brownie; Mr Devine; the Reverend Roberts; Rosie; the cream of Tumdrum society. Mayoress Minty had been invited but had had to decline; she was at the launch of the council's nude charity calendar, which featured photographs of dinner ladies with strategically placed Yorkshire puddings and lollipop men with their giant lollipops; the *Impartial Recorder* had run a full-colour centre-spread preview the week before and it had caused uproar. Mayoress Minty had come out strongly in support: if Northern Ireland had had more nude charity calendars, she'd told the paper, maybe it wouldn't be in the state it was in today, a characteristically provocative and utterly nonsensical statement which had caused more uproar, but the mayoress was sticking to her guns; she'd ordered a hundred copies of the calendar to send out to friends and family; and her own personal favourite, she was telling anyone and everyone who cared to listen, was March, which featured the council caretakers with mops atop their dignity.

The real star of the show at Zelda's meanwhile was the food – they had really pushed the boat out with the food. There wasn't a drop of coronation chicken in sight. It was a meat- and poultry-free feast that would have warmed the heart of even the most red-in-tooth-and-claw of carnivores, let alone a short, chubby, vegetarian librarian from north London.

Israel was seated, broken-nosed and puffy-eyed, at the head table overlooking the vegetarian proceedings, Minnie on his left, George on his right. He'd polished his brown brogues and had borrowed Mr Devine's three-piece tweed suit again, and he was wearing Ted's purple tie. He liked to think he had a certain rakish charm. He didn't, in fact, but he had the glow of someone who knew that the end was near. His old brown suitcase was already packed.

Dishes kept arriving before them, as if by magic, although actually served up by the raggedy-nailed and not entirely clean hands of a troop of fat and miserable-looking schoolchildren in their white school shirts and blouses, employed specially for the evening by Zelda. There was more couscous and fried aubergine than Israel had ever seen.

'It's like the *Satyricon*,' he said jokingly.

'Surely,' said Minnie. 'Wasn't that on the telly? We had to send to Belfast for those,' she said, indicating a plate of deep-fried sweet potatoes. 'And the ... Och, what do you call this stuff?' she asked George.

'What stuff?' said George irritably.

'Och, the whitey stuff there that looks a wee bit like tripe?'

'I don't know.'

'Come here, Israel,' said Minnie, even though Israel was already there. 'What's those sort of wee lardy lumps?'

'Tofu?'

'Aye, right. That's from Derry, that is.'

'Londonderry,' said George.

'Och, don't be so silly,' said Minnie. 'One of them healthy food shops up there.'

'Right,' said Israel, heading off an argument. 'Well, thank you anyway.'

'Don't thank me. Thank Zelda,' said Minnie. 'It was her idea. She wanted to give you a big send-off. Sure, it's not been easy for you.'

'I'm sure he can't wait to get back home,' said George, grinning unpleasantly at Israel.

Well, yes, Israel had to admit ... It had been a busy couple of days.

Unfortunately it had turned out that P. J. Bullimore was *not* responsible for the theft of the missing library books: the police had searched his premises thoroughly but to no avail, so Israel's hunch, like just about all his other notions, had turned out to be entirely wrong. But then again it appeared that Bullimore *was* responsible for having stolen numerous items of furniture from Pearce Pyper and other locals: his Antiques and Collectables Treasure Trove was a trove of other people's treasure. Bullimore was currently helping police with their enquiries.

So Israel may not have recovered the stolen library books and there was still the small matter of the ongoing investigation into his suspected breaking and entering of Bullimore's premises, but he was a local hero, the most famous librarian, probably, in Tumdrum's history. He'd had his picture in the *Impartial Recorder* again, this time with Pearce Pyper, handing back an Art Deco clock that Pearce thought he'd merely mislaid and which in fact P. J. Bullimore had stolen, along with dozens of other priceless items. People had been queuing up to reclaim their fancy reupholstered chairs and their stripped farmhouse pine dressers which had been painted in green gloss the last time they'd seen them and which Bullimore had been selling off at prices they'd never have been able to afford. In recognition of his services to the community, Linda Wei and the Department of Entertainment, Leisure and Community Services had decided that Israel should be released immediately from his contract. He was free to go.

There was a distinctly festive spirit then that night at Zelda's. Christmas was only a week away, and there was a tree, and decorations and much sipping of Shloer and wine and beer and at the point at which the desserts were being served – a range of pavlovas and banoffee pies to rival those in any mid-range provincial pub or bistro –

Zelda swept out of the kitchens and through the room as if on the crest of a wave, hair high and erect, chatting to guests, laughing with them, dangling mistletoe as she went.

Minnie leant over to Israel, mid-pavlova.

'She's kept her ankles, you know,' she said.

'Her ankles?' said Israel.

'Aye. In the old days you couldn't have beat her legs in County Antrim. Look.'

Israel tried to catch a glimpse of Zelda's ankles between the tables: he couldn't quite make them out.

'See?'

'There's lots of ankles, Minnie, I can't see them.'

'She was a mannikin, you know, when she was young.'

'A mannikin?'

'A model,' said George.

'Can't you tell?' said Minnie.

Israel looked and for a moment he could tell, he could tell what men might have seen forty or fifty years ago – a slight sway of the hips as she moved, and a certain way she had of fanning her dress out behind her to best advantage, a way of holding attention by using her body, the way the hair had been carefully arranged. He could tell that many, many years ago Zelda must have been fiercely, bitingly beautiful, even though the edge of that beauty was now concealed and obscured by the effects of age, and also by blusher, and concealer, and eye shadow, and eyeliner, and mascara, and lipstick, and powder. Zelda was still a beauty, but now she was a pantomime beauty.

'She's mink, you know. Upstairs. Mink coats. And pearls. She was amazing when she was young,' said

Minnie. 'She was like our own local Katharine Hepburn, wasn't she, George?'

George couldn't hear her. 'What did you say?'

'Zelda, she was like Katharine Hepburn.'

George looked sceptical. 'I was too young to remember, Auntie.'

'Oh well. She was. She taught me everything I know, you know.'

George snorted.

'About what?' asked Israel.

'Och, you know, the way of the world,' Minnie laughed.

George snorted again.

'She taught me how to smoke: I hadn't even thought of smoking before.'

'You don't need someone to teach you how to smoke, do you?' asked Israel.

'Of course you do, if you're a lady. It's different if you're a fella. It's not as easy as it looks. You have to look bored, you know, if you're a lady, that's what she always said.'

'Right.'

'And you have to cock your head when someone's talking, like you're taking an interest in them. Feminine wiles, isn't it. She used to get it out of all these magazines, you know.'

'What happened after she was a model?'

'Well, she got married, and they lived all over – down south and what have you. Her husband had this canteen business, very successful. Supplying places across the border. And then her husband passed on … you know.'

'No.'

'Her husband was an RUC reservist,' said George. 'He was killed in his car. Shot in the back of the head.'

'Oh, God.'

'She was there in the car with him,' she added.

'God. That's terrible.'

'Och, well ...' said Minnie, as if someone witnessing their husband being murdered in their car were the equivalent of catching a bad dose of the flu.

'How did she cope with that?'

'Same as everyone,' said George bitterly. 'She coped.'

'I had no idea.'

'Well, anyway,' said Minnie briskly. 'Sure, it was a long time ago.'

Zelda had gone to the front of the restaurant and was motioning for Israel to join her. But Israel did not move from his seat: he was thinking about Zelda's husband. Minnie prodded him. Then Ted and John Feely Boyd hoisted him up and out of the seat and up to the front, to the sound of much clapping and cheering.

He stood sheepishly in front of the counter, next to Zelda.

'Speech!' came the cry. 'Speech!'

'I really don't want to,' Israel whispered to Zelda.

'Don't be silly, boy,' said Zelda. 'And stand up straight,' she hissed. Israel noticed lipstick on her teeth. 'Come on! Smile! This is your moment.'

'Up!' she said. 'Head up!'

'Well,' said Israel.

'Speak up!' shouted someone from the back of the room. 'We can't hear you.'

Someone brought a chair for him to stand on.

'Well,' said Israel again, getting up on the chair.

'We still can't hear you!'

'Sorry,' said Israel.

'Stop apologising!' boomed the Reverend Roberts, to peals of laughter.

'Well,' started Israel again, more loudly and confidently, but wobbling slightly.

'Mind! You'll hurt yerself,' called Minnie.

Israel steadied himself.

'Sure he's nothing left to hurt,' said Ted, to more laughter.

'Well,' began Israel again, prodding his glasses, and trying to get a word in edgeways. 'I just want to say thank you to all of you for tolerating my presence among you for the past few weeks. It has been a ... er ... steep learning curve.'

'Steeper for us!' shouted Linda Wei.

'I am particularly grateful to Linda,' continued Israel, with some irony. 'And also to Ted. And to Zelda and Minnie, for arranging this lovely evening.'

He hadn't rehearsed a speech. He thought for a minute that he would say something about how libraries were important to communities, how they brought people together, and represented all that was good about mankind's striving for knowledge and self-understanding. But then he changed his mind. There was no point him telling people what they already knew. Also, unexpectedly, he found himself getting rather choked up as he spoke. So he just said a quick thanks and got down off the chair. He had to dab a few tears from his eye.

There was a rousing chorus of 'For he's a jolly good

fellow!' and then a long couple of hours of banter and drinking, although of course Israel stuck strictly to the Shloer, having learnt his lesson now several times over, and eventually most everyone had gone and said their goodbyes – a lot of handshakes, and manly bear-hugs also from Ted and the Reverend Roberts – and then Israel stepped outside alone into the cold night air.

There was the bus stop and the concrete bus shelter, and the big empty flowerbeds, and the war memorial featuring the unknown soldier, whose rifle and whose plaque had long ago turned green, and the churches, and the shops, and the seagulls picking litter: the town centre just the same as usual, deserted now except for a few parked cars and the mobile library, which was sitting big and bold and proud as you like outside Zelda's, underneath a street light, the sea off in the distance, and hills to either side.

Israel went up to the van, to the rusty creamy red flanks of the van, and patted her, as though patting the rear of a cow – something he must have seen Ted do dozens of times, but not something that he himself had ever before had either the urge or intention to do, but which suddenly seemed to come naturally – and he opened her up and got into the driver's seat.

'Well, old girl,' he said to no one except himself and the van. 'Here we go.'

He drove out past the edge of town then, past Ted's Cabs and the First and Last, and up round onto the coast road, past the sign that said WATCH FOR FALLING ROCKS, past the grey exposed cliff face on the one side and the dark black sea on the other, following the coil of the road, sometimes high above the sea and sometimes right alongside, through the thin little patches of wood, dipping down and along through the pools of leaves and the run-off from the little gullies and streams that flowed down into all the blackness and nothingness below.

He drove over the bridge up by the Devines', and as he hit the bump and came down the van felt different; it felt heavier somehow. Israel reasoned it was maybe heaviness of heart. He couldn't honestly say that he'd come to love this place, and he couldn't honestly say he'd come to love the people, but ... well, maybe it was just because he was leaving; he was the sort of person, after all, who could get nostalgic about yesterday's breakfast.

He thought he'd better check though, just in case it was a real rather than a merely sentimental or imaginary problem with the van, and he pulled over just by the second furze, where he'd made his first pick-up, and glanced around.

The shelves were in now: Dennis had fitted them the past few days, and they were beautiful; you could see the grain even in the moonlight. Linda Wei had gone absolutely mad at first when Israel had told her about the cost of the shelves – she had exploded, a quake of Pringles and Diet Coke – but then soon after he'd been hailed as a local hero and she'd calmed down. So the shelves were a success; the shelves looked great.

And now, tonight, on every one of those beautiful grainy shelves there were books – hardbacks, paperbacks, sitting like old friends gazing down at him in silent amusement.

They were back.

Israel pushed his glasses up high onto his forehead and swallowed hard.

Someone ... Someone must have stocked the van while he was in Zelda's saying his goodbyes. The library was full. It was ... It was ... Well, it was unbelievable.

By the time he drove back to Zelda's the party was over. The last of the parked cars had gone. There was no one around. The door was still open though and he went through the restaurant, calling out – 'Zelda! Minnie!' – past the tables – 'Zelda! Minnie!' – past the counter – 'Zelda! Minnie!' – past boxes in the hallway and on into the parlour. His voice died out. There was no one around.

He went back into the hallway and stood at the bottom of the stairs and called out, more quietly. 'Zelda? Minnie?'

There was still no reply.

Something seemed to compel him to walk up the stairs – either instinct or inspiration, or a growing sense of terror, but whatever it was it kept on compelling him so that when he reached the landing he stepped through the open door to the left, which led into a huge room which stretched the entire length of the building, overlooking the town square. There was an orangey glow from the street lights.

And all along the walls of this vast orangey empty room were bookshelves – row upon row of bookshelves. Empty bookshelves.

He walked back out into the hallway and took a deep breath. He didn't know what to think. He fumbled in his pocket for some Nurofen: he had none left.

He stared for a moment at the photos on the walls: photos of a younger Zelda wearing a fox stole with the head attached, the jaw as a clasp; Zelda again in another photo with a hockey stick; another of her in a car with her hair in a tight scarf; Zelda wearing a fur coat.

'That was my first fur coat.'

Israel nearly leapt out of his skin.

Zelda stood at the top of the landing. She was looking tired. She was removing her make-up.

'Zelda!'

'Sshh,' she said. 'Minnie's asleep.'

She gestured for Israel to move back into the vast empty room.

'Zelda ...'

'Yes?'

'The books.'

'Yes?'

'They're all back, in the van.'

'Yes. That's right.' She wiped creamy cotton-wool pads across her cheeks.

'But ...' And now finally it clicked. 'Hang on. It was *you*? Who stole the books?'

'Well, they're back now.'

'Wait. Why? I mean ... You were North Coast Books?'

The computer downstairs. The boxes in the hall. Oh, good grief.

'*You?*'

'Not just me.' Zelda's pale face shone in the glow of the street lights.

'Who? Who put the books back?'

'Everyone.' She was picking at her false nails, plucking them off, one by one.

'Everyone? What do you mean everyone?'

'Everyone. Everyone here tonight.'

'What? All of you?'

'Yes.'

'Minnie. And …?'

'Ted?'

'Not Ted! No!' laughed Zelda. 'He wouldn't have anything to do with it: he's not half the man he was.'

'Linda? The council?'

'No, of course not.'

'But. The Devines?'

'No, not them either, they wouldn't have anything to do with us. But everyone else.'

'Everyone with the overdue books and …'

'Yes. Of course.'

Israel couldn't believe it.

Zelda stared at him, unmade up, her fingernails bare.

'Why?' said Israel.

'Why do you think? The council robbed us of the library. We weren't going to let them rob us of the books as well. We've all lost enough round here already.'

'But …'

'When they announced they were closing the library we just took the books and set up our own – the people's library.'

'Here?' said Israel, glancing around.

'Yes, here,' said Zelda. 'That's right.'

'You stole the books and kept them here, above the café?'

'We ran it as a proper library. The books were in safekeeping.'

'But you were selling stuff on the Internet?'

'Out-of-date books and duplicates just, I think you'll find, to replenish our stock.'

'Right. I see. '

'No, I don't think you do see. I don't think you have any idea.'

'But—'

'No. No more buts now, thank you. I would love to stay and chat but I'm very tired, I'm afraid: I'm not as young as I was. I suggest you go home and get some rest.'

'But I have to—'

'What?' Zelda arched an already highly pluck-arched eyebrow. 'Tell the police?'

'Yes.'

'That's your decision. The books are all back. No one's been hurt.'

'Yes. But. Why have you given them back now? Why have you told me?'

'I don't know. Because. We decided to trust you. That you'd look after them.'

'But I'm going back now. I'm not staying. I can't stay here. I have to go back to London. My life's in London.'

'Is it?'

'Yes.'

'Your life is wherever you're living, I think you'll find, young man.'

'What?'

'Never mind. But anyway. You have to do what you think is right. Just the same as us.'

'Zelda. I—'

'Goodnight now. And close the door after you please. Quietly now.'

'Zelda ...'

And with that, Zelda disappeared into the darkness of the house.

If a man in a van could ever properly be said to be experiencing a long dark night of the soul, a glimpse of the infinitude of the self, and if he could be understood, in at least some small way, to be undergoing a process of being and becoming, then Israel Armstrong on his last night in Northern Ireland most certainly was. He drove in the van until dawn, until his mind was clear – down the coast road, and along the dual-carriageways, and the ring roads, and the single-track roads of County Antrim – and he parked up eventually back at the strand to watch the sun come up, the books behind him, the vast sea before him.

And when he rang Gloria back in London there was no reply.

The signs went up around town later that day.

This was not what was supposed to happen at all.

NORTH-EAST EDUCATION AND LIBRARY BOARD

MOBILE LIBRARY

Revised Timetable commencing 1 January 2006

CREMARTIN DISTRICT

Barrow Lane (Eastern lay-by)

1st & 3rd Monday in the month 10 a.m.–12 noon

Frankhill Country Park (Main car park)
1st & 3rd Monday in the month 1 p.m.–3 p.m.

Ballyoran (Monument)
2nd Monday in the month 10 a.m.–12 noon

Conwarren, Outdoor Pursuits Centre
2nd Monday in the month 1 p.m.–3 p.m.

MULLAN AND BALLYROGAN

Hill Hall
1st & 3rd Tuesday in the month 10 a.m.–11 a.m.

Ballyrogan Market Square
Tuesdays 2 p.m.–4 p.m.

Ballyrogan Business Park
(Outside Duggan's Software Solutions)
2nd Tuesday in the month 5 p.m.–6 p.m.

TUMDRUM AND DISTRICT

Sea Front, Tumdrum
(Opp. Papa Joe's Ice Cream Parlour)
Wednesdays 12 noon–1 p.m.

Hammond Road, Tumdrum (Outside library)
Wednesdays 2 p.m.–3.30 p.m.

First and Last Public House, Tumdrum (Car park)
Wednesdays 7 p.m.–9 p.m.

LARKIN'S CROSS

Community College (Car park)
Thursdays 10 a.m.–12 noon

Mullan (By Public Toilets)
2nd and 4th Thursday in the month 1 p.m.–3 p.m.

Fiddler on the Green Public House (Car park)
1st & 3rd Thursday in the month 7 p.m.–8 p.m.

PORTSTRAND

Strand School
Fridays 9.30 a.m.–11.30 a.m.

Old Windmill
1st and 2nd Friday in the month 12 noon–1 p.m.

Myowne (Visitors' car park)
3rd & 4th Friday in the month 12 noon–1 p.m.

DRUM DISTRICT

Drum (Monument)
Saturdays 10 a.m.–12 noon

Edenderry Estate (Shops)
1st & 3rd Saturday in the month 1 p.m.–3 p.m.

Killynure, GAA Club (Car park)
2 & 4th Saturday in the month 12 noon–1 p.m.

Contact: Israel Armstrong, Mobile Librarian

E-mail: iarmstrong@nelb.lib.ni,
County Library, Main Street, Rathkeltair,
Co. Antrim BT44 3HR

Acknowledgements

For previous acknowledgements see *The Truth About Babies* (Granta Books, 2002) and *Ring Road* (Fourth Estate, 2004). These stand, with exceptions. In addition I would like to thank the following. (The previous terms and conditions apply: some of them are dead; most of them are strangers; the famous are not friends; none of them bears any responsibility.) I remain extremely grateful to the editors of *The Enthusiast*.

Robert Altman, Wes Anderson, Roger Angell, Ole Anthony, Harold Arlen, Roger Ascham, Simon Ashby, David B., Robert Baden-Powell, Stewart Bailie, Geoffrey Balderson, Bangor Rugby Football Club, John Barry, Paul Bell, William Beveridge, Steve Biddulph, O. Blaiklock, Lawrence Block, Jane Brocket, Buck 65, Lawrence Buell, Burkhard Bilger, Abraham Cahan, Jane Campion, John Candy, Ethan Canin, Joe Carey, Michael Chabon, Chase Organics, Roz Chast, George C. Chesbro, Billy Childish, Angelique Chrisafis,

Agatha Christie, Susan Clarke, Rachel Cohen, Michael Collins, Captain Cook, Jacques Cousteau, Ben Cove, Damien Coyle, J. Creaghan, Yuriy Cubarenko, Matt Damon, Stuart Daniels, Susan David, Richard Deacon, Michael Deane, Mariana Della Barba, Julie Delpy, Johnny Depp, Vittorio De Sica, Fred Dibnah, Terence Patrick Dolan, Placido Domingo, Ariel Dorfman, Christopher Eccleston, Travis Elborough, Aaron Elkins, Victor Erice, Robert Fagles, Dr Feelgood, Federico Fellini, Mrs Finlay, First Bangor Scout Group, David Fitzsimons, Matthew Fletcher, Franz Ferdinand, Sasha Frere-Jones, Bill Frissell, P. Galvin, Finn Garbutt, Frances Garbutt, Luke Garbutt, Tom Gatti, Julian Germain, Ricky Gervais, Fiachra Gibbons, Christopher Guest, Half Man Half Biscuit, Tony Hargreaves, Adam Hart-Davis, Ethan Hawke, Fergus Henderson, Arve Henrikson, Thierry Henry, Willie Heron, I Am Kloot, Rea Irvin, Mahalia Jackson, Ashley Kahn, Keane, Atheline Kelly, Amir Khan, Mark Knopfler, Leon Kossoff, Stefan Kürten, Josh Lacey, Richard Lattimore, Chang-rae Lee, Dan Lepard, Graham Linehan, Sidney Lumet, Robert Lyle, Mrs Magowan, David Mamet, Sarfraz Manzoor, Ellie Martin, Keith Martin, Jay Martin, Rosie Martin, Steve Martin, Wendy Martin, Willy Mason, Eleanor Massey, Arthur Mathews, Duncan McCallien, Ralph McClean, John McCormick, Andrew McEwan, McGrory's Hotel, Moira McIver, Paul McKenna, Eric McKillen, Stuart McLean, Sean McMahon, Brad Meldhau, Louis Menand, Mrs Mills, Julianne Moore, Chris Moyles and Comedy Dave, Bill Murray, Julian Nangle, Willie Nelson, Christopher Nolan, Bill Oddie, Jo O'Donoghue, R. O'Hare, Orhan Pamuk, Gareth Peirce, Gilles Peterson, Michel Petrucciani, Sue Pitt, Stephen

Poliakoff, Adam Pushkin, Rathgael Gymnastics Club, Rathmullan House Hotel, Satyajit Ray, Emily Reeve, M. Reeves, Django Reinhardt, Simon Reynolds, Sheila Rhodes, Paul and Amy Richards, Nicholas Rinaldi, Marilynne Robinson, Tony Robinson, Arundhati Roy, Patricia Rozema, Joe Sacco, George Saunders, Martin Scorsese, Ricardo Semler, Robert Sinclair, Paul Smith, Charles Albert Lucien Snelling, Steven Soderbergh, Aaron Sorkin, Sufjan Stevens, Ben Stiller, Anthony Swofford, Peter Tatchell, Catherine Tate, David Tattersall, P. K. Tattersall, John Taylor, The Thrills, Robert Tressell, Mark-Anthony Turnage, Gus Van Sant, Mordechai Vanunu, Lars Von Trier, Nicholas Walt, Harriet Walter, Emily Warren, Richard Weight, Hannah Westland, Karen Weston, Jo Whiley, Mrs Whiteside, Billy Wilder, Jincy Willett, Frances A. Yates, Viktor Yushchenko, Reiner Zimnik.

The Mobile Library

MR DIXON DISAPPEARS

Read on for a preview of the next instalment of Ian Sansom's *Mobile Library* series, in which Israel Armstrong investigates the curious vanishing of Mr Dixon, a department store manager and amateur magician.

Mr Dixon Disappears is available in paperback from HarperPerennial in August 2006.

1

He was sick of the excuses and the lies. He was tired of the evasions and the untruths, of people refusing to stand up and speak the truth and take responsibility for their own actions. It seemed to him like yet another symptom of the decline of Western civilisation; of night drawing nigh and mere anarchy loosed upon the world, and the centre cannot hold; and chaos; and climate change; and environmental disaster; and war; disease; famine; oppression; the eternal slow slide down and down and down. It was tragedy. It was disgrace. It was entropy, nemesis, apotheosis, imminent apocalypse and sheer bad manners all rolled into one. People were not returning their library books on time.

Israel had been out on the road in the mobile library for a few months now and he reckoned he'd heard just about every possible excuse.

'I'm sorry, I forgot,' people would say.

And 'I've been in hospital.'

Or, 'I liked it so much I lent it to my sister' (or my brother, or my mother, or my father, or my cousin, or my friend, who lives up country, or in Derry, or over there in England, actually, and isn't that where you're from?).

Or, 'Sure, I brought it back already.'

Or, 'No. I don't think so. I never had that one out.'

Or, 'I put it back on the shelves myself. Some other one must've have it out now.'

Or, 'Someone stole it.'

Or, 'I left it on the bus,' or in the bath, or on holiday, or in the car and it's in for servicing.

And, even, once, 'It was a bad book, full of bad language and bad people doing bad things, so I threw it away.' (Well, what the hell did Mrs Onions expect, borrowing *Last Exit to Brooklyn*? Israel had asked her, after he'd got her to pay the replacement cost of the book, and a fine, and had steered her safely back towards her usual large-print romantic fiction, and it turned out she had a cousin who'd emigrated to New York back in the sixties and she'd never visited and she was toying with the idea of a trip over for her seventieth birthday and she'd wanted to find out what it was like over there, and frankly there was no chance of her visiting now after reading that filth; they were going to go to Donegal for a few days instead, to see her sister, down in Gweedore, which was quite far enough, and did Israel know if Frank McCourt had written any others?)

But mostly when they were challenged about their overdue or unreturned books, the good people of Tumdrum would just narrow their eyes and look at you with a blank expression and purse their lips and say, 'Book? What book?'

It wasn't funny. It was cracking him up.

Just about the only thing that kept him sane, in fact, the

only thing that protected Israel from his own sure slide down into surliness and pique, was lovely Rosie, Rosie Hart from the First and Last, who'd been helping him out on the mobile library, in an unofficial capacity. It was a casual arrangement, but it worked. On the days when Ted was busy with his taxi firm ('Ted's Cabs: If You Want To Get There, Call the Bear'), Rosie would come in and give Israel a hand, and help him get loaded up and sort out the tickets and clear out the van and help him find the service points and issue the books, and she was in many ways the ideal helpmeet and librarian: she was young and she was presentable and she did not eat garlic, or shake, or snarl or suffer from perpetual indigestion, or dyspepsia, or rage, or otherwise exhibit any eccentric or anti-social behaviours, and all her bartending experience meant that she was fair but firm and she had an instinctive way with people, while Israel, on the other hand, could sometimes come across as a little … brusque.

If someone came in to the mobile, for example, a borrower – or a 'customer' as Linda Wei, Deputy of Entertainment, Leisure and Community Services at Tumdrum and District Council, insisted on calling them – if a borrower came in and they asked for a book Israel would always start out with good intentions. He'd say, 'Hello! Welcome!' and he'd try to be as cheery as a mobile librarian might reasonably be expected to be, and he might even ask the person if they knew the title of the book they were after, but invariably the person – let's call them Mrs Onions, for the sake of example – would say 'No,' and Israel might manage to remain patient for a moment or two and he might say, 'OK, fine, do you know the name of the author?'

But then of course the person – let's say still they're Mrs Onions – they would say 'Och, no,' and Israel would start to struggle a little bit then, and the person, Mrs Onions, would usually add, 'But you'd know it when you saw it, because it's got a blue sort of a cover, and my cousin had it out last year I think it was, and it's about this big ...' At which point Israel would lose interest completely, would be incapable of offering anything but his ill-disguised north London university-educated liberal scorn for someone who didn't know what they wanted and didn't know how to get it. But Rosie, Rosie would take it all in her stride and she'd try to find every blue-coloured book in the van and if they didn't have it in, sure they could get a few blue-coloured books on inter-library loan, it was no problem at all. Israel just couldn't be bothered with all that; he liked the idea of public service, but he was struggling with being an actual public servant.

Nonetheless, he couldn't really complain. He was settling in. He was always happy to pick up Rosie in the van from Myowne, the mobile home park, in the mornings and they'd do their service run, and then they'd collect Rosie's son Conor at Tumdrum primary school, where they had a little after-school club going, Israel playing chess with some of the children, and Rosie doing a reading and homework hour in the mobile, and even Israel had to admit it wasn't a bad little set-up. It wasn't bad at all.

Until, that is, the disappearance of Mr Dixon from the Department Store at the End of the World.